PRAISE FOR *NO 1*
BY MARK E[...]

T0013310

'*No Place to Run* is that most wonderful of things – a book that opens with a breath-takingly startling premise and then keeps the momentum going until the very last page . . . Just brilliant, Mark Edwards really is in a league of his own.'
—Lisa Jewell, #1 *New York Times* and *Sunday Times* bestselling author of *The Family Upstairs*

'Like a Reacher, but with a hero like the rest of us.'
—Linwood Barclay, bestselling author of *Take Your Breath Away*

'*No Place to Run* is another cracker from Mark Edwards.'
—Elly Griffiths, *Sunday Times* bestselling author of the Ruth Galloway Mysteries

'A tense, nail-biting read.'
—Steph Broadribb, author of *Death in the Sunshine*

'Another intriguing, exhilarating, and compulsive read from the master of psychological suspense. Mark Edwards just keeps getting better and better.'
—Emma Haughton, author of *The Dark*

'This is a belter of a story. A big screen high tension adventure.'
—William Shaw, author of *The Trawlerman*

KEEP HER SECRET

ALSO BY MARK EDWARDS

The Magpies

Kissing Games

What You Wish For

Because She Loves Me

Follow You Home

The Devil's Work

The Lucky Ones

The Retreat

A Murder of Magpies

In Her Shadow

Here to Stay

Last of the Magpies

The House Guest

The Hollows

No Place to Run

WITH LOUISE VOSS

Forward Slash

Killing Cupid

Catch Your Death

All Fall Down

From the Cradle

The Blissfully Dead

KEEP
HER
SECRET

MARK
EDWARDS

 THOMAS & MERCER

Text copyright © 2023 by Mark Edwards
All rights reserved.

Published by Thomas & Mercer, Seattle

www.apub.com

Amazon, the Amazon logo, and Thomas & Mercer are trademarks of Amazon.com, Inc., or its affiliates.

ISBN-13: 9781662508936
eISBN: 9781662508929

Cover design by @blacksheep-uk.com
Cover image: © Kichigin / Shutterstock; © Olga Donchuk / Getty; © Nilufer Barin / Arcangel

Printed in the United States of America

KEEP
HER
SECRET

PART ONE

PART ONE

Chapter 1

'I can't see the others.'

I turned to follow Helena's gaze down the slope of the mountain, a jagged wall of rock blocking my view of the path. I listened, expecting to hear voices, but the wind was blowing in the wrong direction, carrying our fellow hikers' words down to where the Krossa River threaded through the valley. Earlier that day, our party had come over the river in a pair of Jeeps, and our guide, Dagur, had chuckled as he told us about a bus that had got stuck at this very point the previous year, its occupants forced to wade through the bitterly cold water with their rucksacks above their heads while the hapless driver tried to get his vehicle moving again.

There was no sign of Dagur or the other hikers now. Helena and I were alone.

'Do you want to wait?' I asked. 'Go back?'

Helena removed her beanie for a moment, as if exposing her head to the air would help her think. 'No. Let's keep going. They'll catch us up.'

We walked on. Helena pulled her hat back into place over her dark, shoulder-length hair and took her phone out of her jacket pocket. We were approaching the crest of the slope, looking for a spot from which to take the perfect photo that Helena had been seeking all week. Last night, in our hut further down the valley, I had flicked through the pictures we'd already taken on this trip, starting in Reykjavík five days ago before moving out into the wild countryside. Geysers and volcanic rock and wild ponies. There were hundreds of pictures, each one shining with this country's almost ludicrous beauty. The geothermal waters of the Blue Lagoon, where we'd taken a much-needed break from all the walking. The frigid, foaming surface of the Atlantic, where we'd seen humpback whales. Lava fields and black beaches. There were pictures of the group and plenty of selfies taken in front of beautiful backdrops, but mostly there were lots and lots of photos of Helena and me together, grinning at the camera. Great pictures. But none of them quite 'the one'. The perfect photograph Helena was searching for.

A little further up the slope, she stopped walking and said, with a voice full of wonder, 'Look at it, Matthew. Just *look* at it.'

We stood side by side and, for the hundredth time since I'd come to Iceland, all I could do was marvel. This was Thórsmörk, the Valley of Thor, formed by glaciers, one shimmering behind us, another dominating the view ahead. It was easy to see why this place had been named after a god. Easy, too, to imagine that god slamming down his hammer and causing the eruptions that had sent clouds of ash across Europe a decade ago.

There was no sign of any such drama today. Behind the thick grey clouds that skimmed the glaciers' shining peaks, the sky was a rich blue. It was peaceful. Calm. Standing there, gawping at the beauty before me, I felt both thrillingly alive and utterly inconsequential, a speck on the surface of this ancient place.

Something inside Helena's head made her laugh, the skin around her eyes crinkling, and not for the first time in the last few weeks I mentally slapped myself. She was gorgeous. She laughed easily. She was lovely. Why had I ever let her go?

She caught my eye and grinned.

'What's amused you this time?' I asked.

'I can't tell you. You'll never speak to me again.'

'You'd have to tell me something pretty terrible for that to happen.'

Was I imagining it or did her smile slip for a fraction of a second? I was sure that something passed over her face – the shadow of a cloud – but then that infectious smile of hers was back, the gap between her front teeth on full display, and I was grinning too.

'Come on. What is it?'

'All right, well, I apologise in advance and I'd like you to know I've enjoyed our brief time back together. But I was just thinking . . . it's a sight for Thor eyes.'

I groaned.

'I told you you'd never want to speak to me again. Hold on, you're trying to come up with a pun in response, aren't you?'

'Yeah. But everything I've come up with is a bit too Loki.'

She covered her face with her gloved hands. 'That's *terrible*, Matthew.'

'I win though, right?'

She leaned forward and kissed me – eyes bright, lips cold – before pulling away and turning her attention back to the view.

'Here, let me get one of you,' she said after taking a few shots of the landscape.

I obliged, turning my back to the glacier.

'Say Loki!' she said.

I laughed as she took the photo, then asked, 'What exactly are you going to do with this perfect photo, if you ever manage to take it?'

She raised her eyebrows. 'Put it on Instagram, of course. Both my followers will be delighted.'

'But really?'

'I don't know. I guess I just want an image that will always remind me of this trip. Of our first holiday back together.'

She stepped forward and we kissed again. I could almost hear the gods in the valley telling us to get a room. Right now, I was pleased we were on our own, the rest of the group still somewhere further down the mountain.

'So are you satisfied now?' I asked. 'Do you think that's the one?'

'I'm not sure. Let's go a tiny bit higher, up there.' She pointed a little way ahead, where the slope flattened out but the path, well-trodden by thousands of hikers over the years, ended. The ground beyond was rocky and uneven. 'I think we'll be able to see both sides of the valley from there. What do you say?'

I hesitated. 'I don't know. Maybe we should wait for the others before we go further.'

She looked past me down the empty path. There was still no sign of them.

'It's fine, Matthew. Come on, it's the last day of the trip. Let's check out that spot, take a few final pics, and then we'll head back down. I imagine Dagur is treating the whole group to a lecture about rock formation. They'll be ages.'

'I quite enjoy his lectures.' The idea of straying from the path made me nervous. I'd seen that film about the guy who'd slipped on a mountain and had to chop off his own arm.

'Yeah, I bet. Geeks of a feather.'

'Hey!'

She laughed again. 'Actually, I like Dagur. You know who he reminds me of? Indiana Jones, if his degree was in geology not

6

archaeology. And he was Icelandic. And he carried a backpack instead of a bullwhip.'

'In other words, he's nothing like Indiana Jones.'

She mock-sighed and laid her palm over her heart. 'My search goes on.'

We started walking.

'I'm going to be sad to say goodbye to all this,' she said. 'To go back to normal life.'

'Maybe we could stay. Become sheep farmers or something.'

I expected her to come back with some terrible joke or pun, but she appeared distracted, gazing out at the view again, her mind seemingly a thousand miles away. She was frowning.

'Helena? Are you okay?'

'Huh?' She shook the frown off. 'Yes! I'm good. I'm great. Come on, let's get this done and then we can head back down. I've got some chocolate bars in my backpack. Take the best picture ever and I promise to share them with you.'

I looked beyond her. All week I'd happily obeyed yellow signs that screamed warnings about rockfalls and hot water, but there were no signs here; not that I could see anyway. Helena, who had teased me about my cautiousness, noticed me looking.

'See?' she said. 'No warning signs.' She strolled up the path, giving me no choice but to follow, and called back, 'It's safe, Matthew. It's perfectly safe.'

She strode ahead as if she did this every day. I jogged to catch up, my backpack bouncing against my spine. It was remarkable how she was able to move as if she wasn't even wearing one. Must be all the yoga she did. Core strength. She bounded along like a mountain goat while I huffed and puffed behind her, vowing to work on my fitness when we got home. I was going to need to keep up with her.

The sloping path gave way to ground that was flat but rocky. Helena walked straight ahead, turning her head left and right, clearly seeking out the best spot for the photo she seemed strangely obsessed with getting. For the first time, I found myself feeling a little frustrated with her. The wind was even stronger now and I was having to watch where I trod so I didn't trip.

Then I heard Helena say, 'Wow,' and I followed her gaze. I didn't feel irritated anymore. She was right to have led us up here.

'Welcome to the top of the world,' she said when I reached her.

'This is insane,' I said.

'I know, right?'

I had thought the view further down had been spectacular, but this was something else. I could see across the whole valley. The trio of mighty glaciers, crowned with ice. The green foothills of the mountains that sloped down to the stony valley floor, the river gleaming in the sun. Turning to the south I could see all the way to the coast, a sliver of blue on the far horizon. It was like something from Tolkien. A morbid thought entered my head: when I died, I would be happy to have my ashes scattered here. I'd seen the beaches of Thailand, the forests of California, Tokyo lit up at night from the top of a skyscraper. But this beat all of them.

'Here,' Helena said. '*This* is the perfect spot.'

As I'd been marvelling at the beauty around me, Helena had made her way over to the edge of the ridge. Loose rocks lay at her feet; to her left, a boulder came up to her waist.

'Please,' I said. 'Be careful.'

Behind her, the rocks gave way to thin air. Just looking at the drop, at the nothingness beyond the ridge, gave me that feeling in my belly like I'd gone over a bump in the road.

'It's fine.' She held out her phone. 'Take my picture and then I'll take one of you.'

I removed my gloves, tucking them into my jacket pocket, and took the phone from her. She stood at the edge of the cliff, facing me. I held up the phone, centring her in the frame, and paused. The backdrop was postcard-perfect, but Helena was still the most beautiful part of this picture. The colour in her cheeks. The pale blue of her eyes. My skin tingled beneath my coat and I felt a little shiver of anticipation, thinking about getting back to the hut, taking off our hats and gloves and—

'Come on,' she said. 'What's taking so long?'

I smiled to myself.

'Okay, done,' I said. 'Let's get out of here.'

'Wait. Let me see.' She stepped forward and flicked through the pictures. 'My face looks weird. How can it look weird in *all* of them?'

'Helena, your face does not look weird. It's the exact opposite of weird.'

'Which is?'

'Um. Wonderful?'

She rolled her eyes but looked pleased. 'Can you take a few more?'

I couldn't shake the sensation of vertigo. The wind was so strong, and the ground so uneven, that although there might not have been any yellow danger signs around, they were flashing inside my head.

'Please, humour me, okay?'

We were having to raise our voices to be heard above the wind.

'All right. One more quick batch of pictures and then we go down,' I said. 'I don't—'

'Fine then, whatever,' she said. 'If you don't want to do it, I'll take a selfie.' She marched towards the cliff edge.

I was frozen for a second. Was she being reckless, or was I being a drag? Either way, was it worth our first argument since we'd rekindled our relationship?

'I'm sorry,' I said, going after her.

Helena stopped and turned. 'It's fine. I just don't like being told what to do. Lee was always . . .' She shook her head and said, 'Come on, take the photo.'

She stepped back up to the cliff edge, a footstep away from the precipice, and turned towards me, the smile back in place, stretching her arms out like Julie Andrews in *The Sound of Music*. I stood about ten metres away from her so I could capture some sense of the scale of this place in the photo.

What happened next took no more than three seconds. But looking back, as I sometimes do now when I'm unable to sleep, I see it unfolding in slow motion. The beginning of all that followed.

As I took the final photo, the phone positioned in front of my face, a gust of wind blasted my back, knocking me a step forward. Something black flew into the frame of the camera – one of my gloves; the gust of wind must have dislodged it from where it hung from my pocket – and it flew towards Helena.

She reacted instinctively. She brought her hands in protectively and stepped backwards as the glove flew into her face, one foot stamping on the ground behind her.

The ground, which crumbled beneath her.

And I watched, helplessly, as she vanished from sight.

Chapter 2

'So, Helena, Matthew. Have you been together long?'

It was Dagur who asked the question. It was the first night after leaving Reykjavík, three days before Helena's fall. We were all sitting at the long table in the dining hall of the huts where we were staying, having spent the day hiking along the Laugavegur trail. Dinner was meatballs, not dissimilar to those you might find at Ikea, with a plant-based version for the vegetarians in the group, including me.

Not counting Dagur, there were eight of us in our party: three couples and two solo travellers – a young woman from Brighton called Devon, and George, a retired theatre director in his sixties. George had told us that his husband had died a couple of years ago, and he had come here because it was a trip he and Derek had always intended to take together. We were all British except for Sinéad and Laurence Gallagher, a middle-aged couple from Ireland.

George had been telling us about the man who'd been in the seat next to his on the plane over. 'He was so inebriated, I'm surprised they let him on. He came staggering down the aisle then fell on top of me, babbling absolute nonsense. It was like sitting next to Mr Blobby.' He chortled, then did an impression. 'Blobby. Blobby. Blobby.'

Dagur, who had joined us and was sitting next to Helena, looked blank. 'Blobby?'

'Oh,' George explained, 'he was this ridiculous pink character who was on British TV in the nineties. Hung out with a chap called Noel and had a Christmas number one.'

Dagur said, 'I see,' as if we had just confirmed his suspicion that all Brits were insane.

I asked him how he had coped during the pandemic when there'd been no tourists to show around.

'It was not so bad,' he replied. 'I finally got round to writing the novel I've been talking about since I was a young man.'

'How exciting,' Helena said. 'What's it about? Wait, let me guess. It's about an intrepid tour guide in the Icelandic mountains who finds the body of a murdered tourist.'

'I love that kind of book,' said Sinéad, who was sitting across from us, beside her husband. She was a pleasant woman with shaggy silver hair and the experience-seizing fervour of a recent empty-nester. 'Nordic noir. Ritual slaughters in the snow, local folklore, a hunky detective with a dead wife and an impressive beard.'

Dagur laughed. 'Actually, it's a love story.'

'Ooh,' said Sinéad. 'Does it have lots of naughty bits? Can I read it?'

Dagur blushed. 'Not too many naughty bits. What can I say? I'm a romantic.' Then he turned to me and Helena and asked his question. *Have you been together long?*

I replied first. 'Hmm. Not really.'

Helena squeezed my knee beneath the table and said, 'A week and a half.'

Dagur's mouth dropped open and Sinéad almost spat out her meatball. 'What?'

'Yeah. This is basically our second date.'

Everyone around the table laughed like this was a joke.

'A week and a half? Really?' All eyes went to the other end of the table, to Devon. She had been quiet throughout the meal, listening to everyone else and nodding along but not offering much herself. She was in her early twenties and had dark hair, a similar shade to Helena's, cut in a short, choppy style. She was small and striking – around five foot three with a ballerina's physique and big green eyes. Meeting her, I'd expected her to be talkative and confident, but I'd hardly heard her speak during this first day of the trip.

'It's true,' I confirmed.

'That's crazy,' said Dagur, with a laugh. 'But also – romantic.'

'Did you meet online?' George asked. 'On one of those hook-up apps?'

Sinéad raised her eyebrows. 'You know what a hook-up app is, George?'

'Oh yes, there was an interesting discussion about them on Radio Four. I wish they'd had them when I was a young man.' He winked at Devon. 'Your generation is so fortunate. All those hot guys, just a swipe away.'

Everyone else roared with laughter but Devon didn't smile. She kept her gaze fixed on Helena. 'It seems a little crazy to me,' she said. 'To go on holiday with someone you've just met.'

'You mean in case Matthew turns out to be a serial killer?' said Sinéad. 'Hey, Dagur, maybe that could be your next book.'

'I promise I'm not a serial killer,' I said. 'And this might be our second date, but we haven't just met.' I caught Helena's eye. 'We've known each other a long time.'

ᚦ

When I got the invitation to the reunion party, my first instinct was to say no. It came from a guy called Dave Sprouse, whose name popped up on my Facebook page occasionally but who I hadn't seen since I'd left college. Dave was one of those people who liked to keep in touch with everyone he'd ever met – he had over a thousand Facebook friends – and one day in late summer I got a DM from him saying, *Hey, you know it's the twenty-year anniversary of our graduation in a couple of weeks? I thought it might be fun to get some of the old gang together. No pressure, but we're going to meet at the Mulberry Bush from 7pm on Sept 8th. Hope to see you there!*

Like I said, I had no intention of going. I hadn't exactly achieved all my dreams over the last two decades. Aged forty-two, I had been single since breaking up with my long-term girlfriend almost two years ago, my job was mediocre and I lived in a tiny flat in an unglamorous part of south London. I wasn't sure I could cope with a pub full of people I'd known a long time ago bragging about everything they'd achieved and showing me photos of their children and holiday homes. There was a reason I wasn't still in touch with them.

But then the evening arrived. I gazed into my empty fridge, contemplated another night home alone and remembered Dave's message. Before I had a chance to reconsider, I scooped up my keys and wallet and headed down to the South Bank.

The Mulberry Bush had been our local when we were at uni. I'd been back there a few times over the years, so walking in wasn't too much of a trip down memory lane. But then I spotted them. The gathering in the corner of the pub who I had mistaken for a group of middle managers out for a post-work drink – they had once been the fresh-faced youths I'd shared lecture halls and messy nights out with. I almost backed out until one of the group spotted me and beckoned me over, and as I joined them, saying hello to Dave and a couple of other people whose names I struggled to remember, the group shifted and parted to reveal a face and a name that I would never have forgotten.

Helena. My ex-girlfriend.

I could sense her presence as I chatted with Dave and a woman called Fiona who had, like me, studied graphic design. I couldn't concentrate on anything Fiona and Dave were saying. Because the moment I saw Helena, everyone else in the pub had turned black and white, leaving Helena as the only person still in colour.

Had I hoped she might be here? I hadn't really thought about it. Although I had some good memories of the year Helena and I dated, it was a long time ago. I had filed her away in my mental archive along with the girls I'd dated at school. Formative experiences, first kisses, the loss of my virginity. All nice to look back on in a nostalgic way but, yeah, a long time ago. The stuff of youth.

So I was shocked by my reaction to seeing her now. The immediate physical effect she had on me. Quickening pulse. Stirring blood.

I was gripped by a crazy sense of panic. What if she slipped away, Cinderella-like, before I got the chance to talk to her? I tried to focus on what Fiona was talking about – oh yes, she was discreetly trying to let me know how rich she was – until she noticed how often I kept glancing at Helena and, with a roll of the eyes, went to talk to someone else.

By this point, Helena was talking to another woman and I loitered awkwardly beside them while I waited for their chat to finish. Did she know I was there? Did she remember me? So far she had shown no sign of it. And then . . . the other woman got drawn into another conversation and Helena turned towards me, a smile already on her lips, and I couldn't think of a single thing to say.

All I could come up with was, 'I'm so glad to see you here.'

Her smile remained and I noticed her look me up and down, clearly assessing how much I'd changed.

'I know,' I said. 'I look old, don't I?'

'What? No, not at all. I mean, you don't have as much hair as you used to and you're not wearing that awful leather jacket anymore—'

'Hey, I loved that jacket!'

'I know you did.' She laughed. 'But apart from the much-missed and maligned jacket, you look exactly the same.'

'Well. And you . . . you look great,' I said. 'I mean, you really, genuinely do.'

'Thank you.'

She had been gorgeous when I'd known her at college, with all that black hair and those light-blue eyes – eyes that were, right now, looking directly into mine – plus those long limbs and that gap between her teeth. But with the lines on her face that hadn't been there before, and her hair just as black but now cut in a shoulder-length bob, there was no other word for it: she was beautiful.

I found my mind flashing back through time to our first kiss. Where had we been? That's right – a gig at the student union, some indie band who'd vanished after one album. I could hear the music now. Could feel Helena's lips against mine, our bodies crushed together in the heat of the crowd . . .

'Hello? Earth to Matthew?'

I blinked at her. Was I flushed? My heart was pounding.

'Sorry?' I said.

'I was asking what you're doing these days. Do you live in London?'

'Yes. Crystal Palace.'

'And work?'

'I'm a web designer. For MerchBox?'

'Oh. Yeah. I think I've heard of it.'

I smiled. 'I can tell you haven't. We sell merchandise from TV shows and movies. T-shirts and Funko Pops and all that kind of stuff. How about you?'

'I live in Brighton,' she said. 'Well, just outside.'

'And you came up to town just for this?'

Another laugh. 'No, I came up to see the Walter Sickert exhibition at the Tate. Wanted to catch it before it finished. Then I remembered Dave's invite and thought it might be fun to pop along.'

'And now you deeply regret your decision?'

'Oh yes. I'm dying to get away.'

I noticed the glass she was holding was empty. I gestured to it. 'Do you want another?'

She contemplated the glass, then me. To my delight, she took a step closer to me and spoke into my ear. Her breath was warm. And was she wearing the same perfume she used to wear? I remembered she'd had a bottle of Chanel N°5 that her grandmother had given her as an eighteenth birthday present, which she'd been eking out for two years.

'I only really want to talk to you,' she said. 'Shall we go somewhere else?'

It took all my willpower to force myself to play it cool. To not beam like this was the best offer I'd ever had. *I only really want to talk to you.* The sentiment was mutual. Right now, I couldn't imagine ever wanting to talk to anyone else.

We slipped out of the pub without saying goodbye to anyone, and then we were walking along the South Bank. It was one of the last clement evenings of the year, summer resisting autumn's chill, and there were lots of people about. I felt light-headed, almost giddy. Something was happening here, wasn't it? Was I mistaken? It all seemed unreal.

'Are you hungry?' I asked.

'Ravenous.'

We found a pizza place near the London Eye that had a couple of free tables outside. Helena took off her jacket and hung it over the back of her chair, and I noticed her clothes were well cut and expensive, making me feel like a scruff in my jeans and H&M shirt. I was desperate to ask her about her relationship status. She wasn't wearing a ring but I braced myself to hear that she had a boyfriend and that I'd been misreading the signals.

'I came here once with my ex,' I said.

'Oh, really?'

'Yeah. Angela. We split up at the end of the first lockdown after driving each other completely bonkers.'

'I heard that happened a lot. How long were you together?'

'Three years. But we'd only just moved in together when the pandemic happened.'

'No kids?'

'No. I think I've missed that boat.' It was a subject I tried not to think about much. I had spent twenty years as a serial monogamist – a series of two- or three-year relationships with fallow gaps in between. None of these relationships had ever progressed even to within sight of the marriage-and-kids stage. I had been accused of being scared of commitment on more than one occasion. Quite often these days I would see dads out and about with young children and feel a pang, even if it wasn't necessarily too late for me. Other times I'd encounter parents with tantruming toddlers and think I'd dodged a bullet. 'How about you?'

'Kids? No. I never wanted them.' Her voice was flat, so I couldn't tell if she was being honest or if there was some regret there.

'And what about . . . relationships?'

I braced myself.

'I was married,' she said.

Was. That was good.

'To Lee.'

There was a pause. Finally, I said, 'Not *the* Lee?'

18

'Yes. Lee Davidson.'

I sat back. 'You married Lee Davidson? I can't believe it.'

'Well, it happened.'

The waitress came before I could say anything else. I ordered without thinking. When the waitress left, I said, 'And now . . . you're divorced?'

'Not divorced. Widowed.'

I hadn't been expecting that. I had certainly never been Lee's biggest fan – I still couldn't believe Helena had married him – but to hear he was dead . . . 'Oh my God. I'm so sorry.'

'It's fine. I'm fine.'

'When . . . How did it happen?'

We had already ordered a bottle of wine. Helena took a big swallow of it and said, 'Can we not talk about it? I'm having a nice time and I don't want to start getting emotional. Is that okay?'

'Of course.'

She put the glass down. 'Except now I feel like I have to say something, so you don't start treating me like I'm made of crystal. It happened in January. An accident. But I'm fine, honestly. I'd rather not talk about it, not right now. Not when I'm having dinner with an old friend.'

'I understand. I promise not to ask about it anymore.' I raised my glass. 'To old friends.'

We clinked. 'Old friends.' She held my gaze. 'It really is good to see you, Matthew.'

I lost track of how long we stayed in the restaurant. We polished off the bottle of wine and ordered another. By the time the bill came I was several steps past tipsy. I also felt elated. Talking to Helena now was just as easy as it had been when we were younger. Just as easy, but better. She was so funny, so interesting. And there was a connection there. A reconnection. Lots of eye contact. Several times, she touched my arm as she spoke. I didn't want the evening to end.

Fate, it transpired, didn't want us to part either. As we left the pizza place, Helena's phone chimed.

'Oh, for God's sake,' she said, checking the screen. 'All the trains to Brighton have been cancelled. Major signalling failures. They're putting on buses from Kent.'

'Oh no.'

'I don't think I can face it. I might try to get a hotel and go back in the morning.'

'You could always stay at mine,' I said.

She looked at me. 'In Crystal Palace?'

I started to explain the train connections she could take in the morning, but she interrupted.

'I'm not going to have sex with you.'

I laughed. 'It wouldn't have crossed my mind.'

'I bet.'

'Honest.' Of course it had crossed my mind. 'I have a very comfortable sofa. You can have the bed.'

'Is there a lock on the door?'

'Helena . . .'

'I'm joking!' She hesitated, looking along the South Bank, at the buildings opposite, glowing in the darkness. 'Okay,' she said. 'If you don't mind, that would be great.'

So we got a taxi back to mine. And we didn't have sex, or even kiss. We sat up half the night talking, and it was only when Helena tried to suppress a yawn that I noticed how many hours had passed. Shortly after that, she went to bed and I settled down on the sofa. I was too wired and elated to sleep. I kept thinking that maybe she would appear and say she felt bad about taking the bed and invite me to get in with her.

It didn't happen. But a man could dream, couldn't he?

20

'Well, anyway,' said Helena, standing up from the dinner table after I'd given our fellow holidaymakers a very brief account of how we'd met again, 'I need some fresh air. Coming, Matthew?'

It was cold outside. Bracing. It was dark too, with a single light bulb strung above us. Helena wrapped her arms around herself and breathed out a plume of air.

'They all think we're mad,' she said.

'Do you care?'

'No, I quite like it. It's funny.'

She pulled me to her and we kissed.

'I'm so glad I agreed to this,' she said, gesturing towards the low mountains in the distance, faintly visible beneath the star-speckled sky.

That first morning, when she'd woken up in my bed after the reunion party, she had stayed huddled beneath the quilt while I made breakfast and coffee. I knocked on the door to see if she was awake and, walking into the room, sunshine flooding through the window and shining on her hair, I knew without doubt that she was the most stunning woman I had ever seen. I also knew that I didn't want to let her get away again.

We ate breakfast and I gave Helena a spare toothbrush and a clean towel. When she came back from getting dressed she took her phone out and scrolled upwards with her thumb, checking her emails. 'Look at this,' she said, turning the screen towards me to show me a photo of snow-capped mountains beneath a glowing green sky.

The heading read: *See the Northern Lights! Experience the Raw Beauty of this Unspoiled Country!*

Helena read the email aloud: '*Discover magical Iceland, starting with two nights in the cosmopolitan capital, Reykjavík, followed by a four-night hiking trip across the south of the country, from the lava field at Eldhraun to the Laugavegur trail, culminating among the glaciers of Thórsmörk. Along the way, you'll enjoy excursions to the Blue Lagoon and the Kerid Crater. Your specially trained tour guide will ensure the trip is exhilarating, educational and refreshing, guaranteed to blow away the cobwebs.'*

'Wow,' I said. 'I've always wanted to go to Iceland.'

'I remember. We used to talk about it all the time. I thought it was because you had a thing for Björk.'

'It wasn't *just* that.'

'I like the part about blowing away the cobwebs,' she said. 'God, I really want to go.'

I normally would've dismissed the notion the instant it popped into my head, but this was already such a strange morning – my college girlfriend was here in my flat! – that I let it linger. And then I said, 'Shall I book it?'

'I'll be sick with envy.'

'I meant for both of us. You've got a passport, right?'

She hesitated for a moment before saying, 'Yes.'

'Then what do you say? Shall we do it?'

She stared at me for a moment, studying me as if she were trying to see if this was a joke, if I was going to laugh and say, *Ha ha, just kidding!*

'I'm not joking,' I said. 'It'll be fun.'

'Are you actually being serious?'

'I am. What do you think? No commitment. No expectations. Just two old friends . . .'

She was nodding to herself. It was strange; like she was giving herself an internal pep talk.

'This is crazy,' she said. 'But yeah. Let's do it.'

And that was how we found ourselves here, ten days later.

We'd slept together the first afternoon in Reykjavík. We'd checked into our room, looked at the bed, then each other, and neither of us had needed to say anything. Afterwards, we'd lain in bed, Helena's head on my shoulder, and she'd said, 'You don't need to be gentle.'

I had lifted my head to look at her.

'I'm not made of china. I need you to forget that I'm a widow. Okay?'

The second time, halfway through, she'd gasped in my ear and said, 'That's better.'

Now, Helena directed her gaze to the sky. 'Dagur thinks we might see the Northern Lights later this week.'

'That would be the cherry on the cake.' I put my arm around her. 'So you're not regretting it? Coming here with me?'

'Not one bit. How about you?'

'Of course not.'

I kissed her again. Here, in this strange, cold landscape, far from my normal life – with a woman who had just come back into my life – I felt happier than I could ever remember.

Chapter 3

Shock froze me to the spot.

It was one of those moments when your stomach flips and you go into denial – *That didn't really just happen* – followed by desperate bargaining: *Dear Universe, rewind time and I will be a good person forever and ever.*

Except the universe isn't listening, so in rushes the acceptance: *It's real. That just happened.*

Your girlfriend just fell off a cliff.

I dashed forward and threw myself on to my hands and knees before the precipice, not yet daring to look over. Helena hadn't cried out as she'd fallen, but above the wind I'd heard rocks crumbling, and a sliding, rumbling noise as the ground gave way beneath her feet. She was dead. She had to be dead.

My stomach was cold, breath coming sharp and ragged. At last I peered over, convinced that there would be nothing. An empty space. Or, God, a broken body, far below.

She was right there.

She was pressed face first against a forty-five-degree stone slope, the top of her head about four feet below the edge of the cliff. The rock was smooth and grey, with nothing for her to grip on to that I could see, so I couldn't understand what was stopping her from sliding further down to what seemed to be the sheer drop that started about two metres below her boots.

'Helena?'

She was breathing heavily, frozen still, her arms by her side. Yet she wasn't sliding down. It was like a magic trick. Was she standing on a tiny ledge? I couldn't see one; as far as I could see, her feet were dangling. It didn't make sense.

She lifted her face towards me. I wasn't surprised to see that all the blood had drained away, leaving her as pale as a vampire. She looked more bewildered than terrified.

'My rucksack,' she said in a trembling voice, little more than a whisper. 'The belt. It's caught on a rock.'

She looked downwards. I couldn't see it because her body was in the way, but I understood what she meant. As she had slid down the rock face on her belly, a jagged rock that was sticking out from the cliff had hooked beneath the waist strap of her rucksack and was holding her in place, preventing her from plummeting to her death. That's why her arms were by her side – she was gripping the strap.

'You need to stay perfectly still,' I said.

'I fucking know that.' She sucked in air. 'Oh God. Matthew . . .'

I lay on my belly and reached down as far as I could, but she was slightly too low. Even if I had been able to get hold of her wrists, the angle and the lack of something to anchor myself to meant I couldn't have pulled her up anyway. I'd have needed superhuman strength. I had no rope in my backpack. No climbing equipment at all. Nothing she could hold on to. I thought about taking off my jacket, lowering it down to her, but what good would that do?

'The strap,' I said, still lying flat on my stomach with my head over the cliff edge. 'Is it going to hold?'

'I don't know.' Her voice was shaky but I could hear her without too much difficulty. The cliff formed a barrier against the wind so it wasn't buffeting Helena and making it difficult to communicate.

She dipped her chin so she could peer down her front towards the waist strap that was preventing her from falling. But this tiny movement made her body jerk and she cried out. I sucked in a breath, certain she was going to fall, that the strap would give way or become unhooked from the rock. Helena made a whimpering sound but she stayed in place.

'It moved,' she said. 'The strap. It gave a little. It's trying to slide through the buckle.'

I couldn't see the strap but I could picture it. Hers was an old-fashioned rucksack that her dad had bought decades ago. I'd teased her about it. But it meant the strap was a hardy, rough fabric and the buckle that was used to tighten it was metal, not plastic.

'Okay,' I said, 'I'm going to get help.'

I got carefully to my feet – my legs felt like they were made of rubber and I had to take several deep breaths before I could stand straight – and looked at Helena's phone, which I was still holding, the camera app open, ready for me to take another souvenir photo. I double-checked that there was no signal here. There wasn't. But the others couldn't be too far away, surely? I prepared to run down the path to find Dagur or anyone else who could help. My mouth was dry, heart thumping in my ears. I couldn't even imagine how Helena must be feeling right now. Was her life flashing before her eyes? Did she have faith she was going to be rescued? Or was she down there currently making peace with her God?

'Matthew!'

I had just started to run back towards the path. I stopped at the sound of her voice.

'I'll be back with help,' I yelled, turning my head towards the cliff and away from the wind.

'No. Please don't leave me. Matthew!'

I hesitated. I needed to find someone.

'Matthew, don't go. I'm begging you. I don't want to die alone.'

I stopped, agonising over what to do.

'Please,' she repeated. In the wind, her voice was like a whisper.

Reluctantly, I went back, got down on my hands and knees again and crawled to the lip of the cliff, peering down at her.

'The strap's unfastening,' she said, looking up at me. 'I can feel it sliding through the buckle. It's happening slowly . . . but I can't stop it. I can't grip it hard enough.'

'You have to try. Let me go and get Dagur. He's probably got a rope.'

'I can't, Matthew.' There were tears in her eyes now. 'I can't hold it much longer.'

I looked down at the cliff face, trying to see something she could grab on to, but it was hopeless. I had to go and get help and pray the strap would hold long enough. I would regret it forever if I didn't try.

But as I started to get to my feet, she let out a groan and said, 'Oh . . . God, I deserve this. This is my punishment.'

'What?' I had no idea what she was talking about.

'He's going to be there, waiting for me. In Hell.' She looked upwards. Tears streaked her face.

'What are you talking about?'

She repeated what she'd said before: 'I deserve this.'

I was speechless. What did she mean? What did she believe she needed to be punished for? And who did she think was going to be waiting for her in Hell? Was she talking about Lee?

She took a breath and looked up at the sky, still holding on to the waist strap, and I guessed she was saying a silent prayer. I didn't know what to do. Stay here with her, or risk letting her die alone by running for help?

The decision was taken out of my hands.

'Matthew?'

I looked over my shoulder. It was Dagur, jogging towards me across the ridge, the sun behind him, making him glow like an angel.

I called down to Helena. 'Dagur's here. *Don't let go.*'

Chapter 4

Dagur ran to where I was standing, took one look at Helena, shouted at her to stay calm and threw his own backpack to the ground. He opened it and pulled out a long rope. I found out later that it was a confidence rope, something that guides almost always carry with them. As he uncoiled it, moving fast, the rest of the group appeared over the crest of the mountaintop. Sinéad and Laurence, George, Devon and the rest of them, all with stunned, quizzical looks on their faces. Devon came to the front of the group, eyes out on stalks.

'Come here,' Dagur called to the group. 'But take care. Don't go too close to the edge.'

'What's going on?' Sinéad asked.

I pointed to the precipice. My hand was shaking. 'It's Helena.'

They gasped and stared and George said, 'Oh my goodness.'

Devon brushed past me and went up to the very edge of the cliff, staring down at Helena.

Dagur barked at them: 'All of you. Come here. Now.'

He got to his feet and headed straight to the boulder that sat close to the cliff edge. It was a metre tall, and solid. He tied one end of the rope around it, testing it to ensure it would hold firm. Then, as everyone gaped at him, he tied a loop in the other end. I was on my hands and knees again, talking to Helena, urging her to hold on, telling her everything was going to be okay. She was concentrating so hard on gripping the strap and preventing it from coming apart that she didn't react. I could tell it was taking every ounce of strength and determination she had left.

Dagur appeared beside me at the cliff's edge.

'Helena,' he said in a loud voice. 'I'm going to lower this to you. You need to slip it over your upper body so it will pull tight under your armpits. You understand?'

She looked up, eyes wide and afraid. 'I can't let go of the strap.'

From somewhere behind me I heard Devon – who had followed Dagur's instructions and moved away from the precipice – say, in a shocked whisper, 'She's going to die.'

'She's not going to die,' I snapped.

I turned away from Devon to hear Dagur say, 'Helena, reach up with one arm, take the rope, pull it down over your head and arms. You will be okay.'

He didn't wait for her to respond. He quickly lowered the rope and I watched as Helena took one hand away from her waist strap, wincing like she was convinced she would fall and sucking in a shuddering breath as she grabbed the rope. She did as Dagur instructed. It was awkward. Her backpack was in the way. But she managed to get the loop of rope over her head and under one arm before switching hands quickly, seizing the end of the strap and then manoeuvring the rope with her newly freed hand so it pulled tight beneath her underarms. She returned both hands to the strap.

'Okay, good,' Dagur said. 'You don't need to worry about falling. You are attached to a boulder up here. You're going to be okay.'

He gave me a look, as if to say, *How the hell did this happen?*

Then it was straight back to business. 'All of you. Help me. We're going to pull. Like a tug of war, except hold the rope with the palms facing down, like this. Got it?'

We lined up along the rope, with Dagur at the front, closest to the cliff, and Laurence, the heaviest man, at the back, nearest the boulder. I was somewhere in the middle.

Devon stood to the side and Dagur said, 'You too.'

'But I have no upper body strength.'

He looked disgusted. 'It all helps.'

Reluctantly, she took a spot behind me.

'Heave,' Dagur commanded.

I heard a gasp from Helena as the rope went tight. I guessed she weighed about nine stone. Together, with Dagur shouting instructions, we pulled. At first, there was no movement, but with Dagur yelling, 'Pull! Pull!' we slowly, so slowly, dragged her up the slope. Sinéad knelt by the precipice, shouting encouragement to Helena. I don't know how long it took. It felt like hours but it couldn't have been more than a minute or two. Then Helena's head appeared over the lip of the cliff, followed by her hands. She clawed at the solid ground.

'Keep steady,' Dagur instructed, and we held firm as he let go of the rope, grabbed the upper straps of the rucksack that had saved Helena's life and pulled her to safety.

She lay on her side on the ground, everyone gathered around her, Dagur closest. The side of her face was red where she had scraped it on the rock, and her hands were curled in on themselves. She didn't move for a minute as Dagur unstrapped her rucksack and took a silver metallic space blanket out of his own pack and encouraged her to sit up, wrapping the blanket around her. Everyone was chatting, asking her questions, a babble of excitement and relief and shock. A couple of people threw glances at me as if it was my fault. Devon stood close by, pacing like she was the one who was traumatised. *Drama queen*, I thought. One of those people who made everything about them.

Helena's eyes met mine through the crowd. Then she covered her face with her hands and sobbed.

ω

I stood outside on the deck of our hut. I had been so consumed by what had happened during the afternoon that I'd almost forgotten that this was the last day of the trip. We would all be flying home the following morning. Inside, Helena was taking a bath.

We were staying in another group of huts in the valley. They stood in a line, dark wood with green roofs, each of them occupied by a couple or a single person. Mine and Helena's was halfway along the line, with Sinéad and Laurence's hut to our right and Devon's to our left.

Helena had gone straight to our cabin when we returned and we had both avoided dinner. I didn't want to spend an hour being quizzed by everyone else in the group; didn't want to hear the breathless retellings of how 'we' had saved her. As far as I was concerned, the only hero here was Dagur, though when I tried to talk to him about it he insisted he was merely doing his job. He seemed shaken, though. He had almost lost one of his group and I hoped he wasn't going to face disciplinary measures from his employer, though if he did I would tell the powers that be that it hadn't been his fault. We shouldn't have strayed from the path. You didn't need to have watched more than a couple of horror movies to know that.

Dagur had spent much of the time since we'd got back on the phone, presumably filing a report with his boss. He had tried to persuade Helena that she should allow him to take her to the nearest hospital but she refused, insisting she was okay, that apart from some grazes – on her face, hands and knees – she wasn't injured, just shaken.

I kept expecting the media to turn up, tipped off about the accident and rescue by another member of the group. I knew what the reaction would be if this story found its way on to social media. Outrage at the stupidity of tourists. Lots of mentions of Darwinism in action. But on the way back to the hut, Helena had addressed the group, asking everyone to refrain from broadcasting what had happened, at least until they got home. She attempted a joke, saying the fall hadn't killed her 'but an avalanche of social media criticism might'. She was so visibly shaken, so thankful to everyone for saving her, that her plea landed easily.

'What happens in Thórsmörk stays in Thórsmörk,' said George, tapping the side of his nose.

I agreed with him.

Except there was one thing bothering me. Pushing its way to the front of my thoughts.

What Helena had said when she thought she was about to die.

This is my punishment.

From inside the hut, I heard a door click. The gurgle of bathwater draining away.

I went back in.

Chapter 5

Helena was sitting on the bed, wearing a white robe, her hair wrapped in a matching towel. Her skin was flushed pink from the bath.

The room was small and cosy, with an unusual bunk bed: the lower bunk, where we slept, was a double and the top bunk was a single. This morning, when we'd checked in, Helena had joked about how, if we had an argument, I'd be sent to the top bunk.

Getting dressed that morning, she'd played music on her phone: a Lou Reed album.

'You're still into all that?' The music had thrown me back through time and space to her bedroom at college. The smell of patchouli joss sticks. The rush of buses and taxis outside her flat, drowning out the quiet bits on the Velvet Underground albums she always used to listen to. 'Lou Reed and Andy Warhol? That whole scene?'

'Guilty as charged.'

'I remember you making me sit through that film, *Chelsea Girls*. How long was it?'

'Three and a half hours.'

'During which literally nothing happened. I must have really liked you.'

'I guess you must.'

Now, though, after six days in Iceland, I knew one thing for certain: I liked her even more now than I had in the early days of our college relationship. I would happily sit through whatever boring, arty film she asked me to – not that I would be able to concentrate on the screen with her sitting beside me.

Since we'd arrived in Iceland, I'd been trying to figure out what was going on. I usually eased into relationships slowly, warily, then looked up and found that I'd been with someone for six months or a year. More than one girlfriend had shouted at me that one day I would meet someone who would knock me over and rip out my heart, and that they would love to be a fly on the wall, a witness to my misery. I had never thought it would happen. My blood was too cool. But now? When I stood next to Helena I found myself breathing differently. I felt my blood heating up. Was this what it felt like? Was the prediction made by my exes coming true at last? Like I said, I had never believed it would happen. And I certainly didn't think it would happen with someone I'd already met.

'Are you okay?' I asked now, going over to the bed. I touched my own cheek in the spot where hers was grazed. 'How does it feel?'

'It's fine. I had worse as a kid, coming off my bike.'

A faint cloud of steam from Helena's bath hung in the air. Her rucksack was propped up against the wall opposite the bed and her phone sat on the bedside cabinet. The blinds were drawn against the night, but the little window beside the front door was open because the heating in the room was intense.

'I needed that bath,' she said. 'My muscles have finally started to unknot.'

I nodded. I was still standing by the bed, trying to work out how to ask the question that was burning a hole in my brain.

'Maybe you should have gone to the hospital. Get yourself checked out. You might be in shock.'

'I don't like hospitals.'

'I get it. But—'

'Matthew, please. I'm fine.' She gestured to the rucksack. 'Dagur said if it had had a plastic buckle it would almost certainly have snapped when it got hooked on the rock. Did I tell you my dad used it when he went Interrailing around Europe in the seventies? One of the few things of his I still have.'

I knew that both her parents had died young, when she was in the sixth form, before I'd met her. A car accident.

'Can you pass it to me?' she asked.

I picked up the rucksack and handed it to her, then sat on the chair opposite, watching as she pulled out the two chocolate bars she'd mentioned earlier, along with a bottle of Reyka vodka. She set the chocolate aside and unscrewed the bottle cap. Watching her do this made me realise how badly I needed a drink, and I went over to the kitchenette to fetch two tumblers.

Helena poured a double shot into each and raised her glass. 'To being alive.'

I repeated the toast and we clinked glasses. The vodka burned in my chest, the warmth spreading through my veins. It seemed to have a similar effect on Helena. She exhaled through pursed lips. 'That's good stuff.'

'Helena,' I said.

She met my eye.

'I need to ask you—'

'About what I said.'

'Yes.' I was relieved she wasn't going to deny saying it.

She refilled her glass, then mine. She knocked back the second shot. I couldn't blame her. She had almost died today. If ever was a good excuse to get drunk, this was it.

'What exactly did I say?' she asked. 'It's all blurry.'

'You said, "I deserve this. This is my punishment." Then something about how he was going to be there waiting for you in Hell.'

She sat in silence, gazing into her empty glass. She had her legs crossed, and the upper one bounced up and down repeatedly.

'Did you mean Lee?' I asked.

She still hadn't told me how he had died. All I knew was that it had been an accident and that it had happened at the start of the year.

She didn't reply at first. She stared at the carpet, apparently deep in thought.

At last she took a deep breath and finally met my eye.

'I'm going to show you something.'

She shuffled around so her back was to me, then removed the towel from her head. She took hold of the damp hair that had fallen when she took the towel away and pulled it over her shoulder, revealing the nape of her neck. She always wore her hair down so I hadn't seen this patch of skin before, even when we were in bed together.

There was a scar there. Smooth and pink, with a few raised white ripples. It stretched downwards, across the top of her back, fading out just above her shoulder blades. It looked like she'd been burned. Scalded.

'Jesus,' I said.

She let her hair fall back into place and turned to me. 'He did that. Lee.' I could tell she was trying hard to sound calm, but there was a tremor beneath her words.

'He scalded you?'

I could picture him as he'd been when we were students. Handsome. Arrogant. I could see him leaning back in his chair in our shared kitchen in the halls of residence, watching everyone, a little smirk on his lips. It was almost as if he were in the room with us now, in a chair in the corner. That same smirk. The same air of being superior to everyone else.

Helena nodded. 'I was making dinner, waiting for him to get home from work. He always wanted to eat as soon as he got back from the office. He'd text me and tell me when he was leaving so I'd know exactly how long I had to prepare his meal.'

I listened.

'That evening, he texted me when he was only ten minutes from home. I decided I'd just about have time to make pasta. But there was something wrong with the kettle – I'd told him it needed replacing, but he didn't want to pay for a new one – so I had to boil water on the stove. It took ages. Had just come to the boil when he walked in. I was standing chopping vegetables to make the sauce, with my back to him. I didn't turn around. I said something like, "It won't be long," and that's when he did it. Threw the boiling water from the pan at the back of my neck.'

'Oh my God. Helena.'

She was clenching her fists as she spoke, her empty glass beside her on the quilt.

'I tried to run to the shower so I could get cold water on it as soon as possible, but he held on to my wrists so I couldn't get away. I was crying, pleading with him . . .'

'Helena, you don't have to—'

'Let me finish.' She swallowed. 'My clothes had blocked most of the water, which is why the scarring isn't so bad on my back compared to my neck. But I can't describe how much it hurt.'

I could imagine it. I was a clumsy cook and had scalded myself numerous times. The burning pain lasted for days.

'He still made me cook his dinner that night. Wouldn't let me eat anything, not that I was hungry. He said next time it would be my face. It's actually the only thing he did that left a physical scar. The only evidence I have of what he did to me. Everything else' – she tapped the side of her head – 'is in here.'

Lee Davidson. I had always known he was an arsehole. I'd seen it with my own eyes, and it was why I'd been so shocked when Helena told me she had married him, why I hadn't felt sad when she told me he was dead. But this – this was much worse than anything I'd witnessed him do. Anger bubbled up inside me. I pictured Lee's smirking face. Pictured myself hammering at it with my fists.

'Helena, I'm so sorry.'

I moved towards her, but she held up both palms. 'Don't. Not now.'

'Of course. I'm sorry. When did this happen?'

She wrapped the towel around her head again. 'About a year after we got married. Like I said, it was the only thing he did that left a physical mark. I think it scared him, actually, seeing the scar. It was something I would be able to show in court.'

'But it wasn't the only thing he did?'

'No. Far from it.'

I tried to choose my next words carefully.

'What did you mean when you said he would see you in Hell? Obviously I understand why *he* would be there, but you?'

She was staring at the floor again. And suddenly, I knew what she was going to say. Why she felt she deserved to be punished. But I needed to hear the words come from her mouth.

There was a long silence. There were tears in her eyes and I almost told her it didn't matter, that I didn't need to know. But that would have been a lie. I had to know what she'd done.

She refilled her glass and asked me if I wanted more.

'You might need it,' she said.

'Go on then.'

Her hand shook as she poured, but when she looked at me she held her chin high. She looked me straight in the eye.

'I killed him,' she said. 'I killed Lee.'

Chapter 6

JANUARY 2022

Helena watched the beach from the terrace at the side of the house. She had a perfect view from up here. It was a bright, clear winter's morning, and she would be able to see everything. Would know if her desperate plan had worked.

She didn't want to think about what she'd do – what would happen to her – if it didn't.

Right now, Lee would be on the path that led down from their house on the clifftop to the beach. She prayed the effects hadn't started to kick in yet. That he was feeling fine, ready for his morning swim.

There was no one else around. The sun had only just risen and it was freezing, the sea far too cold for any sensible person to swim in, even though she'd watched a large crowd venture into the water just a few weeks ago for their Christmas Day swim. Today, there weren't even any dog walkers around, and there were no boats on the water. The seagulls were as noisy as ever, even though there was no takeaway fish and chips for them to feast on this early in the day, but apart from them it was silent.

As she watched, Lee came into view. He walked quickly and confidently, his towel rolled up beneath his arm. She took a step back, not wanting him to see her watching, but he didn't look up anyway. He reached the beach and strode across the pebbles, stopping to remove his T-shirt and trainers, setting them down along with his towel. He stood for a moment, naked except for his trunks and goggles and the watch he never took off: a Rolex that, he boasted, was waterproof up to a hundred metres. Helena knew, objectively speaking, that Lee had a great body: a muscular chest and arms, strong legs. His dark hair was still thick and lustrous. Other women were always telling her how lucky she was. But all she felt when she looked at him was revulsion and fear.

He jogged into the sea like he was a triathlete at the Olympics. He had his back to her and she couldn't see his face, but she knew from experience he wouldn't wince at the coldness of the water. He acted like it was a pool in the tropics, like the one on their honeymoon – that week in the Maldives when she first began to realise who she'd married.

She watched him as he plunged into the water and swam out using strong overarm strokes. Once he was about fifty metres out, he swam to the east, following the shoreline towards the next jutting cliff. The sea was a chemical-green colour, foamy and opaque, the kind of water that ought to be too cold for anything but seals.

Lee swam confidently, unsuspectingly, and she feared her heart might give out.

Because she would know very soon if it had worked.

ϖ

She had come up with the plan after watching a documentary on TV. Apart from reading, it was the only form of entertainment open to her. She hadn't been allowed to go online since Lee found the messages between her and Julia, the ones they'd exchanged back in October after her miserable forty-second birthday, when the stark realisation that she was getting older and her life was never going to get better had finally given her the courage to act. She had been going to take a train to the Lake District while Lee was at work. Disappear. He didn't even know Julia Joss, an old school friend, existed. An unintended benefit of being persuaded to have a small wedding to which none of her friends had been invited, of being cut off from everyone she had known before she met him, was that Lee didn't know anyone from her past. She would go and he wouldn't be able to find her. She would use a lawyer to divorce him, start a new life. Survive.

I don't know what's happened and I won't ask if you don't want to tell, Julia had written. She had always been a lovely person, a girl who would share her packed lunch with anyone who seemed hungry, who had been so kind after Helena's mum and dad died in that crash. *But you're welcome to stay as long as you like.*

And then, a few days before she was due to go, her phone had beeped when she and Lee were watching TV.

She had flinched, cursing herself. She almost always had her phone on silent when he was around, because messages from other people were likely to send him into a fury. This, he said, was their private time. What was she doing allowing other people to invade their sacred space? It was disrespectful. Showed her contempt for him. Even a spammy text from a junk number could lead to a night of darkness.

So yeah, she always kept her phone on silent.

Except this night, she'd forgotten.

'Who the fuck is that?' he'd asked.

'Just spam,' she'd said, picking up her phone as quickly as possible, seeing – to her horror – that the text was from Julia.

'Show me,' Lee said, snatching the phone from her hand before she could delete the message.

'*Are we still on for Tuesday?*' he read aloud. '*Have you bought your ticket?*'

All the blood had drained from her body.

That night, he'd made her strip to her underwear, then locked her in the walk-in freezer in the basement. She'd pleaded with him not to do it. Sobbed as he'd dragged her down the stairs. Begged as he'd thrown her inside and slammed the door.

Sitting in the freezer in the dark, animal carcasses hanging above her, she had decided this was finally it. This was going to be her 'accident'. She could hear Lee telling the story. Poor, tragic Helena had somehow got herself locked in the freezer while he was away on business. He'd claim that he'd found her body when he got home. She wasn't sure which would happen first: hypothermia or suffocation, but whichever way she went, Lee would get away with it, just as he'd got away with it before. Everyone around here loved him. He was one of the village's favourite sons. The man who'd come back here after a successful spell at college and up in London. Local boy done good.

Such a shame his life was tinged with tragedy. First there had been the fire that had killed his first wife, Lisa, and now wife number two, Helena, had died in a freak accident.

How unfortunate could a guy get?

She wasn't sure how many minutes passed before she slipped into unconsciousness, and later she reflected that dying was just like falling asleep. One moment, the teeming activity of the human brain; the next, oblivion. Except this time she'd woken up from oblivion, in their bed, with Lee beside her.

He hadn't killed her this time. But he was letting her know he could. That it would be easy. She lay there beside his gently snoring body, shaking as hard as she had in the freezer, trying to figure out how she was going to get out of this. The obvious course of action was to go to the police, but Lee had told her as he'd dragged her down the stairs that she could say goodbye to her phone, and she was already not allowed to drive their car. The nearest police station was miles away and, yes, maybe she could walk there while he was at work, but the local cops were all people Lee had grown up with. He made regular donations to police funds. The only evidence she had of his abuse was the scarring on her neck, but wouldn't they ask her why she hadn't reported it back when it happened?

She couldn't risk it. Because she knew what Lee would do to her if the police questioned him then let him go, which is exactly what would happen. They wouldn't arrest him and take him into custody. Perhaps reporting his crimes would make it harder for him to convince the world she'd had an accident, but he would definitely punish her. And she feared the pain more than she feared death.

She had fallen asleep again with all this churning inside her head.

Then she'd woken in the morning with Lee sitting on the bed by her legs, with Drella – their long-haired tabby cat – sitting on his lap. Drella was the closest Helena had to a baby. He was beautiful, affectionate, her only companion. She often wondered if she'd be able to go on if she didn't have him, and it hurt her to see him purring on the lap of the psychopath she was married to. It felt like a betrayal.

'I know what you've been thinking about,' Lee had said, stroking the cat gently. 'But here's what will happen if you go to the police or talk to a lawyer about divorcing me. I will hurt Drella and then I'll kill him.' He rubbed behind the cat's ears. 'After that, I'll do the same to you.'

That had been October. For the next two months, all she could think about was how she was going to escape. She tried to do everything Lee asked, to keep him happy, but it wasn't always enough and, several times, after nights spent in hell, she almost went to the police. But he kept reminding her of his threats, his promises to hurt her and Drella, his assurances that no one would believe her, and she always got cold feet.

Something else happened during this period too. As her fear of Lee intensified, it birthed a new emotion: hatred. Previously, there had always been a part of her that had tried to cling to the love she had once felt for him, but she could no longer do it. He had strangled that love, replaced it with fear and disgust. Now, picturing him in pain gave her great pleasure. She imagined him dying in a car crash on the way home from work, his body broken and bleeding amid the twisted metal, and would feel immense disappointment when he walked through the door. She would stroke Drella, and tell him about all the things she wanted to befall her husband, feeling like some crazed Bond villain.

It wasn't a huge step from fantasies of something happening to Lee to thoughts of causing his death herself.

Ideas about striking first.

Then, on a quiet day shortly before Christmas, working her way through that day's list of chores – Lee pinned it every morning on the noticeboard in the kitchen, and would inspect her work each evening – Helena allowed her mind to drift. How could she do it? She fantasised briefly about slitting his throat in his sleep, but then she would only be swapping one kind of prison for another.

The answer was obvious. She needed to do what he'd done to Lisa, and what she was sure he was planning to eventually do to her: make it look like an accident.

She wondered if there was anything growing in their garden that could be used to poison him, but without access to the internet she couldn't research what deadly nightshade looked like or what to do with it.

Perhaps she could leave something at the top of their wooden staircase for him to trip over. Soap or oil on the top step? But she couldn't see that working. As the day wore on she began to think about starting a fire in the night – which would be poetic justice, after Lisa. He often smoked weed before bed, collapsing into a deep sleep, and Helena wondered how easy it would be to make it look as if a fire had started by accident, until she remembered the smoke alarms Lee had installed in every room. She'd have to tie him to the bed . . . And there was also the risk she would end up killing herself. It was ridiculous. It was hopeless.

By the end of the day, she had come to believe it was impossible. Until she watched the documentary.

ᖧ

She spent a lot of time watching trash, surfing through channels looking for anything that would distract her. That December evening, Lee announced during dinner that he was going straight out afterwards. A networking meeting. She was delighted and relieved. An evening of freedom in front of the TV. She channel-hopped until she landed on a programme called *Spiked: The Date Rape Epidemic*. Helena almost skipped it because the subject was so grim, but quickly found herself drawn in by the testimony of a young woman who was talking about what she'd been through. It was a familiar but awful story. She'd been in a bar with her friends and someone had slipped something into her drink. She'd woken up in an alleyway, unable to remember what had happened.

'Rohypnol,' said the voiceover. 'It tastes of nothing, can easily be put into a drink, and starts to work after around twenty to thirty minutes. The victim feels drowsy and disoriented before losing consciousness.'

Helena leaned forward, rapt.

The show's narrator said that Rohypnol, commonly known as roofies, passed through the body quickly so it was hard to detect in blood unless the victim was tested within twenty-four hours. Combined with the amnesia that was commonly caused by the drug, this made it hard for victims to know if they had been spiked.

'By the time I started to feel drowsy,' said the young woman who was being interviewed, 'it was too late to do anything about it. It came on so quickly.'

The narrator repeated that it generally took between twenty and thirty minutes for the drug to kick in and render the person who had imbibed it unconscious.

Helena did the maths.

Every morning, at first light, Lee went for a swim in the sea. It was something he'd done every day since they'd moved in together, unless he was away for work. It was a ritual. Helena had to set an alarm that went off thirty minutes before sunrise, so she could get up and make the coffee he always drank before he set off. While he was gone, she would cook his breakfast and have it waiting for him when he got back.

It was a three-minute walk from the house down the cliff steps to the beach. Another five minutes for Lee to swim out to sea. He was usually out there for twenty to thirty minutes.

If she could get hold of some Rohypnol and put it in his morning coffee, the timing would be perfect. The dose would have to be large enough to immobilise him. It would have to kick in when he was out of his depth. It wasn't guaranteed – she knew that the speed and effectiveness of drugs could vary according to all sorts of factors, like the weight and tolerance of the drug taker – but in theory . . . there was a very good chance it would work.

By the time the show had ended she had dismissed the idea. It was too likely to go wrong. The dosage, the timing, the risks associated with buying illegal drugs. It was all too much. But lying in bed, she couldn't stop thinking about it. Lee was going to kill her, she was sure of it. And the only time he was vulnerable was when he went for his swim.

When the next morning arrived, she had convinced herself it was worth trying.

Each day Lee allowed her to go out for a thirty-minute walk while he was at work (*Don't want you getting fat, do we?*), and he would call her on the landline to ensure she didn't stay out for longer. The one time she'd been gone for more than thirty minutes – she'd been cornered by a charity mugger she couldn't get away from – he'd punished her by forcing her to stand with her arms out in front of her until her shoulders cramped and tears streamed down her face. So she was always careful not to be out any longer than was permitted.

One of her thirty-minute routes took her through a small park on the other side of the village, past a children's playground that had been shut for months because the equipment was in need of repair. Its gate was padlocked, and tape was strung around the swings and the slide.

Most days she would see a guy in a baseball cap standing by the treeline behind the playground. After seeing a couple of guys approach him surreptitiously, she'd realised he was a drug dealer.

It took three days for her to gather the courage to approach him and ask if he had any Rohypnol, using the term the narrator in the documentary had used: 'roofies'.

The dealer had looked her up and down like he couldn't believe this seemingly prim and proper woman was asking for such a thing, an amused look on his face.

'*You* want roofies?'

She tried to sound confident. 'Yeah. I do.'

'I don't have any on me. I've got weed, Molly, some uppers and downers, ketamine.'

'It has to be Rohypnol,' she said, realising she was whispering. 'It's . . . a Christmas present. To myself. I want to knock myself out, sleep through the whole thing.'

He laughed. 'I don't blame you. All right. Come back tomorrow.'

She was terrified that, for some random, spurious reason, Lee might tell her she wasn't allowed out the next day. Or what if tonight was the night when Lee arranged *her* accident? He'd been in a bad mood recently, spending longer hours at work than usual, having whispered conversations on the phone when he was at home – presumably with his business partner, Henry. But she barely saw him that evening. He was downstairs in his home cinema, watching movies, and for once he didn't make her sit there with him, pretending to enjoy whatever violent film he had on.

The next day was Christmas Eve. Lee had told her he was going for a pub lunch with his business partner Henry, and as she hurried to the park, she was convinced the dealer wouldn't be there. But he didn't let her down. He handed her a little bottle and she took it home, burning hot in her pocket, and hid it in a box of tampons.

She would have done it the next day, except it was Christmas morning and the beach was busy with people who only went swimming once each winter (how Lee despised those people). Lee spent most of Christmas and Boxing Day in the basement, drinking whisky and watching movies in the home cinema. She cooked him dinner with all the trimmings, because that's what he'd made her do every other year, but he hardly touched it, said he had no appetite. Something was up with him – work problems, she guessed.

Weirdly though, a few days after Christmas his mood flipped. He talked to her like she was a human being. He didn't yell at her or insult her or make any sexual moves on her at all. She briefly wondered if he'd had a bump on the head that had transformed his personality. Whatever the reason for his change in behaviour, she found it too hard to conjure up the hatred needed to kill him. The Rohypnol stayed in the tampon box in the bathroom.

And then the old Lee came back.

It was the ninth of January, a Sunday. She'd had a long lie-in, Drella purring beside her on the bed, but she sensed Lee's mood the moment she got up and found him downstairs, bored and restless, prowling the house like a caged bear. This was when he was at his most dangerous. Scared, she went straight to the kitchen and began to fix a late breakfast. He came in and watched her, criticising what she was doing, telling her what a shit cook she was, how she was an ugly, lazy bitch and he was sick of looking at her, then accused her of conning him into marriage.

Before he strutted from the room after this barrage of insults, he looked her up and down and said, 'It would be a blessing for both of us if you had an accident.'

Hands trembling, she went to the bathroom, locked the door and took the little bottle out of the tampon box.

She would do it the next morning.

ထ

She watched the sea. Saw him swim out until he was nothing more than a black speck in the water, moving towards the next cliff along the shoreline.

She went inside. She needed to cook breakfast while she waited – *Act like it's a normal day, Helena* – but she dropped an egg as she took it out of the carton. Yolk splattered across the floor tiles. When she crouched to clean it up she saw a splat of red among the orange. She squeezed her eyes shut and pinched the bridge of her nose, trying not to faint.

She stood and went over to the window, with its panoramic view of the sea.

51

There was no sign of him.

She waited. Five minutes. Then ten. No movement in the water. She forced herself to go over to the stove and fry bacon, crispy, just the way he liked it. Drella sat on the counter opposite and watched her. She realised she was crying, tears dripping into the pan, sizzling and spitting as they hit the oil. Her hands shook as she put everything on to Lee's plate and set it on the breakfast bar.

'He'll never hurt you now,' she said to the cat, lifting him into her arms and pressing her face into his fur.

It had worked.

It had actually worked.

Chapter 7

I watched Helena get up from the bunk bed. At some point during the last hour, the towel had fallen off her head and her hair now stuck out at angles, wild and messy. She walked over to the kitchenette, where she rinsed out her glass and filled it with water from the tap. I could see the scarring on the back of her neck. That, and the story she had just told – her truth, her confession – made my heart hurt.

'Before I did it,' she said, turning and coming back towards me, 'I was worried they'd find him quickly and do the autopsy immediately.'

'But that didn't happen?'

I'd hardly spoken during the past hour. All I'd done is listen, occasionally expressing horror as she described her life with Lee. I'd had to fight back the urge to hug her, to attempt to comfort her. I knew she didn't want that. Not while she was talking. It was the first time she'd ever been able to tell her tale. To unburden herself of her secrets, describe the nightmare she'd lived through.

'What *did* happen?'

'Give me a moment.' She was hoarse from speaking so much. Twice during the retelling her voice had broken and the tears had come. I'd tried to tell her to stop, that I didn't need to hear it all, but she'd shaken her head and said she needed to get to the end.

She drank the rest of the water and looked up at the ceiling, blinking like she was fighting back fresh tears. She remained standing.

'I waited half an hour, then I went down to the beach. I needed it to look like I was concerned. I didn't know if anyone was watching – someone else looking out of their window, perhaps – so I ran up to his clothes, ran down to the tideline, called his name, then ran back to the house and used the landline to call 999. It didn't take long for the police to come. They called the coastguard, too.'

She cleared her throat. 'I don't know how, but word soon got out. Maybe someone saw the coastguard's boats. People started gathering on the beach – dozens of them. I sat in my living room with a policewoman and told her about Lee's daily swim, how I'd started worrying when he didn't come back. I had to act like I was hopeful. Panicked and fretful, which was easy, but also upset. I was half convinced he was still alive, that he would come walking out of the sea like the fucking Man from Atlantis, asking what all the fuss was about.

'The police kept asking if I had someone who could come and sit with me, and I let out this wail. "Lee's all I have!" It was true. Apart from my cat, he *was* all I had.'

'Not anymore.'

She looked at me. It was impossible to read her expression.

'So . . . what happened next?' I asked again. 'I take it they didn't find the body straight away?'

'No. Apparently the cold water made it sink to the seabed and stay there. His body didn't turn up for three weeks.'

'Oh my God.'

She sat back down on the bunk bed. 'He was eventually swept up on a beach a little way along the coast. A dog walker found him.'

Three weeks in the water. I guessed he would have been in a terrible state after that. Not that I felt sorry for him.

'Did you have to identify him?'

A shake of the head. 'No. They said they wouldn't put me through that. They just showed me photographs of his watch and the trunks he was wearing. The watch was engraved with his initials. They still needed to make sure, though, so they sent someone round to collect his toothbrush so they could check the DNA matched.'

'And . . . how did you feel? When it was confirmed he was dead?'

She looked me square in the eye. 'I was glad. I'd spent the past three weeks convinced he'd survived somehow. That he would come back having figured out what I'd done. But of course I had to pretend to be grief-stricken, had to organise the funeral, deal with all the well-wishers. Thank God he didn't have any family.'

I remembered Lee at university, telling girls he was an orphan, hoping it would get him a sympathy shag. It had often worked.

'I didn't know how I was going to get through the cremation. I think I channelled all the stress of the last few years into this *performance*. Crying. Calling his name. Everyone was staring at me. Women were sobbing. The girls he'd gone to school with, and their mums. There was part of me that wanted to scream at them all, tell them who he really was – a monster, a man who hated women – that they should be glad he was dead. But my tears were real. It's just that they were tears of relief.'

She stared me, as if daring me to judge her, to condemn her.

But all I wanted to do was put my arms around her and hold her, tell her it was okay. How could I blame her for what she'd done? I had seen the scars. It was absolutely clear that she was telling the truth. This wasn't some story she had concocted. Not only were the scars right there, but her voice, her body language, the little details . . . even the world's greatest actor, or the world's biggest liar, couldn't pull off a performance like that.

And I remembered Lee. It didn't surprise me at all to hear what he had been like in private. It didn't jar with the image of him that I carried in my head.

'Wait,' I said. 'You said he did something to his first wife – Lisa? Did he admit that?'

'Not exactly. He dropped major hints, though.'

'Hang on.' I pressed my fingers to my temple. 'You need to explain the timeline to me. When was Lee married before?'

There was a hint of impatience in her voice as she said, 'So, we left uni in 2002. I met him again in 2012.'

'How?'

'What? Oh. I bumped into him in a bar and he recognised me.' She squirmed, like she found it more uncomfortable talking about the start of their relationship than the end.

'And in the meantime, he was married?'

'Yeah. Lisa Hoxton, her name was. Australian, moved to the UK when she was twenty. I think he actually met her in one of those Aussie pubs in central London. The way he told it, it was one of those instant-passion things. They got married within three months. This was when he was living in Tunbridge Wells, before he moved back to Sussex and set up his house renovation business.' She paused. 'One night their house caught fire. Dodgy electric wiring, he said. Lisa didn't get out in time.'

'Jesus.'

'Yeah. When we started dating it made me feel sorry for him. In fact . . .'

'What?'

'The first time I went to bed with him was after he told me about Lisa dying. My God, I was so naive. So stupid.' She shook her head. 'Later, when we'd been married a while, when I knew what he was really like, he told me about the life insurance, how he'd used it to start his business. And when he talked about the *accident* – she did air quotes with her fingers – 'he'd say it just like that.

'And to complete the timeline for you, I married him in 2014. He'd already gone into business by then and was living in Sussex in a rented flat, which was where we were for the first three years we were together. He built our house outside Brighton during this period and we moved into it in 2017.'

Then she puffed out air and said, 'So. What are you going to do?'

'What do you mean?'

'Are you going to go to the police? Report me for murder?'

I leaned over and took hold of her wrists. Her skin was cold. 'Oh my God, of course not. It hadn't even crossed my mind.'

'Really?'

'Helena. What you went through . . .' I stopped, tried again. 'You did what you had to do. I'd have done the same thing.' I stopped again, shook my head. 'Actually, I don't know if I would have. I don't think I'd have had your guts.'

Maybe I should have been horrified by what she'd done. She had taken the law into her own hands. She had murdered a man. Come up with a plan and executed it. But I was only horrified by what she'd been through.

'You don't think I'm evil?' she asked. 'A black widow?'

I couldn't help but laugh.

'What? That's what they'll call me if it ever comes out that I killed him. Evil nurses are always called dark angels. Wives who murder their husbands are called black widows. I'll end up on one of those "women who kill" shows.'

I laughed again, but there were tears pricking my eyes now.

'When you told me you'd married Lee I was shocked, but I didn't want to say anything negative about him. You'd just told me you were his widow. I can be straight now, though. I never liked him. No, it was more than that. Don't take this the wrong way, but I was actually quite disappointed in you when I heard you'd married him.'

There was a flash of annoyance in her eyes before she said, 'He made me think he was someone else.'

I moved over to sit beside her and we hugged. She pulled me hard against her, with her face pressed against my shoulder. Her hair was damp on my chin. We sat like that for a long time, her heart thumping against my torso, my brain racing, reacting to what she'd told me, pulling up images: Helena locked in a freezer; Helena hurrying home to ensure he wouldn't punish her. I saw Lee running into the sea. Saw him slipping beneath the waves, paralysed and unable to save himself. Had he known he was dying? Had he realised Helena had done it? I had so many other questions I wanted to ask her, but I was going to force myself to wait. I had questions for myself too – like, was there something wrong with me? Was it wrong that when I pictured a man drowning I felt glad?

'What was that?' Helena said suddenly, pulling away from me.

'Huh?'

'I heard a noise. Outside.'

I hadn't heard anything – I'd been too deep in thought – but I followed her as she crossed quickly to the hut door and yanked it open. There was no one there. But there was something happening outside.

'Oh!' Helena exclaimed, and she stepped through the door. What was going on? I followed her out on to the deck and saw what had made her gasp.

The Northern Lights.

Shafts of vivid green filled the sky, the stars fading into the background as ribbons of yellow joined the green and danced in a shifting myriad of patterns. I felt my mouth drop open and stole a glance at Helena, who appeared stunned, as if this was a hallucination. To our left, a group of our fellow hikers had come outside to watch. George waved at me and gestured to the sky, and Laurence saw us and jogged over.

'Incredible, huh?' he said.

'Did you knock on my door?' Helena asked.

'Me? Oh, sorry, I should have, shouldn't I? You might have missed this and that would have been a tragedy.'

He stood with us and our attention returned to the sky. I guessed the noise Helena had heard was someone coming out of their hut and shutting the door. The whole hiking group was out here now, enraptured. Sinéad had come over to stand beside Laurence. Devon was here too. She looked over at us and I waved, which made her turn her head sharply. Such an odd young woman. Maybe she still blamed me for Helena's accident.

The lights pulsed and shimmered above the silhouettes of the mountains. It was hard to believe it was real, a phenomenon easily explained by science rather than a show put on by God. It was enough to make anyone believe in the divine.

It had been the most insane twelve hours. The view from the top of the mountain. Helena's fall and rescue. The revelation that had followed. And now this.

An unforgettable, crazy day, following an intense two weeks. Standing there beside Helena, I didn't think that, as long as I lived, I would ever have another one like it.

Chapter 8

I lay awake half the night, beside Helena, unable to sleep. I couldn't stop going over everything she'd told me. I listened to her breathing and wondered if she was haunted by nightmares. Dreams of what she'd done or what she'd been through. How could she not be? When I finally fell asleep I had my own bad dream: Lee, skin half rotted away, crawling through the surf with seaweed clinging to the remnants of his flesh. His mouth opened and closed noiselessly and something had eaten his eyes. Then I awoke to find Helena had wrapped herself around me, an arm flung across my chest, and as I pulled her even closer she made little noises in her sleep, eyelids flickering in the half-light.

I studied her face. There was no denying it: I was falling in love with her.

Did she feel the same about me? For her to tell me what had happened with Lee – well, that must mean she trusted me. That she felt close enough to me to share her darkest secret. Right now, that was enough.

I kissed her head and she stirred but didn't wake. Her naked skin was hot against mine; the palm of her hand was on my chest, above my heart. We would be going home right after breakfast, but I wanted to stay like this forever. Entangled. Close.

I was lying to myself when I'd thought I was falling in love with her.

I had already fallen.

Even though she's a killer? whispered a little voice in my head.

Perhaps there should have been a part of me, at the very least, that was repelled. To take a life – it was something I could hardly even imagine. And it hadn't been a faceless stranger; it was someone I knew, or had known.

My answer was: he'd asked for it. Helena had been convinced he was going to kill her. She'd been acting in self-defence.

Couldn't she have gone to the police? asked the voice.

Maybe . . . It was certainly what she *should* have done, but she had addressed this, hadn't she? Lee had taken her phone away from her and she had no access to a car. The closest police station was miles away.

Surely she could have overcome those logistical issues?

Perhaps she could have. But it wasn't as if they would have immediately thrown him into a cell, even if they'd taken her report seriously. He would still have been able to hurt her. And he had threatened to kill her cat.

Lee had brutalised her for years. Controlled her life. Cut her off from everyone else. To Helena, he'd been a monster with terrible powers. If he'd told her going to the police or a lawyer would be a big mistake, she would have believed him.

She'd been trapped. Scared. Desperate.

He had driven her to it and there was no question in my mind: the bastard had had it coming.

I pulled her closer and she stirred again, opening her eyes for a moment and smiling at me. She was so beautiful. And there, with her in my arms, I made a silent vow that I would do all I could to make her happy. To protect her.

And I would never spill her secret.

I got back to my flat in Crystal Palace just after two that afternoon. Helena had headed back to Saltdean. We had kissed goodbye at the train station, and watching her go I'd felt a shot of something very like panic to be parting from her. Was this lovesickness? Whatever it was, I felt turned inside out in a way that was at once awful and wonderful. On the train home I caught my reflection in the window. I was grinning. I must have looked crazy.

As I got off the train, I realised I'd left my phone in airline mode. Connecting to the network, it emitted a series of beeps as numerous texts arrived. One was from my boss at MerchBox. More importantly, Helena had messaged me.

You don't have my journal, do you?

I replied immediately: *No!? Why, have you lost it?*

A flurry of messages followed. She was sure she had put it in her shoulder bag that morning, which had been with her ever since: in the minibus that had taken us back to the airport, and on the plane. Everything else was in there except the journal.

It doesn't have any . . . secrets in it, does it?

No. Nothing about that thing anyway! But it's annoying.

I'll check my suitcase as soon as I get home xx

She replied with a couple of kisses. Back at my flat, I opened my bag and tipped out the contents. No journal. I texted Helena to tell her, then remembered I'd had a message from my boss, asking me to call her.

MerchBox had enjoyed a great couple of years. Business had boomed during the pandemic: not just because high street shops were shut but because so many people had rediscovered their love of shows like *Star Trek* and *Buffy* when they'd run out of new Netflix shows to binge. I was one of two in-house designers, responsible for both the look and feel of the site but also creating illustrations based around the brands we sold. We were about to launch a new line based around Hammer horror movies and classic sci-fi. I assumed that was what Samantha, my boss, wanted to talk to me about.

I sent her a text telling her I was free to talk. Almost immediately she sent me a Zoom link.

Samantha was slightly older than me: a redhead with a smattering of freckles across her nose. She had played a minor character in a British sci-fi show in the early 2000s and had then spent a few years making guest appearances at conventions, which was where she'd got the idea for the website. She still got a lot of fan mail and requests for signed photographs.

'Hey, Matthew,' she said when she popped up in her box. 'How was Iceland? Amazing, I bet?'

She was in her home office. There was a poster from the show she'd been in behind her. We exchanged small talk about my trip for a minute.

'So, are you calling about the new range?' I asked. 'I've got some cool ideas.'

She frowned. 'I'm sorry, Matthew. I'm just going to come out with it.'

Five minutes later, when the call ended, I was stunned. I sat staring at my laptop screen wondering what had just happened. They were 'scaling back'. Order numbers had dropped sharply over the summer. They had decided it would be wiser to cut the core in-house team and outsource most of the work. I would be paid a month's gardening leave, plus a small redundancy payment.

'You can keep your fifteen per cent site discount though,' she'd said.

I'd heard myself say, 'You can shove your discount up your arse.'

Her eyes had widened in shock. That kind of reaction really wasn't like me. Before she could speak, I'd ended the call.

The thrill of telling her to shove her discount lasted a couple of seconds. I was unemployed. I hadn't been jobless since I'd left university. When Angela and I split up, I'd bought her share in the flat. How was I supposed to pay the mortgage? I checked my bank balance. It wasn't a pretty sight. If I was frugal, I could last three months, maybe four. I would have had an extra month if I hadn't just spent so much on the trip to Iceland.

I navigated to an employment website but I couldn't face the thought of a job hunt right now. I shut the laptop and stood up. Suddenly, the walls felt too close together, the sight of my dirty clothes spilling from my rucksack made me sick, and the prospect of spending the rest of the day – and God knows how many days ahead – stuck here on my own was too awful to bear.

It was early afternoon. I messaged a couple of my friends asking if they wanted to meet up for a drink, but they were busy working. That was another thing. Some of my friends had had kids during the last few years and were never available. Some had moved out of London. Others had decided they were more Angela's friends than mine. And I really didn't want to see any of my now-former colleagues for a bitch-fest about Samantha, or fake sympathy from those who'd kept their jobs.

There was only one person I wanted to speak to or see.

I tried to second-guess her reaction to me phoning. Despite everything, it was still early days in our relationship and I didn't want to be too overbearing or smothering. I knew from experience that there was nothing more off-putting to a woman than being clingy or needy.

But I'd just lost my job. I needed to talk to someone. So I FaceTimed her.

She answered almost immediately.

'Long time no see,' she said with a small, quizzical smile. From the background, I could see she was sitting in her kitchen.

I told her what had happened.

'Oh Matthew, that really sucks. What are you going to do?'

'I don't know. Set up an OnlyFans account and charge people for naked photos?'

'Hmm. Well, there *are* a lot of weirdos out there.'

'I knew you'd make me feel better. Hey, who's that behind you?'

'This?' She pointed the camera at the large, fluffy tabby cat that was standing on the counter. 'This is Drella. He's very cross with me for going away.'

'He's gorgeous.'

'Isn't he?'

'Drella. Wasn't that Lou Reed's nickname for Andy Warhol?'

'You remembered! Yes, well, it's what his superstars called him.'

'A mash-up of Dracula and Cinderella, right?'

'So you were listening to me back at uni. Huh. Like I said, he's a bit sulky because I left him with the cat sitter, but it's nothing a few tins of tuna won't fix.' She trailed off and returned the camera to her own face. 'Listen, if you're at a loose end, why don't you come here? You can meet Drella.'

'Really?'

'Well, assuming he agrees.'

'I meant, are you sure you want me to come and visit you? I don't want to come on too strong.'

She rolled her eyes. 'Matthew, I'm not interested in all that game-playing bullshit. Get your bum on a train to Brighton and I'll see you later. Okay?'

'Okay.'

I was grinning again, my newly unemployed status forgotten. Instead of miserable, I felt intoxicated.

Chapter 9

I took the train, and then an Uber from Brighton station to Saltdean, arriving in the late afternoon.

Driving up to the house, I opened my phone to double-check the address. *This* was where she lived? But, of course, it matched the description she'd given when she'd told her story the night before. High on a cliff overlooking the sea, the house was classic Art Deco, painted entirely white on the outside, with large windows and a flat roof. All clean lines and geometric shapes, the windowpanes divided into grids, with stained-glass details on the yellow front door. The front of the building was divided in two by a long, vertical window with a yellow frame to match the door, and a staircase was visible through the glass. The house looked like it had been airlifted here from Miami.

There was a garage to the right of the house and a passageway that, I assumed, led to the back garden. Just beyond the driveway, behind me as I stood facing her front door, were the steps that led down the cliff to the beach below. The beach where Lee had left his clothes before his last swim. Today, late in September, the sky was gunmetal grey, seagulls wheeling in a thin shaft of sunlight, and the sea was a dark, foamy green. It was so easy to imagine a man drowning out there, with or without a bloodstream full of drugs.

'I'm now ashamed that I ever allowed you to come to my flat,' I said as Helena opened the door. 'You didn't tell me you lived in a mansion.'

'It is not a mansion!'

'Okay. But it's the kind of place that gets featured in magazines. It's incredible.'

Helena was dressed head to toe in black, all soft wool and natural fabrics. Standing in the doorway of her house, the breeze from the sea stirring the dark hair that fell to her shoulders, she took my breath away.

'Come inside,' she said.

I paused on the doorstep.

'It really is an amazing house,' I said.

'Lee designed it to match the older houses around here. It's meant to look like it was built in the thirties. There used to be an old wreck of a house on this site but Lee tore it down and started again. The whole thing is high-tech and eco-friendly. You can't see them from here, but there are solar panels on the roof.'

'To go with the car?' There was a Tesla parked on the drive.

'That was Lee's. I was going to sell it, but you know what? I love it.' She dropped her voice. 'And it gives me great pleasure thinking how pissed off Lee would be to see me driving around in his baby.'

She led me into the entrance hall and closed the door, and I put my arms around her, pulling her in for a kiss.

'Easy,' she said with a laugh, pulling away.

'I've missed you.'

Another laugh. 'It's only been a few hours!'

There was a framed photo of Helena and Lee on the wall in the hallway. She saw me notice it.

'It's there for show,' she said. 'I thought people might find it weird, suspicious, if I took down all the photos. Not that I have many visitors.'

I studied the picture. 'He didn't change much – from when I knew him at college, I mean.'

'No. Not externally, anyway.'

'Not on the inside either, by the sounds of it.'

She sighed. 'Perhaps you could have warned me about him.'

'Helena, I had no idea—'

She cut me off. 'It's fine. Come on, I haven't started the tour yet.'

I followed her through a door into a large living room dominated by expensive-looking burnt-orange sofas and a huge TV. It was immaculately clean and tidy, almost like a show home. Then she led me upstairs and showed me the bedrooms. The main bedroom, which had an enormous picture window with the most incredible view of the sea, was the only room that looked lived in: clothes thrown over the back of a chair, make-up and other beauty products on a dressing table, the rucksack that had saved her life spilling its contents across the carpet. At the end of the landing there was a door that led out to the terrace from which Helena had watched Lee head out on that fateful day. The terrace could also be reached from steps that led up from the garden.

Back downstairs she took me into the kitchen. It was all state-of-the-art, with a breakfast bar, granite counters and an American fridge-freezer the size of a Cadillac, but with Art Deco details everywhere, like the patterned green-and-white floor tiles. Drella was curled up in a cardboard box on the floor. He lifted his head to blink at me then went back to sleep.

'I've tried to interest him in all these expensive cat beds, but he prefers that box.'

'Cats,' I said.

'Do you like them? You're not allergic or anything?'

I crouched down and gently stroked the top of Drella's head. 'I love cats. And this is a particularly beautiful one. Look at those ears!'

Drella jumped out of the box and sauntered out of the room.

'Compliments embarrass him. Are you hungry? I didn't have any lunch.'

She rifled through her cupboards and opened the fridge.

'And when she got there the cupboard was bare,' she said. 'Sod it. Let's go out.'

She told me there was a decent pub about a fifteen-minute walk away, in Rottingdean. We took the path that led along the top of the cliff before sloping down towards the promenade.

'That used to be a pub,' she said, nodding at an abandoned white building that stood on its own a short distance away. 'The Smuggler's Arms. Sadly it closed down years ago.'

We went down some steps and walked along the undercliff. There was a fresh breeze, and waves sloshed against the sea wall, the spray leaving puddles on the path. There were a few people around: a man walking a black dog on the beach; joggers; a beleaguered-looking dad trying to coax his young children along.

'Did your journal turn up?' I asked.

'No. I called the travel company in Iceland and the airline. They're both going to have a look, but I bet it fell out of my bag on the plane and the cleaner put it in the bin. Luckily there's nothing really important in it. Just impressions of Iceland. Thoughts.' She cringed. 'God, I'd hate anyone to read it.'

'Anything about me in there?'

'Maybe.'

'About how gorgeous and funny I am?'

'Something like that.'

I went to take Helena's hand and she looked around nervously.

'You're worried someone will see us and think badly of you?'

'I don't know if I'm being stupid. It's just a small place. They all knew Lee. I don't want tongues to start wagging about my new boyfriend. *Ooh, it didn't take her long.*'

'I get it. It's been, what, eight months?'

'Yeah. I should still be in mourning. I really can't afford . . .' She didn't need to complete the sentence. 'If anyone asks, we're old friends. Okay?'

We walked on in silence for a minute. Not holding hands.

'I still can't get over your house,' I said, refusing to let an uncomfortable silence grow between us.

'It is a lovely house. But I'm going to put it on the market soon.'

'Really?'

'Can you blame me? It doesn't exactly hold happy memories for me.'

Chastened, I said, 'Of course.'

'I wanted to put it up for sale straight away, but there's been all this legal red tape with Lee's will which has only just been resolved and, to be honest, I didn't have the energy. Would it shock you if I said I sank into a period of depression after he died?'

'Not at all.'

'I spent the first two months barely able to get out of bed. I only just managed to feed and wash myself. Dealing with anything legal or administrative, like transferring the energy supply into my name, was enough to send me back to bed for a whole day.'

'PTSD,' I said.

She nodded. 'That's what the doctor said. Why she advised me to see a counsellor. Of course, they think it's grief – they told me to see a bereavement counsellor – not a reaction to everything I went through mixed with a nice, nonsensical portion of guilt.' She looked away, blinking against the breeze. 'I know it sounds stupid, but there actually is grief there. Like I'm grieving the man he pretended to be when we first met. The life I thought I'd have.'

I waited, sensing she had more to say.

'So I hid away for a few months. And I actually did go to see the bereavement counsellor, and it actually did help.'

I nodded.

'And then, well, I decided I needed to get back out there, see people again.' She paused. 'I was a little disingenuous when I told you I only remembered the reunion at the last minute, and that I only went to London to see that exhibition. In reality, as soon as I got Dave's invitation I thought about going. I . . . This is embarrassing.'

'What?'

She pushed her hair out of her face. 'I hoped you'd be there.'

I couldn't help but grin. 'Did you?'

'Please don't laugh at me.'

'I'm not laughing! I'm thrilled.'

'How about you? Were you hoping I'd be there?'

'Yeah, of course.'

It was a little white lie, and I wasn't sure if she believed me.

'Did you ever try to look me up over the years?' she asked.

Now I felt uncomfortable. I could make something up about searching for her on Facebook or – what was the name of that site everyone used to be on? – Friends Reunited. But I didn't want to tell her any more untruths. The thing was, my memory of the end of our relationship was extremely foggy. I knew we'd broken up after going to a gig, that I hadn't exactly covered myself in glory. But the exact details eluded me. To make things more complicated, I didn't want Helena to know that I couldn't remember, especially as I got the impression she could recall every detail.

'I didn't think you'd want to hear from me,' I said. 'Angela always said ex-boyfriends were exes for a reason.'

'Hmm.'

'What?'

'Nothing. Let's just leave it at that.' A smile played at the edge of her lips. 'You seemed pleased to see me, anyway.'

I really wanted to kiss her, but there was a stream of people coming along the path now. Any one of them could be the local gossip.

We walked on. 'So,' I said. 'You don't want tongues wagging about your new boyfriend, huh?'

'What . . . Oh, I said that, didn't I?'

'You did.'

'I guess I'm not sure what else I should call you.'

'Boyfriend sounds good to me. *Secret* boyfriend sounds even better.'

She winced and laughed at the same time. 'Oh God, I feel like a teenager. Seeing each other in secret. It's ridiculous.'

'It is. But it's exciting too, isn't it?'

ω

The pub was on the outskirts of Rottingdean, close to the pebbled beach. In the distance, I could see a hill with a windmill on its crest. There was a substantial beer garden with views of the English Channel and, perhaps because our bodies had become acclimatised to the chill of Iceland so the weather here was comparatively mild, we chose to sit outside. We ordered food and a bottle of red wine, then I went inside to use the bathroom. When I came out, Helena was on her phone.

She turned the screen towards me, showing me the Facebook app.

'I had a friend request from Devon,' she said, passing me her phone. 'She's posted some photos from the trip. We're in a couple of them. I have my eyes half-closed.'

'And I have my mouth half-open. Flattering. Did you accept the friend request?'

'Yeah.'

I handed the phone back to her and checked mine to see if I'd had a friend request from Devon too. Yep, there it was. I hesitated for a moment – I didn't expect to ever see her again – then clicked Accept.

The tables next to ours were empty, so I felt able to talk openly, albeit in a low voice.

'I have to ask: what happened in the aftermath of Lee's death? I assume the police or the coroner looked into why this person who was such a strong swimmer drowned? Did they do toxicology reports?'

She glanced around. 'They wanted to, but because of how long the body had been in the water, they decided it wasn't going to help them much. I wasn't worried, though. I was confident the Rohypnol would have left his body by then.'

'So why did they think he drowned?'

'The report was inconclusive. His body had been in the water too long for the tests to tell them anything useful. A lot of people were talking about rip currents. But then the police started talking about drugs.'

She had hardly touched her food, just pushed it around, the battered cod crumbling to pieces on her plate.

'When they came to the house to talk to me about what might have caused such a strong swimmer to drown, I told them that yes, he was a user, and that I thought he kept his stuff in the safe but that he'd never given me the combination, which was true.

'They sent someone in to bust it open,' she continued. 'There were a couple of wraps of coke in there, some cannabis, some speed too, a couple of bottles of something I didn't recognise. It seemed he was a bigger user of drugs than I'd realised. It was helpful. It painted a picture.'

'What about the dealer?' I asked, speaking low because there were more people around us now. 'They didn't talk to him, did they?'

'No. I was worried about that but I never heard anything about it. I think he worked for the Crowleys.'

'Who are they?'

'The local crime family. I think every town has one. Lee went to school with one of them. Jamie Crowley. If, as I suspect, the dealer was one of his guys, he would have known I was Lee's wife, if not at the time then certainly after his death was in the papers. In fact, Jamie came to the funeral.'

'Really?'

'Yeah. Weird bloke. He smiled and shook his head through the whole thing, like Lee's death was an ironic joke. Anyway, he never said anything to me but they must have known I'd bought the Rohypnol that may or may not have been responsible for his death. Like I said, they couldn't do any worthwhile toxicology reports, so it was just a theory, but I know Jamie Crowley wouldn't have wanted the police asking him difficult questions. I've walked through that park many times since and haven't seen the dealer there once.'

She picked up her cutlery and finally dove into her fish and chips. I watched her eat, thinking about what she'd told me. I wouldn't have admitted this to Helena, or anyone else for that matter, but there was something sexy about it. The way she had outsmarted her husband and the cops. It was impressive as hell. It *thrilled* me.

'This is so good,' she said, jabbing her fork at her food. 'Did I tell you Lee used to count how many calories I consumed? He'd measure out my food. I used to be curvier than this. Of course, once he'd starved me he started moaning that I had no tits and suggested getting me a boob job "for my birthday".'

'If he wasn't already dead . . .'

She raised an eyebrow at me. The meal had come with a thick slice of white buttered bread, and she used it to construct a chip butty, smothered in ketchup. 'Whenever I eat something like this now, or drink alcohol, I see his horrified face in my head and it makes it taste twice as good – even if it has gone a bit cold. I'm going to get dessert too. They do a great— Oh shit.'

'What is it?'

'It's Henry. He's coming over.'

I turned to see a tall man with grey hair, late fifties I guessed, coming towards us, a big smile on his face. He wore a white shirt and a cream blazer, expensive but rumpled. He looked like he ought to be hanging out on the French Riviera, not at the British seaside.

'Don't say anything,' Helena said quietly, putting on a smile as Henry arrived at our table. She stood to greet him. 'Henry!'

'Helena.' He put his hands on the tops of her arms and kissed both her cheeks. I could smell his cologne from where I was sitting. 'So lovely to see you.'

'You too.'

He glanced down at the remains of the food on Helena's plate. 'Mmm, that smells rather good. Making my tummy rumble.' He patted his belly. 'And you look well, Helena. A lot better.'

'I feel better. I mean, I'm getting there.'

'That's *wonderful*. So sorry I haven't been round to see you. It's all been rather manic recently, what with having to run things on my own.'

'No need to apologise.'

He seemed to notice me for the first time. He looked at me, then at Helena, then returned his focus to me. 'Hello.'

'This is Matthew,' Helena said. 'An old friend from college.'

Henry stuck out his hand and I got to my feet to shake it. His grip was just this side of painful. 'Good to meet you.'

'Henry was Lee's business partner,' Helena said.

'The untalented one,' Henry said.

'Too modest. Managing the money side of things required talent.'

'Hmm, maybe.' I could see the compliment pleased him enormously. He turned to me again. 'You're not an architect, by any chance?'

'A web-designer-slash-illustrator.'

'Ah.' Henry smiled at Helena, showing a set of teeth that displayed a history of smoking and tea drinking. 'I'd better be getting on. See that young lady over there?'

He nodded at a curly-haired woman sitting just inside the back door of the pub, wearing a business suit.

'That's Kathy Leed from Channel Homes. You know, the estate agent? She's been hassling me to meet up for ages and I finally gave in.' He winked. 'A free dinner, you know.'

'I might need her services soon,' Helena said, looking over at her.

Henry raised his eyebrows. 'Oh? You're thinking of selling?'

Helena hung her head a little. 'There are a lot of ghosts in that house.'

'Of course, of course. Well, let me get you her card. Better yet, I could ask her to call you? I have your number.'

'Um . . .'

'Yes, I'll do that,' said Henry. He seemed strangely energised by the thought of Helena selling the house. He leaned forward to kiss her cheeks again and shook my hand for the second time. 'Great to meet you, Matthew.'

He strolled away and I watched him take his place at his table, opposite the estate agent. Helena and I resumed our conversation. But every time I looked up, I noticed something: Henry, looking in our direction. More specifically, in Helena's direction. The first time he saw me notice, he smiled and raised his glass. The second time, he acted like he'd been caught peeping. But it still didn't stop him. He couldn't keep his eyes off her.

Chapter 10

After dinner, Helena took me for a walk into Rottingdean. It was a lovely place, full of old houses and narrow streets, lots of BMWs and Audis around. Helena told me how Rudyard Kipling had been a resident here and showed me the house where he'd lived.

'He seems like an interesting character,' I said as we walked back towards Helena's house along the cliff road.

'Who, Kipling?'

I laughed. 'No, Henry. Do you get along with him?'

'He's always been very civil to me, but I don't know him particularly well.'

'He fancies you.'

She made a spluttering noise. 'Don't be daft.'

'He does. I could tell from the way he kept staring at you. Did he come sniffing around after Lee died?'

'Matthew!'

'Sorry. I was just trying to find out if he's likely to challenge me to a duel.'

'You're such an idiot. Also, he thinks we're just old uni friends.'

'Hmm.' I wondered if anyone would believe that was all we were, despite the lack of public displays of affection.

We passed the lido, which had just closed for the evening. Across the street was an underpass that led to what seemed to be the most popular part of the beach. I could see rock pools to the left, where the tide had gone out. It was dark now and the wind had picked up, the air growing chilly.

'Do you own half of the business?' I asked.

'No, I sold it to Henry. My lawyer said I should hang on to it, but I didn't want anything to do with it. To be honest, I let Henry have it for a nominal amount because I just wanted rid of it.'

I didn't like the idea of Helena being ripped off, but didn't blame her for wanting to cut all ties with Lee.

'You wouldn't sell the house for a bargain price though, would you?'

'Why, are you interested?'

I laughed. 'I could just about afford to buy the downstairs bathroom.'

'I don't even know what the house is worth,' Helena said. 'It will be interesting to get it valued.'

'And do you want to stay local?'

'I really haven't thought about it. Maybe I'll move into Brighton. But do you know what I'd really like to do? Use the money to have an adventure. Go on a round-the-world trip. There's so much I want to see and do. I've got a cousin in New Zealand. I've never been to Asia or South America. I'd like to see the Arctic before it all melts.'

'What happened in Iceland hasn't put you off travelling?'

We were climbing the hill that led up to her house, and she stopped beside a bench and looked out to sea.

'You know what? It really hasn't. Do you know why I agreed to go to Iceland with you? I wanted to do something impetuous, push my boundaries. And the moment we got off the plane I knew it was the right decision. Like I was an animal that had been in a zoo for years, and here I was being let back into the wild. That's why I became so obsessed with taking the perfect photo. I wanted something that encapsulated that feeling. Me, at the top of the world, framed by all that raw beauty. The perfect image to represent my freedom, my escape.'

She looked at me. She was out of breath and her eyes were a little wild.

'I can't imagine how you felt, hanging from that cliff,' I said.

She wrapped her arms around herself. 'I thought it was the end. I thought I was going to be robbed of my fresh start.' There was a long pause and then she said, 'I've put a huge amount of trust in you.'

'Helena, I swear I'll never tell anyone.'

'You say that now. But what if I make you angry? What if I hurt you?'

I admit I hadn't thought that far, but said, 'I can't imagine you making me so angry that I'd want to punish you that badly. But if I did, so what? You could just say I was making it up. There's no evidence, is there? It would be my word against yours and, without proof, no court would convict you.'

There was no one around and it was dark, so I felt able to take her hands in mine. 'And you don't need to worry anyway. I'm not going to tell anyone. As far as I'm concerned, you did the right thing. Illegal, but right. I would have to be an absolute arsehole to snitch on you. I promise, Helena: I'm going to take it to my grave.'

She searched my eyes as I spoke. I was sure she would have seen through any insincerity. But I was telling the truth.

'No one is ever going to find out what you did,' I said. 'You're safe. You don't need to be scared.'

'That's a relief,' she said after a while, a little smile creeping across her lips. 'It means I'm not going to have to kill you to protect my secret.'

'I . . .'

She slapped my arm lightly. 'Your face. You look like you think I'd really do it.' She leaned in closer and whispered, 'The black widow strikes again.' I must have looked scared or shocked because she laughed again. 'Don't worry, Matthew. You're a good guy. You have nothing to be afraid of.'

We were almost at the house now. As we approached it, she said, 'Can I ask one more thing?'

'Of course.'

'Can we not talk about Lee? Let's pretend I never told you. Better yet, let's pretend I don't have a secret, or even an ex-husband. Let's just try to have fun, okay? I'd prefer not to relive my brush with death either.'

As soon as we got indoors, she went over to the framed wedding photo and took it down, opening a cupboard and slinging it inside.

'That's better,' she said. Then she leaned in and kissed me. Her skin was cold but her lips were warm. The moment she touched me I felt insanely turned on, and I pulled her against me, kissing her harder. Suddenly I felt frantic, desperate to have her, right here, in this house where she had lived with Lee, this house where she had plotted to kill him. The words she'd spoken in the street – about being a black widow, about being dangerous – had not only scared me, they had excited me. Whatever that might tell me about myself, or what I was becoming, was beside the point just now. I needed my hands on her.

'Come on,' she said, smiling beneath my kiss. 'Let's go upstairs.'

ꙍ

A noise woke me.

It was pitch-black outside. We were in the second bedroom, not the one she had shared with Lee. She'd told me she would rather not sleep with me in there, that she wouldn't be able to relax. That she'd feel like Lee's ghost was watching. That really wasn't something that appealed to me, so I hadn't argued.

There was that noise again.

It sounded like somebody moving around down by the front door. Naked, I crossed to the window and peered out. I couldn't see anything, just the roof of the car. I stood there in the dark bedroom and listened. All I could hear now was Helena breathing and the hum of electricity.

Wide awake, I gathered my clothes and went into the en-suite bathroom, where I had a quick shower and got dressed. When I came out, Helena was sitting up in bed, looking at her phone.

'Are you all right?' she asked.

'Absolutely.' Should I tell her about the noise? I decided it would only unnerve her, and I was sure it had just been the wind or a cat. Strange sounds in an unfamiliar place. My imagination stoked by the knowledge that, out there, within view of this room, the man who'd once lived in this house had died.

'What time is it?' I asked.

'Just gone ten p.m.'

'Shit. My body clock is going to be totally screwed.'

'Welcome to my world. I've been almost nocturnal for the last year. What do you want to do? Go downstairs and watch a movie? There's a home cinema in the basement.'

She had the duvet pulled up over her, naked shoulders exposed, make-up smudged and hair tousled. I wanted to get back into bed with her, to do again what we'd done a couple of hours ago. I moved towards her and Helena smiled and said, 'Easy, tiger. Later.'

'Can I at least kiss you?'

'Oh, go on then.'

I sat on the bed and we kissed. Helena's breathing changed and she pulled me against her, and then there was no going back.

I had never known anything like this. That heat between myself and another person. The desire that obliterated everything else; a fire that fed on itself. Towards the end, when we were both close, I thought I heard another noise outside – the scrape of footsteps – but I didn't stop. I couldn't stop.

Afterwards, Helena laughed and said, 'So much for just a kiss. Now, give me some privacy to make myself decent and I'll see you downstairs.'

ω

When she'd given me the house tour earlier, she hadn't taken me into the basement, so I wasn't one hundred per cent sure how to get to it. From the ground floor, I went along a short hallway that led towards the back of the house. Sure enough, there was a door halfway along, on the left, that opened to reveal a set of steps leading down. I went down and found another door at the bottom. It was locked but the key was there in the keyhole. I turned it and went through.

For the second time that day, I had a 'wow' moment. The basement was almost as big as my flat in London – and, I soon discovered, was divided into several distinct spaces or rooms.

The first space I found myself in was a den, with exposed brick walls and floorboards that were covered with a couple of large, colourful rugs. There was another burnt-orange sofa, a massive TV with an Xbox beside it, and a Sonos smart speaker attached to the wall.

There were three more doors leading off from this central den. One of them was made of steel and was, I realised, the door to the walk-in freezer that Lee had locked Helena in. I had a quick look inside and discovered it was mostly empty. I'd never heard of anyone having a walk-in freezer in their home before. I would have to ask Helena about it.

The second door, on the far wall, opened to reveal a large storage room which was stacked high with more boxes, crates full of CDs, old clothes and assorted other junk. Nothing particularly interesting.

I closed the door and moved on to the third. It opened to reveal the home movie theatre.

I think I whispered 'Oh my God' as I went inside. I had fantasised about having a room like this in the dream house I was going to own one day. There were two plush velvet sofas and a row of seats facing a screen that took up a whole wall. The room was carpeted like an old-fashioned cinema and had a black ceiling dotted with stars. At the back of the room there was a projector that was attached to a UHD DVD player.

'Ridiculous, isn't it?'

Helena had come into the room behind me. She was wearing candyfloss-pink silk pyjamas, her hair tied back in a ponytail.

'Completely ridiculous. But also, amazing.'

'Have you chosen a movie?'

She crossed to the rear of the room, where there were shelves full of DVDs and Blu-rays. Hundreds of them, maybe over a thousand, took up the entire back wall.

'He was always talking about getting rid of all these and going digital, but he'd spent so much on his collection he couldn't bear to do it. I was planning to put them all on eBay but it's such a hassle. I might just donate them to a charity shop when I move.'

I scanned the DVDs. He had everything. All the recent blockbusters, including all the Marvel movies, but also a deeper, more interesting selection than I'd expected. I didn't recall Lee being into cinema. He had all of Stanley Kubrick's films, many of them in fancy box sets. There was a vast horror section, including many of the 'video nasties' that had been banned in the early eighties. Helena saw me flicking through them and said, 'I really can't handle horror. I used to love it. I grew up watching *Scream* and Freddy Krueger, but these days . . .'

'I understand.'

On the top shelf, I noticed a row of DVDs that, from their titles, were clearly porn. A glance at the titles told me everything I needed to know: this was hardcore S&M. Bondage videos, probably filmed in the days before the internet had made DVDs like this redundant. Helena saw me looking and shuddered. 'I definitely need to get rid of those. They're vile. All of them.'

She turned away and I flicked through the more mainstream collection, not wanting to think about Lee forcing Helena to watch porn with him – and very probably worse. It turned my stomach and I suddenly wanted to get out of there, go back upstairs.

But Helena said, 'Matthew, I'm fine. Let's just choose something.'

'Okay.'

The films were organised by genre, rather than title or chronology. On the bottom shelf, I discovered a film noir section. *The Postman Always Rings Twice. Double Indemnity.*

'How about this?' I said, pulling out a 1950s movie called *Black Widow*, starring Ginger Rogers.

'Very funny.'

She crouched beside me and traced the spines of the DVDs with a finger. So many classics: *Gilda, Touch of Evil, Strangers on a Train.*

'I love this stuff,' she said. She slid *Double Indemnity* out. 'Lee actually got me to watch this with him. Jesus, I'd forgotten that . . . He actually looked at me a long time and grinned. "You can just forget it," he said. "You're not smart enough to pull it off."'

She pushed the box back into place like it was hot.

'I thought we weren't going to talk about it,' I said.

'I know, I know. Hey, what about this one? I haven't seen this since I was a teenager.'

She held up the box for *Bonnie and Clyde*. Faye Dunaway and Warren Beatty in sepia, leaning against a truck, guns in hand. 'Grab some popcorn – it's in that box over there. And you might want to get a couple of beers out of the mini-fridge in the den.'

I went to fetch the beer. I wasn't sure if I wanted even more alcohol, but the last couple of days had been so surreal, flicking back and forth between agony and ecstasy, that I just went with it. I could give my liver a break tomorrow. When I got back into the cinema room, Helena was on one of the sofas with the film cued up. I joined her, passed her a beer, and settled back as the opening credits rolled.

ᛦ

An hour later, with Helena dozing on my shoulder and Clyde wrestling with a sheriff in a lake, the doorbell rang upstairs.

At first, absorbed by the movie, I thought it was part of the film. A background noise. Then it rang again. I realised there must be a buzzer down in the basement, in the den, because otherwise I wouldn't have heard it.

I nudged Helena.

She murmured something then opened her eyes, lifting her head from my shoulder. 'What is it?'

'There's someone at the door.'

'What?'

The buzzer sounded again.

Helena blinked at me. She looked exhausted. 'What time is it?'

I checked my watch. 'Just gone half eleven. Do you want me to go up and answer it?'

'Wait.' She pulled herself into an upright position, stretched and yawned, then picked up her phone. 'I have a video doorbell. I can see who it is through the app. It's probably a lost pizza delivery guy.'

She thumbed her phone screen and opened the app, touching a button so she could see who the camera was pointing at.

Confusion creased the skin between her eyebrows.

'It's Devon.'

It took me a second. The county? Why was she . . . Oh! 'Devon from Iceland?'

We both said it at the same time: 'What the hell is she doing here?'

'Jinx,' said Helena, and we headed up the stairs to find out.

Chapter 11

What *was* Devon doing here, at this time of night? It made no sense. Following Helena, who was fully awake now, up the stairs and into the short passage that led to the entrance hall and the front door, I remembered the noises outside earlier. I recalled, too, that both Helena and I had accepted friend requests from Devon that evening.

The last time I'd seen her had been at Gatwick Airport, waiting by the baggage carousel. It was hard to believe it was still the same day now – that we'd only returned to the UK that morning. Devon had been on the same flight as Helena and me. We'd chatted briefly while we waited for our bags. She and Helena had talked about transport links to Brighton, and Helena had been worried she'd end up feeling obliged to get the train with her, making awkward conversation. But then Devon's bag had come through and she'd strolled off, saying, 'See you later.'

And now here she was, seeing us later. How did she know where Helena lived? I guessed it wouldn't be too hard to find out. This was a small village. All Devon would need to do was ask around.

Helena opened the door. Standing in the shadows in the dark hallway, and partially obscured by the open door, Devon didn't see me straight away.

The porch light was on, illuminating Devon. She was wearing the black Canada Goose anorak she'd been wearing in Iceland, as well as jeans and white Adidas, her hair tied back. What struck me immediately was how she was thrumming with nervous energy, almost shaking with it. Her expression was deadly serious.

'Devon?' Helena said. 'What are you doing here? Is everything all right?'

'Can I come in?'

Devon still hadn't noticed me.

'What is this about?' Helena asked.

Devon slipped her hand into her pocket and took out something that she held out to Helena. 'I found this in my bag.'

Helena gasped. 'My journal!' She took it. 'I can't believe it. How . . . ?'

'I think it must have happened on the minibus to the airport. Do you remember there was that bit where we went over a bump in the road and we all jerked in our seats? My bag fell over and everything spilled out of it – the novel I was reading and all my paperwork, a magazine – and I guess when I scooped it all up . . . well, your journal must have fallen out of your bag too and I picked up the whole lot.'

This all came out in a breathless rush.

'Did you notice it was missing?' Devon asked.

'Yes . . . You didn't need to come all this way, though, this late at night. You could have just messaged me.'

'I know, but I used to keep a journal too, and I know how anxious it would have made me if it went missing. And don't worry, I didn't look through it.'

Helena flipped through the journal, then said, 'I'm being so rude. Come in.'

'Are you sure? I was just going to get an Uber back.'

'Of course I'm sure.'

Devon smiled to herself as Helena turned and gestured for her to enter, reaching out to switch on the light as she did so. It was a curious smile, the kind that appears when someone gets what they want. Helena, with her back to Devon temporarily, didn't see it – and it slipped the moment Devon saw me.

'Oh. *You're* here.'

'Hi Devon,' I said.

She looked from me to Helena. 'Have you guys moved in together?'

'What? Oh. No, Matthew's just staying over.'

Devon seemed nervous now, and was clearly fighting not to show it, like someone walking into an important job interview. Her eyes darted around, taking in her surroundings, and a gleam of sweat appeared on her upper lip.

'This is a beautiful house,' Devon said. 'Did you say your husband was an architect? I guess you inherited the whole thing when he passed.'

'Well . . . yes.'

There were spots of colour in Devon's cheeks, and it struck me how young she was, her coat swamping her and making her look like a child.

'I didn't get the chance to say it in Iceland,' Devon said, 'but I'm so sorry for your loss.'

Her eyes flicked to me for a microsecond, like she was trying to gauge my reaction.

Helena said, 'Thank you,' sounding confused. She had put the journal on a side table and I saw her look at it. Was there stuff about her marriage to Lee in there? And had Devon been lying when she said she hadn't read any of it? It seemed highly likely.

'Would you like a drink?' Helena asked. 'Wine? Beer? Or a hot drink?'

'Hmm. Wine would be good.'

'White okay? Matthew, do you want to get a bottle out of the fridge?'

'You might need to show me,' I said, wanting to talk to her. I didn't like what was going on. The expression on Devon's face when she'd come in, the questions she was asking – I didn't trust her.

But Helena either wasn't picking up on the hints I was shooting at her or was choosing to ignore them. 'You know where the fridge is. Come on, Devon, let's go into the basement. Matthew and I already have drinks down there.'

The two women went through the door that led downstairs. Devon glanced at me over her shoulder, wide-eyed and innocent as a newborn, and I wondered if I'd read her wrong. It also struck me that Helena wasn't wet behind the ears. I was sure she would be suspicious of Devon too. She didn't need me whispering warnings to her.

Feeling a little more relaxed, I went into the kitchen and took a bottle of Sancerre out of the giant American fridge, then searched the cupboards for glasses. When I joined the women in the basement, Helena was perched on the sofa in the den, while Devon was doing what I'd done earlier, looking around in amazement.

'This is bigger than my flat,' she said.

'That's what I said.' I poured a glass of wine and handed it to her. 'You said you live in Brighton, right? On your own?'

'Oh no, I have a flatmate. Robin. We've lived together since uni.' She drifted over to the bookshelves, which displayed a few architectural models, including one of this house, and a couple of sports trophies. 'Was all of this his? Your husband's?'

'That's right,' Helena said.

'He was talented.' Devon traced the edge of the model house with a finger, then took a sip of the wine, which she then placed on the coffee table near Helena's feet. 'I'm surprised you haven't boxed all this stuff up.'

'That's the plan. Eventually.'

'Does it not upset you?' Devon asked. 'Seeing his stuff everywhere?'

Helena had stopped smiling. 'I don't come down here often. But I think it's quite common. For the bereaved to be unwilling or unable to get rid of their spouse's possessions.'

'Oh yes, we did something about that in my degree.'

'You studied psychology, right?' I asked, recalling something she'd said on the trip.

'That's right. Do you still have all his clothes upstairs in his wardrobe? Wait, I'm guessing you have walk-in closets here. Nothing as common as a wardrobe.'

The temperature in the basement had dropped several degrees.

'Why are you asking all these questions about my husband?' Helena asked.

'Oh. I'm sorry. I didn't mean to upset you.' Devon's voice was flat. She didn't sound sorry. What exactly was going on here?

'You're not upsetting me,' Helena said. 'I just think it's a bit weird, that's all.'

Devon had moved away from the shelves but still hadn't sat down. She stood in the middle of the den. I went over and sat next to Helena, pouring us both a glass of the Sancerre.

'Why don't you take a seat?' Helena said to Devon, nodding at the small armchair beside the sofa. 'You're making me feel tense.'

'Oh, I'm sorry,' Devon said, still not sounding it. But she finally sat down. 'So you two knew each other at college?' she said, pointing a finger at Helena then me. 'In London, was it?'

Had we shared that detail in Iceland? I couldn't remember. But I said, 'That's right. Helena was studying history of art and I was doing art and graphic design.'

'Who's your favourite artist?' Devon said to Helena.

I was beginning to wonder if Devon was on drugs. In Iceland, I had thought she was quite introverted and strange, but she had seemed harmless enough. Maybe she *was* harmless. Maybe she was simply socially awkward. She was like an alien who had been told the best way to communicate with humans was to fire questions at them.

'My favourite artist? Andy Warhol.'

Devon frowned. 'He was the famous-for-fifteen-minutes guy, right?'

I knew how annoying Helena found it that this quote had become the thing most people remembered Warhol for, but she managed to hide it. 'That's him.'

'Do you have any of his paintings?'

Helena laughed. 'I'm not that rich.'

'But you are wealthy, right? I mean, look at this house. If your husband was an architect and built this place, he must have been successful. I'm guessing he was insured too, right?'

Both Helena and I stared at her. 'You know it's not polite to ask questions like that?' I said.

Devon looked puzzled. 'I was just wondering if Helena was downplaying her wealth. It's nothing to be ashamed of. I wish I was rich. As it is, I live in a shitty house in Moulsecoomb with damp patches all over the walls. You've got a Tesla outside. I can't even afford a crappy second-hand car.'

'What job do you do?' I asked.

'I've just graduated,' she said. 'I'm still figuring that out. I was thinking of becoming an influencer.'

I laughed. 'Maybe you should get a proper job while you wait for the influencer thing to take off.'

'That's what Robin says.'

'Does she?'

'He. Robin is a guy.'

'Oh. Sorry. Your flatmate but . . . not your boyfriend?'

'God, no.' She screwed up her nose.

I checked my phone. It was close to midnight. Devon had only taken two sips of her wine. How long was she planning to stay?

'Robin sounds wise,' I said. 'Saying you should get a day job, I mean.'

'You reckon? I think it's unfair.' She looked straight at Helena. 'Some people don't have to work to get rich.'

Helena stood up. 'What is the matter with you?'

Devon didn't reply. The nervous energy she'd had on the doorstep was back, to the point where she was almost shaking.

'I'm very grateful that you brought my journal back, but since I invited you in you've been nothing but rude. I think it's time you called an Uber and went home.'

Devon didn't move.

'Do you need me to call one for you?' Helena stalked off to the home cinema and came back holding her phone. 'What's your address?'

Devon got to her feet. She took a deep breath, looked straight at Helena and said, 'I know what you did.'

My insides turned to ice. This was it. What I had known was coming from the moment she turned up. I stood – the three of us were on our feet now – and looked at Helena, astounded by how calm she seemed. But when she spoke there was a catch in her voice. The slightest tremble.

'What do you think I did?'

There was another long pause.

'You murdered Lee. You put Rohypnol in his coffee so he would drown when he went for a swim.'

There was a long moment of silence. I felt compelled to break it, forcing out a laugh. 'What the hell are you talking about?'

Devon held herself up straight. Now that she'd spat the words out she seemed more confident. Less like she was going to explode from the tension inside her.

'There's no point denying it,' she said.

My immediate thought was that Helena had written something in her journal, something she had either forgotten or didn't want to admit to, and that Devon had seen it in there.

But Devon said, 'I heard you. Last night, in your hut. I came to tell you about the Northern Lights – I didn't want you to miss it – and I put my ear to the door just in case you were in bed. I overheard you.'

'What, exactly, do you think you heard?' Helena said.

'I just said. You confessed to killing your husband. You talked about going down to the beach where he'd left his clothes. How you'd given him Rohypnol. You're a murderer. It was premeditated, and if you were caught you'd go to jail.'

It sounded very much like she'd rehearsed this speech.

There was another very long silence. Twice I went to speak but stopped myself. I was afraid of making this situation even worse. Of saying the wrong thing.

'I deny it,' Helena said finally, keeping her eyes fixed on Devon's. 'I never said any of that.'

Delivering her speech seemed to have made Devon braver still. 'Is that really the way you want to play it?'

'I honestly don't know what you're talking about. I never said any of that, did I, Matthew?'

She turned her face to me. It was remarkable how innocent she looked. If I hadn't known better, I would have sworn she was telling the truth. I guessed lying was a skill she'd had to learn living with Lee. A self-defence mechanism. It was disconcerting but, again, it was kind of impressive.

'Of course not,' I said. 'It's utter nonsense. I'm trying to figure out if this is meant to be a weird joke.'

Devon tutted, shook her head slightly, then took her phone out of her pocket. She poked at the screen.

Helena's voice came from the phone's speaker.

'*That's what they'll call me if it ever comes out that I killed him. Evil nurses are always called dark angels. Wives who murder their husbands are called black widows. I'll end up on one of those "women who kill" shows . . .*'

It was a surprisingly clear recording, I thought, before remembering the front window of our cabin had been open that evening. It was indisputably Helena's voice. If that clip was played in front of a jury, they would have no doubt who and what they'd heard.

'That's just an excerpt, obviously,' Devon said. 'I have the whole part where you talk about the Rohypnol, calling the police, crying tears of relief.'

Helena had her hand over her mouth, her eyes wide.

'Don't think about taking my phone from me and destroying it,' Devon said. 'I have a backup, ready to give to the police.'

She didn't look nervous anymore. She looked delighted with herself. Smug.

I could hear her breathing. I felt like I was suspended in time. Paralysed by what was happening in front of me.

Helena said, in a slow, measured voice, with a tremor only someone who knew her well would be able to detect, 'What do you want, Devon?'

I answered for her, since Devon had already told us. 'She wants money.'

Devon seemed disappointed she hadn't been able to deliver the line herself.

'And what will happen if I give in to this blackmail?' Helena asked her.

Devon suddenly seemed slightly less sure of herself. Less cocky. Perhaps she had been expecting Helena to break down and beg her not to reveal her secret. 'I'll delete the recording. Destroy the thumb drive in front of you. I'll go away, never tell anyone what I know. I'll forget all about it.'

Helena pressed her fingers against her temples. 'How much, exactly, will buy this silence?'

'I'm not greedy. I'm assuming most of your money is tied up in this house. I want half a million.'

I stared at her. 'Five hundred thousand?'

Devon gave me a filthy look, as if she was furious with me for being here. 'I could ask for a lot more. But like I said, I'm not greedy.'

'Devon, you're right about most of my money being tied up. Do you think I have half a million pounds just lying around?'

'No. But I reckon you could get it without having to sell this place.'

'Even if I could, how exactly would I explain it to the bank? To the Inland Revenue?'

'I've thought of that,' she said. Suddenly it was like we were in a meeting, listening to her pitch. This was a completely different Devon to the one we'd met in Iceland, where she had been so quiet. 'We'll say I pitched you a business idea while we were in Iceland and you agreed to invest. An angel investor, I think they call it.'

'What is this business idea?' I asked, and Devon looked at me like I was stupid.

'Does it really matter? A website or something. Funding for my influencer business.'

Helena and I exchanged a look, agonised on my part, thought-ful on hers, like she was actually considering Devon's proposal.

'Let me get this straight,' Helena said. 'I pay you five hundred thousand pounds, you delete these audio files and smash up the thumb drive, and then you promise never to bother me again?'

'You got it.'

'And you haven't played the recording to anyone else? Told anyone about it?'

'No.'

'You'd really go to the police?' Helena said, a curl of disgust on her lip. 'Even knowing what I went through?'

Devon scoffed. 'What you say you went through.'

'What?'

'Seems to me you wanted this big house and all his money to yourself. You just spun Matthew this bullshit story about Lee being a bastard to you so he wouldn't run a mile.'

Now it was Helena's turn to shake. I could see it coming from deep within her. Anger. Outrage.

'How dare you,' she said, 'come into my home, try to blackmail me, then accuse me of lying about what I went through.'

She took a step towards Devon, and for a second I thought she was going to hit her. I moved towards them as Devon said, 'This is your last chance. Otherwise I'm walking out that door and going straight to the police.'

'Fuck you,' Helena said.

Devon reeled. I could see it on her face. She had convinced herself Helena would cave in to her demands immediately. On top of that, she must have thought Helena would be here on her own. I guessed she must have heard us at the airport, talking about going back to our separate homes. Surely she must have considered back-ing out when she realised there were two of us.

Or maybe she actually felt safer with me here. She knew Helena had killed before. She probably thought my presence would stop Helena from doing anything extreme.

Devon's mouth opened and closed and then she said, 'You really want to go to jail?'

'Go screw yourself.'

'All right. Fine.'

Devon moved towards the door and Helena stepped into her path.

'Get out of my way,' Devon said. She tried to shoulder her way past, and Helena grabbed hold of both of Devon's arms. Devon tried to pull back, but Helena held on. 'Let go of me!'

'Give me your phone,' Helena demanded. She was trying to get her hand into the pockets of Devon's coat, which meant she had to let go of one of Devon's arms. This allowed Devon to break free and dash for the door.

I ran across to block her, and as she saw me, Devon's mouth opened with shock and she swerved, trying to go around me. She was too slow. I reached out to grab hold of her and she jerked to a halt, throwing herself backwards – straight over the coffee table.

She went down, hard, banging the back of her head on the mini-fridge.

She didn't move.

For the second time that night my insides froze. *She's dead*, said the voice in my head that liked to taunt me with worst-case scenarios. Both Helena and I rushed over to her and crouched beside her.

There was a red mark on the side of her head where it had hit the fridge, but she was breathing. Thank God.

Helena reached into Devon's coat pocket and took out a colourful cloth purse, a packet of chewing gum and a set of house keys.

'Check the other one,' she said.

I did as I was told, pulling out a phone, which I passed to Helena, who considered it for a moment, then held it up to Devon's face to unlock it. She passed it to me. 'Do you know how to change the settings so it doesn't keep locking?'

'Yes.'

I went into the settings and changed the auto-lock to 'Never'. At the same time, I disabled the passcode so we wouldn't need to point it at Devon's face if we had to use it again.

'Good.'

She stood and moved towards the door. Noticing that I hadn't moved, she said, 'Come on.'

'What, we're going to leave her down here?'

'What do you suggest we do? I need time to think.'

I hesitated. 'There's no other way out of the basement?'

'No.'

At my feet, Devon stirred, making a groaning sound and moving a palm to the mark on the side of her head.

'She's not going to die,' Helena said. 'She might have a bit of a headache, but that's all. Come on.'

I wasn't sure if Devon might have concussion. But I was too panicked to think straight. The last thing I wanted was her walking out of here and going to the police.

I followed Helena out through the basement door and she locked it behind us. Halfway up the stairs, in a daze, I heard Devon call out, 'Hey.'

Helena ignored her. She ushered me through the top door and locked that too.

I followed her into the kitchen, where she went straight to the sink, filled a glass with water and downed it.

'Helena,' I said.

She turned to me and the glass slipped from her hand into the sink, and the thudding, splintering sound it made as the glass hit the metal and shattered was far louder than it should have been. Without thinking, Helena put her hand into the sink to pick up the shards, then snatched it back, hissing with pain. She lifted her fingers to her face. Blood ran down her arm and beneath the sleeve of her pyjamas.

From beneath us, the banging started. The banging, and the yelling.

And I knew without a shadow of a doubt: nothing was ever going to be the same again.

PART TWO

PART TWO

Chapter 12

Helena sat at the table in the kitchen, the finger she'd sliced open wrapped in a tight bandage. It was three in the morning and Devon had finally ceased banging on the basement door. At least the banging and shouting was evidence that she wasn't too badly hurt, but every muffled thud had connected directly with my frazzled nerves. Helena was the same. Every time Devon thumped or yelled, Helena winced like someone had prodded her. So it had been even more of a relief when Devon had fallen quiet.

What now? I kept thinking. *What are we going to do now?*

I had cleared up the broken glass, speckled with Helena's blood, and was finding it hard to keep still. When I'm agitated, I have to keep moving. Find something to tidy or clean, some dull task that keeps my hands active and my mind occupied.

'Please, Matthew,' Helena said. 'Sit down. I can't think straight with you pacing around like a polar bear.'

'Sorry.'

I sat, though my leg immediately began bouncing restlessly. Why had Devon fallen quiet? Was she exhausted? Had she fallen asleep? Or did she have concussion? She had been knocked out temporarily. Really, she should see a doctor.

Except we had locked her in Helena's basement.

If we let her out now, she would not only tell the police about Helena's confession, she would tell them we had imprisoned her against her will. Helena and me. And I had been the one who had caused her to trip and bang her head, hadn't I?

I wasn't sure if failing to go to the police the moment Helena had told me about killing Lee was a crime, but this certainly was.

'Matthew!' Helena leaned over and put her hand on my knee. 'Stop shaking your leg.'

I forced myself to keep my limbs still.

'Thank you. Now please – *please* – try to stay calm. Okay?'

'Okay.'

She exhaled and went back to looking through Devon's phone. She had already been into the voice memo app, played the recording of her confession aloud, then deleted it.

'Okay,' she said. 'When I deleted the recording, it gave me the option to remove it from the cloud backup too, so obviously I did that. And . . . Matthew, are you listening to me?'

'Huh? Yes, of course.'

'You need to focus. All right?'

'All right. I'm focusing.'

She raised her eyebrows at me, then went on: 'I've looked through her texts and emails and she doesn't seem to have sent anyone the recording from her phone, and she hasn't sent any messages about it. Not that I could find, anyway. She uses WhatsApp a lot.'

'Okay, good. Great. I think we should turn it off now.'

Helena nodded and powered down the phone.

I had watched enough crime dramas to know the police were able to trace the location of mobile phones. Something to do with them bouncing a signal off the nearest transmitter . . .

I caught myself. Why was I thinking this, about the police looking for her? Surely it wasn't going to go that far? Certainly not yet, anyway. 'We need to fix this situation before anyone starts wondering where she is,' I said, barely aware I was speaking aloud.

'I know that.'

'You seem remarkably calm.'

'Do I? Well, I don't bloody feel it.' She curled her injured hand into a fist and immediately uncurled it, wincing.

'Does it hurt?'

'Of course it hurts.'

She got up and went over to fill the kettle. As she took a mug down from the cupboard, she did the same as she'd done with the glass, dropping it. It banged on to the counter but this time it didn't break. It made her step back, though, and press her palm to her chest.

'Please. Sit down,' I said. 'I'll make it.'

I waited for the kettle to boil, glad to have this task to occupy me. I spooned sugar into both our mugs, found the milk in the fridge. When the tea was ready I set the mugs on the table and sat opposite Helena.

She let out a groan of despair. 'Oh God, what have I done?'

I reached across and squeezed her unbandaged hand. 'Not just you. *Us.*'

'You're not the one who has an awful secret to hide.'

'Helena, we're in this together, okay? We're both responsible for her being in the basement. And we're going to work together to get through this.'

She sipped her tea, scowling at the mug. 'Fucking Devon. What kind of person does something like this? Did you see how pleased with herself she was?' I could see her jaw flexing as she clenched her teeth. 'I'd like to have wiped that smug look off her face.'

'I think we did.'

'Ha.'

We were both silent for a minute. Drella slunk into the room but must have felt the stress hanging in the air, as he turned around and walked straight back out.

'This is what I'm thinking,' Helena said, after taking a deep breath. 'The recording is the only evidence. She could go to the police and tell them she overheard me say I drugged my husband, but I will simply deny it. I've got no criminal record. I never told anyone about the domestic abuse I suffered. As far as everyone else is concerned, I had the perfect marriage and no reason to kill my husband. To the police, I'm the epitome of a normal, law-abiding citizen.'

'There isn't anything about it in your journal, is there? Nothing she might have photographed?'

'No. I'm not an idiot.'

I almost told her not to snap at me, to remind her we were on the same side, but I took a deep breath of my own. I understood how tense she was. Us falling out now would be the worst thing that could happen. 'I know you're not. Look, let's focus on getting out of this mess. The taped confession is the only thing that could lead to you getting convicted. So we need to find it, delete it, destroy it. Make sure we delete any copies she made. Then we can let her go and deny anything she says.'

'It sounds so simple.'

'That's because it is. As long as she hasn't made multiple copies and sent them all over the place.'

'Oh God.' She put her face in her hands.

'But I don't think she would. She's arrogant. She obviously came here thinking you would cave straight away. What did she say? She said she would delete the recording and destroy the thumb drive she's backed it up on. *The* thumb drive. Singular. She clearly thought that was the only precaution she needed to take. The best way to do this is to go to her place. Look at her computer and delete any copies she's saved on there, check her history and see if there's any sign that she's uploaded it somewhere or sent it to anyone.'

'Yes. Good. That sounds good.'

Devon's purse, which I had removed from her pocket, lay on the table alongside her house keys. I opened it. There was nothing inside except a debit card and a few coins. We had her keys but didn't know her address.

'It must be on her phone,' Helena said.

We both looked at the mobile that lay beside the empty fruit bowl. It was an old iPhone, a few generations before the current model, with a pink plastic case. The screen had a crack in one corner. I was reluctant to switch it on again because it seemed to me like it would be turning on a beacon that would bring the whole world running to our door.

We didn't have much choice, though. We needed to find Devon's address.

I picked it up and turned it on. It took ages for the Apple logo to appear and for the screen to finally come to life. The wallpaper image on the phone was of Brighton Beach, the pier in the background and a man standing on the tideline with his back to the camera, naked but for a tight pair of Speedos. Someone Devon had taken a fancy to, apparently.

I opened the Contacts app and found Devon's name at the top of the list. There was her phone number, her email and an address. But it wasn't a Brighton address. It was an address in Chester.

I showed Helena.

'I'm guessing that's her parents' address,' I said, aware that a lot of students still used their parents' place as their home address.

'Take a look at her emails. Or she must have some shopping apps. Amazon or ASOS or something.'

And there it was, in an email from Amazon. She'd ordered a backpack shortly before the trip to Iceland. A cheap one.

'Moulsecoomb. Of course, that's where she said she lives.' Helena tapped the address into the Maps app on her own phone. 'Yes. It's on the outskirts, quite close to the university.'

Devon's phone chimed, making me jump, and I dropped it.

'Oh my God. My nerves are shot.'

Helena picked it up and, sitting side by side, we both looked at the screen, the hairline crack that snaked from one corner towards the centre more visible now the phone was lit up with a WhatsApp message.

Hey. Where are you?

'Robin,' Helena said. 'That's her housemate.'

Another message arrived almost immediately.

It's 3am. You're not in your room. I'm worried about you so call me OK?

'What shall we do?'

She didn't respond.

'Helena?'

'Give me a second! I'm trying to think.' She took a deep breath, squeezed my hand. 'Sorry. Just . . . let me concentrate, okay?'

As she said that, there was another WhatsApp. *Message me back as soon as you see this, OK?*

Helena typed like a teenager, using both thumbs. *Hey, stop worrying! I'm good.*

She sent that message and immediately began typing another. 'Robin is typing' appeared on the screen, but only for a couple of seconds. He was clearly waiting to see what Devon said. As was I.

I hooked up with someone. No one you know before you ask. I might hang here for a day or two. Get some sleep!

She hesitated. 'Should I put a kiss? Any emojis?' She scrolled up through Devon's messages to Robin. They were usually plain, unadorned with kisses and smileys. Helena sent the WhatsApp as it was.

A reply came back almost immediately. Robin *was* an emoji user. The reply contained a shocked face, then a thumbs up. Finally, he sent a few words: *Stay safe, OK!*

'Robin's a worrier,' Helena muttered, before firing back a final reply: *Stop worrying. All is good. See you soon!*

She tapped on the little image beside Robin's name at the top of the messages and brought up a larger photo of him. He was a skinny guy with a thatch of messy brown hair and a friendly smile. Like Devon, he was in his early twenties, but his sticking-up hair and sportswear made him look like an overgrown schoolboy. His full name was Robin Barker.

There were no more messages from him.

'That was a risk,' I said. 'Devon described him as her flatmate, but for all we know they could have been sleeping together and you might have sent him into a jealous rage.'

She was distracted, looking through some of Devon's other recent messages.

'When I was checking earlier to see if she'd mentioned me to anyone, I saw something about a party . . . That was it. Shit.'

She was looking at a message from Devon's mum that said: *I've sent the train fare to your bank account, plus a little extra so you can buy your dad a present. See you Saturday xxxx*

'It's her dad's birthday on Saturday,' Helena said. 'She needs to turn up for that.'

'Which means we've got . . .' I'd lost track of the days. We'd come home from Iceland on Tuesday. It was the early hours of Wednesday morning now. 'Three days. That's fine. This will all be sorted long before then.'

Helena got up, took the phone over to the counter and put it on to charge.

'You're leaving it on?'

'I think that's the best idea, don't you? If Robin messages, or Devon's mum, we'll be able to reply and reassure them.'

A look of horror crossed her face.

'What is it?'

'Just . . . What have we done, Matthew? What are we doing?'

I pulled her into an embrace.

'We don't have any choice, do we? She came here threatening to destroy your life. This isn't our doing.'

'But we have a young woman locked up in my basement.'

'Which, right now, is better than you being locked up in prison.'

I held her for a little while and then she yawned – a long, deep yawn that made her eyes water.

'We should try to get some rest,' I said. 'And don't worry. In the morning, we're going to sort all of this out. We'll fix it.'

I watched her head off towards the stairs. While I waited for her to use the bathroom, I went down the hallway to the door that led to the basement and listened. All was silent.

I said it to myself several times, until I almost believed it.

Tomorrow, we'll sort all this out.

Chapter 13

I had intended to sleep only for a few hours, but the next thing I knew it was nine o'clock and someone, somewhere, was banging.

For a blissful moment, I didn't know where I was. Didn't remember what had happened. Then it all came flooding back to me. I was at Helena's. The thudding wasn't someone knocking on the front door – a postman delivering a parcel; a happy reason to get up – but Devon demanding to be let out.

I sprang out of bed and pulled some clothes on. I was tempted to shake Helena awake but she looked so out of it I decided to leave her. Let her remain in the blissful ignorance of sleep for a little longer.

The banging got louder as I went down the steps to the basement. Here, it was like being inside a drum, rattling my insides as Devon thumped thumped *thumped.*

'Stand back,' I called, before unlocking and opening the door carefully because I thought she might rush at me. Of course, I was confident that slight, diminutive Devon wouldn't be able to overpower me, but she might have found something to use as a weapon. Something heavy or sharp. 'Take six steps back from the door, then speak to let me know where you are.'

'Go fuck yourself,' she said.

She certainly had spirit. But I could tell from her voice that she was standing away from the door. I slipped through and immediately locked it behind me, shoving the key deep into my jeans pocket.

Devon stood in the centre of the den, in front of the coffee table that she'd tripped over. She had found a blanket somewhere – in the storage cupboard, presumably – and had it wrapped around her shoulders.

The first thing she said was, 'I need the toilet.'

I cursed Lee. Why hadn't he put a bathroom down here instead of a stupid walk-in freezer?

'I can't let you upstairs.'

'Please, Matthew.' She adopted a wheedling voice. 'I'm desperate.'

I should have foreseen this problem. But what can I say? This wasn't a situation I was accustomed to. There was no manual.

'Wait here,' I said.

I went back out through the door and locked it, up the steps, through the second door that also needed locking, then into the main part of the house, where I ran straight into Helena.

'What's going on?' she asked. She was wearing a white towelling robe. I could hear the kettle boiling·in the kitchen. 'Is everything all right?'

I wanted to snap that of course it wasn't. There was a young woman locked in her basement. But I took a deep breath. Losing my shit was not going to help anyone.

'She needs to pee. Urgently.'

'Oh yes. Of course. Hang on.'

I followed her into the kitchen and waited while she went into the utility room that led off it. She came back with a black bucket. 'She'll have to use this.'

I stared at the bucket. It made what we were doing seem even more horribly real. *You're kidnappers*, said the voice in my head. *Abductors.*

'We're going to make her pee in a bucket?'

'Do you have a better suggestion?'

I didn't. I took the bucket and Helena said, 'She'll need these too.' She gave me a loo roll and some hand wipes.

'I hate this,' I said.

'I know. I do too. But just take it to her before she has an accident.'

'Are you not going to come down too?'

She wrinkled her nose. 'In a little while. Now, go on. Quick.'

I hurried down the steps. The look Devon gave me when I came through the door, locking it behind me immediately, could have melted the plastic bucket, which I set down on the floor.

'Don't complain,' I said, before she could say anything. 'This is the only option for now.'

'Give me some privacy, at least.'

'I'll bring you something to drink. And food. Are you hungry?'

She didn't reply. She had picked up the bucket and was looking around for somewhere out of sight of the door. Watching her made me feel wretched. How had I got myself into this? I fled the basement and ran back up the steps.

Helena was standing by the window in the kitchen, looking out. It was raining, the sky swollen with dark grey clouds.

'Can you remember how she takes her coffee?' I asked.

'I don't think I ever knew.'

I was sure I'd seen her order coffee at a roadside café in Iceland, near the geysers. She had asked if they had soya milk or oat milk. I checked the fridge. It was almost empty.

'I need to go shopping,' Helena said from behind me.

There was a little milk, about to hit its expiry date, a loaf of bread that Helena had taken out of the freezer, some butter. I made toast and put it on a tray along with black coffee, a little jug of milk, some butter and a knife.

'What is this, room service?' Helena asked.

'We can't let her starve.'

'I was kidding. I'm just . . . God, I'm angry with her. Part of me wants her to go hungry and thirsty. Doesn't want to worry about whether she takes cow milk in her coffee.'

'I get it.'

Helena pointed in the vague direction of the basement. 'She put us in this situation. She heard me tell you what Lee put me through, how desperate I was. Yet she still came here demanding money and threatening to go to the police.'

'I know. But we have to be civilised, Helena, while she's here. We can't let her starve. And we're not going to put a knife to her throat and make her tell us where all the copies of the recording are.'

'Yeah. Because even if we did, we don't know if she'd tell the truth.'

'Not just that.'

Helena let out a big sigh. 'I think you should talk to her on your own, because if I see her right now, I might be tempted to get that knife.'

'Helena . . .'

She waved a hand. 'Don't look so worried. You're right. We need to be civilised. We're not the bad guys here. We're not Bonnie and Clyde.'

We looked at each other and I wonder if she felt it too. That there was something appealing about being Bonnie and Clyde. Something exciting. But that excitement quickly drained away when I thought about the reality of our situation. This was not a movie. This was real life.

'I'm going to get dressed,' Helena said. 'Are you going to be all right?'

'Don't worry. I'm not going to let her out.'

ϖ

I took the tray down the stairs and went through the 'stand back' routine again, before stepping through and placing the tray on the floor. The bucket was at the far side of the room. I told Devon to stay by the sofa then got the bucket, keeping it at arm's length, and put it out on the steps before locking the door. I picked up the tray and set it on the coffee table.

'I wasn't sure if you're a vegan,' I said.

'I'm not.'

I had put a glass of water on the tray too. She snatched it up and downed it in one go, then, sitting on the sofa, she buttered the toast and bit into it, devouring the first slice like she hadn't eaten in weeks. After taking a big mouthful of coffee, which she'd added milk to, she looked up at me.

'If you let me out of here, I promise I'll go away and you'll never see or hear from me again.'

'That would be nice, but we both know it's not true, don't we?'

'It is—'

I stopped her. 'I wish I could trust you, Devon. But I know for a fact you'd either go straight to the police or demand Helena pay you a vast sum of money. And then what? Even if she pays you, there's nothing to stop you from just continuing to ask for more, or sending that recording to the police. You could probably do it anonymously.'

She glared at me.

'We're not going to hurt you,' I said. 'We're just going to keep you here, where you can't cause any trouble, until we're sure all the copies of the audio file have been deleted. We've already removed it from your phone and the cloud. Now I need you to tell me where the thumb drive you mentioned is. I'm also going to need to know which computer you used to make the backup.'

'Why should I tell you that?'

'Because once all copies of the recording have been destroyed, we'll let you go.'

She picked up the second slice of toast and nibbled at it.

'All right. Let me out and I'll fetch them. You can watch me destroy them.'

'I'm not an idiot, Devon.'

'You come with me, then.'

'No. You're staying here. Just tell me where the thumb drive is. And what did you use? A laptop? A desktop computer?'

She smiled – there were toast crumbs caught in the corners of her mouth – but she didn't speak.

'Do you not want to get out of here?'

'I want my money. Give me that and I'll tell you exactly where the copies are.' Her smug expression had made an unwelcome return. 'You're both going to prison now, Matthew. You're holding me here against my will. False imprisonment, I think they call it.'

This was so exasperating. I understood now exactly why Helena hadn't wanted to come down here. I had thought Devon would be so keen to get out that she would at least pretend to tell me where the copies were. I had thought I'd have to deal with lies and trickery, not an outright refusal to cooperate.

'I can't believe you think Helena will give you that money,' I said.

'It's owed to me.'

'Owed to you? For what?'

She narrowed her eyes. 'It's the price of my silence.'

I took a step towards her.

118

'I'm not scared of you, Matthew. People are going to come looking for me and they'll find me. You've only just got together with Helena again after a twenty-year gap, haven't you? How are you going to feel when you're sitting in separate jail cells? You want to wait another twenty years before you get to screw her again?'

Keep calm, I told myself.

'Fine,' I said. I turned and walked to the door. It was time to stop letting her dictate the run of the game.

'Where are you going?'

I paused and spoke to her over my shoulder. 'If you're not going to talk, there's no point me staying down here.'

I unlocked the door, went through, locked it behind me again. In my haste to get up the steps I almost kicked the bucket over. Liquid sloshed towards the top and I leaned against the cool wall for a minute, waiting for my pulse to slow.

ω

Upstairs, Helena was sitting at the kitchen table with Drella on her lap, clearly getting some comfort from stroking the cat, who was purring loudly. I was surprised by how quickly Helena had showered and got dressed.

I relayed my conversation with Devon to her. She didn't seem at all surprised.

'She's arrogant,' she said. 'But it doesn't change anything. We still need to go to her house, look for copies of the recording. It wasn't like we could have trusted anything she said anyway.'

She got up, Drella dropping to the floor and shooting out of the room.

'Wait,' I said. 'I think one of us needs to stay here. We can't leave her here on her own. I'll go.'

'Are you sure?'

'Of course.' I snatched up Devon's house keys. I had already memorised her address.

'Have there been any more messages from Robin or anyone else?' I asked as I went out through the front door.

'No. Nothing.'

'That's good, I guess—'

The doorbell rang.

Both Helena and I jumped like a gunshot had gone off.

And almost immediately, Devon started banging on the basement door. *Thud thud thud* from below. Shouting too: 'Hello? Help me! Hello? They're keeping me prisoner!' The words were faint but still distinguishable.

Helena and I rushed to the front window. A woman was standing on the path, gazing up at the house and making notes in a little reporter's notepad. She didn't see us watching and didn't appear to be able to hear Devon, who continued to bang on the door and yell for help.

'Do you know her?' I whispered.

'I think it's the woman Henry was with at the pub.'

'The estate agent?' I struggled to remember her name. Kathy something. Leeds? No, Leed.

'Oh, that arsehole. He must have told her I want to put the house up for sale.'

The doorbell rang again. The banging from downstairs intensified and Devon shouted, 'Help! Help me!'

'Oh, Jesus Christ,' Helena said. 'She's going to hear.'

I had a vision of us having to drag Kathy Leed into the house, wrestle her into the basement and lock her up with Devon. The next person who turned up too, then the next, until we had the whole village down there. It was enough to make me hysterical.

'What the hell are you giggling about?' Helena pointed towards the living room. 'Quick, go and put the TV on, and turn it up loud so it drowns Devon out. I'll get rid of Kathy.'

She strode off towards the front door and I did as she asked, hurrying into the living room, switching on the TV and finding a music channel. It was an oldie: Missy Elliott getting her freak on. I turned it up loud so the bass filled the room. As soon as the music was on, Helena went out through the front door.

I went back into the kitchen and picked up Helena's phone, opening the app that allowed me to watch the world through the doorbell camera. I could hear everything through it too, though I had to turn the volume up to full. Here in the kitchen, Missy Elliott was almost as loud as she was in the living room.

Kathy had taken a few steps back and was looking up at the house, as if she was already appraising it, working out its value. I saw her frown in the direction of the living room, and then the back of Helena's head appeared. Even on the tiny phone screen I could see how hunched and tense her shoulders were.

'Can I help you?' Helena said, her voice coming loud and clear through the app.

Kathy Leed was about thirty-five, with a round, friendly face and curly hair. 'I'm so sorry to intrude,' she said with a smile. 'Henry Magrane passed me a message, saying you wanted me to call you about putting your house on the market? I was driving by on my way to the office and I thought, why not come and see you? Have a chat in person?' She did that thing where she made every sentence sound like a question.

Even above the music, I could still hear Devon banging on the door and shouting for help. Would Kathy be able to hear it outside? She gave no indication that she could. But if Devon increased her volume during a lull in the music, or if Kathy somehow got inside . . .

121

'Are you all right?' Kathy was saying now.

There was a pause before I heard Helena reply. 'I'm fine. I'm just not ready to have this conversation right now.'

'Oh.' Kathy's smile disappeared. 'I'm sorry, I thought . . .' She trailed off, then stole a glance over her shoulder at the sea. 'I was so sorry to hear about Lee.'

'Thank you.'

'He was always such a pleasure to deal with,' Kathy said. 'I'm sure you can imagine we meet a lot of . . . difficult people in my job? Lee was always so civil. So polite. He was one of the good guys?'

'He was,' said Helena.

Spots of rain appeared on the lens of the doorbell camera, and Kathy looked up at the sky.

'Tears from Heaven?' Kathy said, with a sad shake of the head.

How I wished I could see Helena's face.

Kathy tilted her head to one side. 'So tragic. And I totally understand if you're not ready to talk to an estate agent now. It's just that Henry said—'

'Why don't you leave me your number?' Helena said, sounding strained. 'And I'll call you.'

'Of course.'

There was a lull in the conversation as Kathy fished in her bag for a business card. At that exact moment, the Missy Elliott track ended and Devon let out a long yell. Kathy's gaze flickered towards the house. Had she heard? I held my breath. *Surely* she had heard. We *were* going to have to kidnap her too . . . But then, to my immense relief, she smiled and said, 'I'm so sorry to have bothered you. As soon as you're ready, just give me a call. Okay?'

She patted Helena's arm and hurried back down the drive to her car. Helena stood there until Kathy had driven away, then came back inside.

I had turned the TV off. Devon was still banging on the door downstairs.

'Do you think she heard?' I asked, as soon as Helena came in.

'I don't know.'

I gestured to the floorboards. 'Could *you* hear her?'

Helena had her hands in her hair and her eyes were wide, unblinking. She looked like she was about to have a panic attack. 'No. All I could hear was the music. There was traffic noise out there too, from the main road. Seagulls squawking.'

I exhaled. 'Then we should be okay.' I paused. 'Do you still want to sell the house?'

Helena threw the business card Kathy had given her on to the sofa. 'Oh yeah, I can see the listing now. Detached clifftop house. Three bedrooms, two reception rooms. Large basement area complete with home cinema and kidnap victim.'

I went to laugh but saw she wasn't smiling.

'Hey, come on.' I pulled her into a hug. She felt brittle, like she might shatter into a thousand pieces. I said her name and she relaxed a little, but extracted herself.

'I can't bear this. We have to get her out of here. I can't go through this every time someone rings the bell. What if that estate agent comes back, or Henry has spread the word that I want to sell? They'll all be round. Every bloody estate agent in the area.'

Devon had finally fallen quiet. Given up. For now, anyway.

'We're going to fix this,' I said. 'If I can find the copies she made now, we won't need to worry about anyone else coming round.'

Helena nodded, still tense, looking like she might cry. Then she took a deep breath and held herself straight.

'You're right. Let me find you the car key.'

ω

It was more of a fob than a key. I had never driven an electric car before, and Helena had to give me a quick lesson to show me how the Tesla worked. I leaned over to input Devon's postcode into the navigation bar on the enormous screen, but Helena stopped me.

'The car stores everything that's been put into the satnav. We don't want any record that we've been to her flat, do we?'

'Good point.' I felt stupid. I was going to need to raise my game if, God forbid, this went on any longer than a day.

'I have a road map. Hang on.'

She went into the garage and brought out a tatty AA road atlas.

'Wow. Old-school. I haven't used one of these in years.'

'It's not far. About five miles. It might be best to avoid driving into Brighton, so go this way.' She showed me on the map. A longer route, but it avoided going into the city.

She leaned through the open car window and planted a quick kiss on my lips.

'I'll be as quick as I can,' I said.

'But no speeding. You don't want to get stopped by the police. For one thing, you're not insured to drive this car.'

I wondered if this was the slippery slope people always talked about. Break one law and you soon found yourself having to break others.

She paused, then said, 'Matthew . . .'

'What is it?'

'You can walk away from all this, you know? None of this is your problem. You aren't responsible for anyone's death. It's not you who's being blackmailed.'

'I know, but—'

'Let me speak. I feel wretched about getting you involved in all this. Burdening you with my secret was bad enough, but now all this.' She made a sweeping gesture towards the house. 'If you want to go home and forget we ever saw each other again, leave me as someone you'd probably forgotten, a face from the distant past, I'd understand. I wouldn't blame you.'

Was I tempted? There was a gnawing, fizzing sensation in my stomach. My head hurt. I felt sick. But the prospect of leaving her, of making her deal with this on her own, the idea that I might never see her again – that was worse.

I took hold of her hand. The bandage on her finger was damp. 'I told you, we're in this together. I'm not going to leave you to deal with this alone. Besides, I'm implicated too now, aren't I?'

'If I get arrested, I can tell them you had nothing to do with it.'

'No, Helena.'

Her voice cracked a little. 'Are you sure?'

'Yes. One hundred per cent.' I wanted to say it: *I love you*. But even now, with the craziness and the intensity of what was going on, it felt too soon. Too soon for her to hear it, I mean. Not for me to feel it.

Chapter 14

Helena watched Matthew drive away, then went into the kitchen, opening the fridge and gazing forlornly into it. She had never been very good at cooking for herself. After Lee died, it had been a blessed relief not having to prepare meals for him every day. When she remembered to eat, she would get takeaways or have something simple: beans on toast, a tin of soup. Warhol had survived on Campbell's soup for twenty years, and if it was good enough for him . . .

Right now, though, she was starving. And she was going to have to feed Devon, wasn't she, no matter how tempted she was to let her go hungry. Why did Devon deserve to be fed, after what she'd done? Helena found herself clenching her fists again, even the one with the bandage, almost enjoying the pain, and she had to take deep breaths to fight off the waves of fury that threatened to overwhelm her.

A walk would do her good; calm her down. A walk into the village to get some shopping in. Two birds killed with one stone.

It wasn't as if Devon was going to go anywhere, and she didn't think the estate agent would come back. The postman had already been, bringing nothing but junk mail. No one else ever called.

She passed Matthew's jacket, hanging on the end of the bannisters, as she went out. Then she passed the spot where her and Lee's photo had hung until yesterday.

Lee would have been furious if he'd known she was back with Matthew. Livid. It made her smile, thinking how unhappy it would have made him. Matthew, here in the house Lee built. Lee watching them from his place in Hell.

She unlocked the front door. When they'd moved in to this place, one of the first things she'd asked Lee was why this door needed a lock on the inside as well as the outside. He'd said it was for security. She'd soon realised it was so he could lock her in.

Still, it was handy now. It meant she could keep this door locked, with the key in her pocket, in case Devon got out of the basement.

Outside, she slipped the key into her bag and walked down the hill, her head down against the strong wind that blew in from the sea. The sky was almost black and it was freezing. She wrapped her arms around herself and hurried on.

ω

June 2001. A house party somewhere near Hampton Court. One of the guys on her course, Simon, lived out there and had invited everyone for a post-exam blowout.

The house was huge, with a long garden that sloped down to the river. It was a scorching day, the garden full of students, beers chilling in massive buckets of icy water. Some of the girls on Helena's course were stripped down to their underwear, sunbathing on the bank. She had been too shy to join them, and anyway, sunbathing – who wanted skin cancer?

She had only been with Matthew for a month. They'd met one night in the student union. A pound a pint, the DJ playing early-nineties music that filled her with nostalgia. Primal Scream. Suede. The Shamen. Helena had been pretty drunk that night, dancing with the girl whose room was next to hers, and then Matthew had appeared, dancing next to her. They'd made eye contact. Half an hour later they were snogging in the corner.

She liked him. He was cute, into music and art and especially films. He was a good kisser and didn't care about football. When she looked at him she got a strange, fluttery feeling in her tummy.

She'd lost her virginity to him, aged twenty-one, in his room in the house he shared with some other students from his course. It had been nice. Better than she'd been led to expect. And it had continued to improve.

Now, here they were at the party, their second-year exams behind them. Matthew fished a pair of bottles out of a bucket, cracked them open and passed one to her. They joined a large group who were sitting on blankets on the grass, passing a joint around. Nearby, a boom box blasted out Eminem's *Marshall Mathers LP*, an album she had already heard too many times, and a few students were dancing and attempting to rap along.

Next week they would all be going their separate ways for the summer, and Helena didn't know if she would see Matthew until they returned to college. She couldn't afford to stay in London and needed to go home to Rye, to stay with her aunt and uncle. Matthew would be going back to his parents' place in Bromley.

'Right,' said one of the boys in the group. 'I'm dying of heatstroke here. Who fancies a swim?'

They all looked down the slope towards the river. The water sparkled in the afternoon sunshine. Several more students jumped up and began to join the sunbathing girls by peeling down to their underwear.

'Fancy it?' Matthew said, turning to her.

'I don't know.'

'Come on, it'll be fun. It *is* boiling.'

'And the water will be freezing.' What she didn't want to tell him was that she was wearing her period pants. She really didn't want to strip down to her undies. 'You go ahead. Maybe I'll join you in a bit.'

'Come on, Hels,' he said.

'Yeah, come on, Hels.' That was Melissa, a girl from Matthew's course. She was pretty, with red hair and huge boobs which were trying to escape from her bra right now. Of course she had stripped off at the first opportunity. 'Don't be boring.'

Helena forced the smile to remain on her face. 'I'm happy sitting here drinking my beer.'

'Leave her, Matty,' Melissa said. *Matty?* 'If Helena wants to be boring, let her.'

She ran down to the riverbank, boobs bouncing, and jumped in, shrieking and trading splashes with the guys who were already in the water.

Matthew shrugged, then turned and followed Melissa down to the water. Moments later he was in the river too, yelling as the others splashed him.

Helena saw a shadow fall over her, and a moment later Lee sat beside her.

She didn't know him well. He had briefly dated a girl on her course and she'd chatted with him at another party. He was reading architecture and had told her he was from Sussex too: a place called Saltdean that Helena had only vaguely heard of. Matthew had been in the same halls of residence as him in the first year and didn't like him; said he'd thought of himself as a 'player'.

'You didn't want to join them?' Lee said, opening his own beer, wrestling off the cap with his fingers.

'I'd rather stay dry.' She winced. 'That makes me sound as uptight and boring as Melissa thinks I am.'

'Don't worry about her. She's just a . . .'

'Bitch?'

He laughed and said, with a wink, 'Hey, I'm a feminist. I would never use that word.'

In the water, Melissa had jumped on to Matthew's back and he was carrying her around, her breasts pressed against the back of his neck, her chin resting on his head. Melissa was shouting instructions at him and getting him to charge at her friends.

'You sure you don't want to join them?' Lee asked.

'I'm sure.'

They sat in silence, listening to the music. Helena could see Lee trying to think of things to say, rifling through his head for conversational gambits like someone in a record shop flicking through albums; rejecting all of them.

'Helena,' he said, 'we're both from Sussex, right? If you find yourself at a loose end this summer . . .'

He didn't finish the sentence. Matthew was running up the bank towards them, wearing just his boxers and leaving a trail of wet footprints behind him. Water clung to his body and even though she was pissed off with him she got that flutter in her tummy again. He ran right up to them and, when he stopped, water sprayed off his body. Some of it hit Helena but most of it landed on Lee.

'Hey!' Lee sprang to his feet. 'Watch it.'

His fists were clenched.

Matthew put his palms up. 'Chill out. It's just a bit of water.'

Lee looked furious and for a moment Helena was convinced he was going to punch Matthew in the face. But then he saw her staring, obviously horrified, and he got hold of himself.

'Whatever,' he said, and he stalked away.

Matthew sat down, looking over his shoulder at Lee. 'Was he trying it on with you?'

'That's a bit rich.'

'Huh?'

'You and Melissa. You were all over her.'

He looked genuinely shocked. 'No I wasn't! Wait – you think I fancy her?' He shuffled closer to her. 'I promise you, Hels. I have no interest in her whatsoever. She's too obvious.'

'Yeah, obviously hot.'

He took her hand. His fingers were cold. 'No. You are.' He leaned in and she let him kiss her, aware that Lee was watching them. Aware, and liking it.

ω

She was still reminiscing as she went around the little supermarket that Saltdean residents used to stock up on essentials. Shortly after they were married, Lee had brought up that afternoon and told her she had humiliated him.

'What, by kissing my boyfriend instead of this guy I hardly knew?'

'He was an arsehole.'

'He was my first love.'

She hadn't seen the punch coming. This was at the stage before she'd learned not to answer back. She'd just stood there, mouth open in shock, and then Lee had grabbed her wrists and twisted her arms behind her back.

'I'm your first love. Your only love. Me, not that wanker. Say it.'

She'd said it. But over the following years, Matthew's name had come up over and over. Whenever she was crying or cowering because of some awful thing Lee had done to her, he would say, 'Perhaps you should call your first love, Matthew, see if he'll rescue you.'

She was standing in the booze aisle, holding a bottle of vodka. Her basket was already filled with bread, eggs, pasta, fresh fruit and vegetables, and some ready meals.

'Helena!'

Henry's voice almost made her drop the basket.

'Sorry.' His brow creased with concern. 'I didn't mean to startle you.'

She managed to fire up her brain. 'It's okay, I was miles away. In a daydream.'

He smiled. 'A pleasant one, I hope. Far away from here, on a tropical island, something like that?'

'God, wouldn't that be nice?'

They both laughed.

Henry wasn't wearing a suit today. He was in shorts and a polo shirt, wiry grey hair protruding from between the buttons. Helena had thought, at first, that Lee and Henry made strange business partners. Henry was older, posher, privately educated. He'd grown up in the countryside around dogs and horses – he still lived in a house in the woods he'd inherited from his grandparents – and seemed happiest in wellies, carrying a shotgun. He was into boating too. He had a little pleasure cruiser that he would take out regularly in the summer. He used to joke about Lee's daily swim. 'You'd never get me in that bloody water. I'm happy to stay on top of it.'

But she'd soon realised their partnership worked precisely *because* they were so different. Henry's accent and old-school charm opened doors that Lee could never have got through on his own, even as ruthless and forceful as he was. And Lee had taken up some of Henry's favourite hobbies, joining him on grouse shoots and other country pursuits Helena didn't want to know about.

'I think I owe you an apology,' Henry said. 'I didn't realise Kathy would turn up on your doorstep.'

'It's fine.' Helena was keen to get back.

'Have you changed your mind about selling?'

She scrambled for something to say. 'I slept on it and decided to hold fire.'

'Oh? Any reason?'

She wanted to tell him to piss off and stop being so nosy. But he had been so kind to her after Lee's death that she found it impossible to be impolite to him. She could hardly tell him the truth, though. *Oh, I can't have anyone coming into the house right now because there's a young woman locked in the basement.*

'I just . . . feel guilty, I suppose. Lee built that house. He loved it.' It sometimes amazed her how easily she could lie.

Henry made a clucking noise with his tongue. 'He'd want you to be happy, though. I'm sure he would totally understand if you wanted to move. It can't be easy seeing the place where . . .' He trailed off. 'Sorry.'

'Don't apologise. You're right. But it's not just that.' She really wanted to close down this idea that she wanted to sell the house. Or delay it for a while, anyway. 'I was looking round and thinking I ought to make a few improvements and repairs before I put it on the market. I've let a few things slide since Lee died.'

He smiled softly. 'That's understandable. What kind of things?'

'Um, well, one of the showers is playing up and . . .' She groped for something to say. 'It's slightly embarrassing, but Drella went through a phase of peeing on the carpet upstairs and there's a lingering smell I can't get out. So I might have to replace the carpet before the house goes on the market.'

She cringed inwardly at the lie. Her cat was an angel. He had never had an accident in the house.

'I know a good carpet fitter,' said Henry. 'I'll send you his details. Want me to come and have a look at the shower? Which one is it?'

'The, um, one in the en-suite. But please. I really don't want to put you out.'

'It would be my pleasure,' he said. 'I quite enjoy getting my hands dirty once in a while.'

'Honestly, don't worry about it.'

'I'd like to help you—'

'Henry, no!'

His eyes widened a little. Had she shouted? She felt herself go pink.

Henry put his palms up. 'Subject closed.'

And then she saw him spot something over her shoulder. Something unpleasant, from his expression. She turned.

It was Jamie Crowley, browsing the shelves of chocolate bars. He had his back to them but he was wearing the brown leather jacket he had been wearing every time she'd ever seen him. She turned back. Henry's face was almost comical. He looked appalled to see Crowley here, as if the local gangster's presence in the supermarket was deeply offensive.

'Come on,' he said to her. 'Are you ready to pay?'

He ushered her to the checkout. Jamie was still trying to decide between a Boost and a Mars Bar. It was surprising to see him buying chocolate, as he looked like the kind of guy who spent his weekends doing military fitness workouts and drinking protein shakes. She didn't usually go for big beefcake types, especially criminals, but even she sometimes found herself wondering what Jamie looked like with his shirt off.

Helena paid, and when they were outside she said, 'What was all that about?'

'All what? Come on, let me give you a lift.'

He had already unlocked the car and was reaching for the bags. Helplessly, she let him take them and place them in the sports car's tiny boot, then got into the passenger seat.

'How are you finding that Tesla?' he asked as they drove up the hill. 'Miss the sound of a real engine?'

'Not at all.'

He made some more small talk and she gave half-answers, finding the act of having to pretend everything was fine and dandy agonising.

When they were almost back, he said, 'Jamie Crowley . . . Was he looking at me?'

'What? Why would he be looking at you?'

'Oh, no reason. But . . . have you seen him much lately?'

'No, not for ages. Why are you asking?'

She felt a gnawing panic in her belly. Had Jamie Crowley's guy, the drug dealer, said something about her buying Rohypnol? Had it got back to Henry? No. That wouldn't make Henry seem afraid of Crowley, would it? It had to be something else.

'Just . . . If you see him sniffing around, call me, okay?'

'Henry, you're scaring me.'

They reached her house and he pulled on to the drive. Suddenly, he smiled and patted her hand. 'Nothing to concern yourself about.'

He jumped out of the car, leaving her speechless as he fished the shopping out of the boot.

'Want me to come and have a look at that shower? It wouldn't be a problem. Get that and your carpet issues fixed and there's no reason you can't put the house on the market.'

He started towards the house. She had to stop him. She stepped into his path and took the shopping from him.

'Matthew's in there. Asleep.'

Henry frowned. 'Your old uni pal?' He looked towards the house. 'Is he staying here? Oh. I see. He's more than a friend, then? Is it serious?'

Her face had gone hot and, no doubt, bright pink. She started to babble. 'I know it's only eight months since Lee passed, but I've known Matthew a long time and—'

'Helena. You really don't need to explain yourself. I just hope Matthew realises what a lucky man he is.' Another glance at the house. 'I also think it gives you another reason to sell up. If I were Matthew, I'd feel very strange about staying over at another man's house.'

Halfway through his final sentence, Henry's phone pinged. He looked at it, holding the phone at arm's length in the manner of a middle-aged person who was resisting reading glasses.

He went pale.

Before Helena could say another word, he was back in the car, the engine running already. Through the window, he said, 'So sorry, just remembered I've got an appointment. Catch you later!'

He drove away, the engine purring as he sped off up the drive and on to the road. She stood there for a while, wondering what on earth was going on. Was Henry losing his marbles?

She decided to park the worry. She didn't have time for it right now.

She had other things to fret about.

Chapter 15

I left the village slowly, getting used to the feel of the car. It was mid-morning, and although the roads were busy, the ominous sky and strong winds were keeping most pedestrians indoors. The weather and the churning grey sea reminded me of childhood trips to the seaside from our home in south London. Hastings and Margate and Eastbourne. It was always either blazingly hot, with my sister running screaming from the wasps that seemed to believe she was their queen, or – more often – pissing down. I had strong memories of sitting in the back seat of the car, eating chips, with the smell of vinegar and the sound of the windscreen wipers squeaking back and forth.

Both my parents were gone now, and my sister, Lucy, who had been beside me on the back seat, had married a Kiwi and moved to New Zealand. I pushed the memories away. I needed to focus. Reminiscing about the good old days was hardly going to help.

The road took me north through pretty-but-damp country-side, then briefly on to an A-road, past the football stadium and south into Moulsecoomb. Although I'd been to central Brighton many times, I'd never had any need to visit this residential area that, Helena had told me, was popular with students because it was just about within walking distance of the university. It was a hilly, run-down place that, this morning, had the feel of a ghost town.

Devon's house was on a quiet street away from the main road: a semi-detached new-build with windows that needed cleaning. There was no car parked out front, which I took as a good sign. If Robin was home, I was going to have to wait until he went out – and who knew when that would be.

I pulled up, suddenly very aware of how conspicuous Helena's car was. This was not a wealthy area and the cars were mostly six- or seven-year-old hatchbacks, plus the odd white van. I hesitated. It was broad daylight, and although there was no one around, any curtain-twitcher could be watching. If anyone asked I would tell them I was a representative of the landlord. But I also decided it was still safer to park a short distance away. I drove into what proved to be a cul-de-sac, reversing into a parking spot so the car was facing the road, in case I needed to make a quick exit.

I walked up the path to the front door. I could see into the living room from this position. There was no one there. I couldn't hear a TV or any music coming from inside. The chances were Robin was at work but I needed to be sure. I knocked lightly on the door. If he answered I would say I was from a neighbouring street and was looking for my missing cat.

There was no reply. No sounds came from within.

Using Devon's key, I unlocked the front door, and found myself in a hallway where a bicycle was propped against the wall. There was a faint smell of Mexican food, and I poked my head into the kitchen to see piles of washing-up next to the sink, and an Old El Paso taco kit box on the counter. I now knew what Robin had made himself for dinner last night.

My heart was beating fast. I had never gone uninvited into someone's house before. It was yet another first on a growing list of things I'd never had any desire to do.

Devon had told us she was broke and, so far, this place backed up her claim. Though it wasn't terrible. I had lived in a similar place when I first left uni, except it had been in London and therefore nose-bleedingly expensive.

I went into the boxy living room, which contained a small Ikea sofa, a TV and a bookcase. A breeze entered the room through a window that gave me a view of a small back garden, but despite the open window the room still smelled stale. Robin had left his dinner plate from last night on the coffee table, along with a couple of empty beer cans and an ashtray which contained the remains of a spliff. He was a slob. I wondered if he relied on Devon to clear up after him – if he was an overgrown man-baby.

There was no laptop nor any other devices in the living room. No desktop computer. That made sense. They were still living like students. Devon's stuff would be in her bedroom. Now I just needed to find it.

I crept up the stairs. No creaks. All I could hear was the faint whirr of the fridge and that electric hum you get in silent houses. I found myself on a short landing with three doors. One was closed, one stood open to reveal a bathroom and the other was ajar. I tiptoed across the carpet to this last door and pushed it open gently to reveal a bedroom. It was immediately obvious it was Devon's room from the women's clothes that hung from a metal rail, the bra that had been flung over the back of the desk chair, and a couple of perfume bottles on the dressing table.

I looked around. A window gave a view of the rooftops of other houses. There was a desk, a small bookcase that looked like it came from one of those cheap places favoured by landlords, and the aforementioned hanging rail. A single clean glass sat on a bedside table – she had a double bed, neatly made, that took up most of the room. It was far cleaner and tidier in here than it was downstairs. More grown-up. There were several framed black-and-white photos of cities on the walls: Paris, Rome, New York. Her backpack, the one she'd been carrying around Iceland, was on the floor beside the bed.

I opened the desk's top drawer and rifled through assorted stationery, a box of condoms, old keys and bank cards and what looked like a broken Fitbit. I opened the second drawer down. This one contained a tangle of wires. Charger leads. Techie detritus. But nothing that would save Helena and me from our predicament. Finally, the third drawer was stuffed full of old notes from her psychology degree. Printed essays and old timetables.

All that was on the desk was a pile of more paperwork and a sketchpad. I quickly leafed through the paperwork. Bills, bank statements, nothing helpful. I looked inside the sketchpad and found some drawings from Iceland. Mountains. Wild ponies. A crater we had visited, with people gathered around it. I was impressed. She was good. I turned to the next page and found myself looking at a sketch of Helena in her hiking gear. I picked it up for a closer look. It was a skilfully rendered pencil drawing, but there was something wrong with it. It took me a moment to realise she'd made Helena less attractive than she was in reality: her eyes slightly too far apart, her lips a little thinner. Not such a great artist after all.

I put the sketchpad down, reminding myself I needed to get out of here as quickly as possible. What if Robin came home? He might have just popped out to the shops. I had to find the thumb drive and the computer. Perhaps, I thought, the drive was still in the computer. Yes, that would make sense, if she'd made the copy immediately before coming to Helena's.

But where was this bloody computer? There were two chargers plugged in beside the bed: one for her phone and the other clearly for a laptop.

I peered at the bookcase shelves. There were lots of self-help books, most of them with the themes of being brave and following your dreams, and a few novels: *The Hunger Games* and the Harry Potter books. There were a couple of cookery books aimed at students, and a number of psychology textbooks from her recently completed degree. It really made her youth hit home. She was barely more than a kid.

There was no laptop on the bookcase. No sign of an iPad or tablet either. Surely she *had* to own a laptop. I looked beneath the bedclothes and even under the mattress. I searched the whole room. It wasn't here. It made no—

Music came on along the hallway.

I went stiff. Robin was home! He was in that bedroom with the closed door. He was playing that Olivia Rodrigo song 'Good 4 U', and I could hear his voice over the top of it, singing along badly.

His door clicked open, filling the hallway with the music, and I ducked behind Devon's door. I stood ramrod-straight, holding my breath. What if he came in here? My entire body had gone cold, and adrenaline and cortisol raced through my veins. I didn't want to have to attack him. But what if he attacked me? He'd call the police. They'd come to Helena's house, find Devon, arrest us both, throw us into separate jails . . .

He came out of his room, still singing – like a seal barking into a megaphone – and I heard another door slam shut. He'd gone into the bathroom. I waited to see if the shower came on, but no, I couldn't hear anything. I guessed he was just using the toilet.

I had to get out of here.

As quietly as I could, I left Devon's room and jogged down the stairs. I almost tripped, and the thought went through my head that Robin would be completely freaked out if he emerged and found a stranger lying at the bottom of the stairs with a broken neck. What would Helena do if I didn't come back? But I kept my balance – my neck remained unbroken – and I let myself out of the front door and ran along the empty street to the Tesla.

It was only as I drove away that I realised what I'd done. I'd left Devon's house keys on her desk. I hadn't found what I'd come for, and now I wouldn't be able to get back into the house.

Chapter 16

'Well?' Helena said as soon as I came through the door.

I told her what had happened. All but the part about having left the keys behind. I just couldn't say the words.

'Are you sure he didn't see you?'

'Yes.' I went into the kitchen. My heart was still thumping. I opened the fridge door, eyeing the wine and wishing it wasn't too early for a drink. There was a saucepan on the stove and a bowl on the counter.

'I was making her lunch,' she said. 'Pasta.'

'Okay. Good. It will give me a chance to talk to her. Ask her where her laptop is. Do you want to come down with me?'

'Not really.'

I waited for the food to be ready and filled a glass of water for Devon. Helena was quiet, stirring the sauce into the pasta, seemingly deep in thought. Her anger appeared to have burned itself out but I wasn't sure if I preferred the glumness that had taken its place. She seemed flat. Exhausted.

She filled a bowl for Devon and sighed. 'I can come down with you if you want. I mean, I don't trust myself not to shout at her, but I will try.'

I picked up the bowl. 'It's fine. Why don't you try to rest? Helena?'

She had zoned out, staring into the middle distance. I decided it was best to leave her to it.

I found Devon sitting on the sofa in the den, arms wrapped around herself. There was a book open beside her, though I couldn't see what it was from where I was standing.

'Are you all right?' I said as I carried her lunch into the room.

Devon lifted her eyes to meet mine. 'What do *you* think?'

'I brought you lunch.'

'I don't want it. I'm not hungry.'

'Devon, you have to eat.'

Balancing her plate against my hip, I locked the door and started towards the coffee table, but stopped when she sprang to her feet.

'I told you, I don't want it. Don't come near me.'

'I'm not going to—'

Hurt you, I was going to say. But she didn't let me finish. Instead, she stalked off into the home cinema. I set her food on the coffee table and went in after her, finding her standing on the far side of the room, as far from me as she could get.

'I told you not to come near me,' she said.

I put my hands up in a placatory gesture. 'Okay. I'll stay over here.'

She narrowed her eyes, and the look she gave me contained so much loathing that I felt it burn my skin.

'Neither of us is going to hurt you,' I said.

'Did you go to my house? I assume that's where you've been. Did you find my laptop? Going to let me go now?'

'No, Devon. I couldn't find it. Robin was at home and I had to make a quick exit.' I met her eye. She had just confirmed that her computer was a laptop and she hadn't mentioned the thumb drive. Did that mean my suspicions were correct – that the drive was still plugged in to the computer? 'You do want to get out of here, don't you?'

'Duh.'

'Then why don't you just tell me where your laptop is? Then we can let you go. *Only* then.'

She frowned. She looked so like a spoiled little girl who'd just been told she couldn't have the toy she wanted, it was almost funny.

'Come on. Where have you hidden it?'

She didn't reply. She did, though, look a little puzzled, as if she was shocked I hadn't been able to find it. I could almost see the cogs of her brain whirring. Mine were whirring too. If she thought the laptop was in plain sight, did that mean it had been removed? Or had she misremembered where she'd left it?

'I need you to help me, Devon. If you want to get out of here.'

She grunted. She clearly wasn't going to tell me. I was going to have to get back into her house and search.

'Does Robin have a job?' I asked.

More silence.

'Devon, I need you to tell me when he's likely to be out, so I can go in, get the laptop and we can end this whole thing. Then we can forget all about everything that happened here and everyone can move on with their lives. Wouldn't you like that?'

She parroted my words back at me in a mocking voice: '*Wouldn't you like that?*'

I took a deep breath. 'What do you say? Are you going to tell me when Robin will be out and where your laptop is hidden?'

She finally looked me in the eye. 'No.'

I clenched my fists. 'Come on, Devon. None of us wants this situation to go on any longer than it has to.'

'Oh, causing you stress, is it?' She pointed upwards. 'Poor Helena finding it hard to cope?' The edges of her lips lifted into the beginnings of a smile. It seemed she had decided that our inability to find the laptop and thumb drive gave her more power. 'I'm not going to help you, *Matthew*. I want my money. I've actually put it up to seven hundred and fifty thousand now. It's going to go up another hundred thousand for every day you keep me here.'

'Don't be ridiculous.' I was trying to be patient with her. To stay calm. But I was tired and stressed and I couldn't keep the anger out of my voice. 'Do you really think you're in a position to make threats?'

'Do *you*?'

'What?'

'Think *you're* in a position to make threats? All I want is my money. Tell Helena to give it to me and I'll leave and I promise never to contact you again. I won't tell anyone that you kidnapped me. I'll destroy the thumb drive and that will be that.'

I started to say, *You're the one who's locked in a basement*, but managed to bite my tongue. It was like dealing with a child, and although I didn't have kids I knew that one of the golden rules of parenting was *Don't make empty threats*.

'You say you're not going to hurt me,' she said. 'And you're making out that it's because you're nice or whatever. But it's because if anything happens to me, the police will come looking. My DNA is all over this place.'

'And how will they know you came here?'

'My phone, obviously. You must have figured that out, right? At some point someone will report me missing, and the first thing the police will do is check where my phone is.'

Not for the first time in the past twenty-four hours, I cursed that bloody phone.

'You only have one way of getting out of this unscathed,' Devon went on. 'Give me what I'm asking for. Then I promise you can watch me destroy the thumb drive. You and Helena will be free to get on with your lives. Everyone will be happy.'

146

I opened my mouth to respond, then paused. What would I do if it were *my* money? If I was the one with the bigger secret? Would I pay, just to get this over with?

I didn't know.

Devon walked around the perimeter of the room towards where the projector and shelves full of DVDs were. The projector had gone into standby mode last night, so the screen was blank. But Devon touched a button so it sprang back to life, sending its beam across the space, Faye Dunaway and Warren Beatty appearing before us.

'Is this who you think you are?' Devon said with a sneer. 'Bonnie and Clyde? A pair of lovers, breaking the law together?'

Her words made goosebumps ripple across my skin. Because she was uncomfortably close to the truth. Not that I was going to admit it to her. I could barely admit it to myself.

'If you believed that, I think you'd be a lot more scared of us.'

'Huh. Didn't Bonnie and Clyde end up going down in a hail of bullets?'

'Eventually.'

She fiddled with the zoom wheel on the projector, bringing the actors on screen in and out of focus.

'When they find out you've got me here, that you're keeping me prisoner, that's what will happen. Armed police. A shootout. I've seen it on TV.'

'And then you definitely won't get your money.'

'Oh I will. One way or another. I bet the papers will pay a lot for my story. I'll probably get a book deal too. *How I Survived the Black Widow's Lair.*'

She continued to rotate the zoom wheel back and forth, so that Bonnie and Clyde shrunk and grew, shrunk and grew.

'Stop doing that!' I shouted.

Devon snatched her hand away from the projector like it had bitten her, and her eyes went wide. But there was still the trace of a smile, like she was pleased to have pushed me. To have broken through my wall of calm.

I had to get out of there before I said or did something I would regret.

As I unlocked the basement door, Devon came out into the den.

'Don't forget to tell her,' she said. 'Three-quarters of a million.'

ϖ

I found Helena on the sofa, lying there staring at the ceiling. Her eyes were bloodshot, the skin around them smudged grey. She sat up as I came into the room, and pushed her hair out of her face. She was wearing a baggy grey T-shirt featuring Warhol's Marilyn Monroe portrait. She'd had one almost identical when we were students. It struck me how much Helena's life was still tied to that period of her life. She had married a man she'd first encountered at uni, and now she was back with me. She still liked the same things. When this was all over, I would encourage her to sell this place, move on, make a fresh start. Obviously I wasn't going to persuade her to dump me, but it would be good for her to find some new interests, new friends.

But right now, that future seemed a long way away. I recounted everything that had been said in the basement.

'For fuck's sake,' Helena said, sitting up and rubbing her face.

'Where is her phone now?' I asked.

'Still plugged in, in the kitchen. Why?'

I went to fetch it. I wanted to see if there were any more messages from Robin.

There were.

148

I read the messages aloud: *Hey. Did you come home? I thought I heard you but then you weren't there?*

Five minutes later: *Did you get my message? Please reply!*

Then another: *Seriously. I'm getting worried. Call me!*

And finally: *I went into your room to see if you were back and your keys were . . .*

I stopped reading. Shit.

'What was that?' Helena asked.

Shamefaced, I read out the rest of the text: *Your keys were on your desk.*

Helena stared at me. 'You left the keys behind?'

I groaned. 'I thought Robin was about to catch me. It was a highly stressful situation, Helena. I'm worried about what he's going to do. We have to pray he doesn't report her missing.'

'Praying isn't going to help. Give me the phone,' Helena said. I passed her Devon's mobile and she tapped out a message with both thumbs.

Stop worrying! I'm fine. Popped back for a change of clothes, that's all. Planning to spend the next couple of days holed up in bed. I'd give you the deets but it might make you sick.

The reply came immediately: *I wish you'd let me know you were home.*

Helena: *I was in a rush. Didn't want to wake you.*

Robin: *The house feels weird. Like someone's been in here.*

Helena hesitated, then typed: *Yeah, me!*

I just hope you're being safe.

Helena made an exasperated noise. 'God, this guy is in love with her.' She typed out a final reply: *Alright Dad! Stop worrying about me. I'll see you later this week. Xx*

'I thought she didn't put kisses on her texts,' I said, as Helena laid the phone down.

'I think it's fine. Hopefully that will keep—'

We both heard it at the same time. A car, coming up the drive.

'We need to stop whoever it is from ringing the doorbell,' I said, jumping up. I really didn't want a repeat of what had happened when the estate agent had come round, with Devon shouting and banging. I ran to the front window. 'It's someone in a Porsche.'

Helena was already heading to the front door. 'It's Henry.'

'Lee's partner?'

'He must have driven home then straight back here again. What the hell does he want?'

'What do you mean, "driven home"?'

'I'll explain later,' she called back from the front door.

Henry had pulled up and was getting out of his car. It was a beautiful vintage Porsche. A Carrera in bottle green. He went straight to the back of the car and opened the boot, taking out a canvas bag. As he reached up to shut the boot, he caught my eye through the window. He nodded and I nodded back. Then Helena appeared on the front step and said, 'Henry?'

The windows were double-glazed and I couldn't hear them talking, and I didn't know where Helena's phone was so couldn't listen in through the doorbell app. All I could do was watch, my muscles stiff with tension, convinced Devon would start making a racket at any moment.

But Devon remained quiet. I watched Helena and Henry through the window. He opened the canvas bag and I saw it was full of tools, as if he'd turned up to do some odd jobs. It was maddening not being able to hear what they were saying. I watched Helena shake her head, and Henry kept smiling but he was clearly disappointed. He kept glancing at the house. A chill rippled across my flesh. Was he suspicious? Did he know about Devon? No – how could he?

Eventually, after an excruciating five minutes, Helena came back inside and I heard her double-lock the door behind her. The Porsche remained where it was, with him behind the wheel, looking at his phone.

'What was all that about?' I asked when she came into the living room. She looked as tense as I felt. Pale and sick.

'He was offering to fix the shower.' She let out a weak laugh at the sight of my puzzled face and quickly explained how she had bumped into him earlier. 'I told him it was broken when I was trying to think of a reason why I wasn't ready to sell the house. That and the house stinking of cat pee.' We both looked over at Drella, who was sleeping innocently on the armchair.

'But you managed to put him off?'

'I told him you were good at that kind of thing – fixing showers – and that you'd sorted it while I was at the shop.'

'I *am* quite handy,' I said.

'Good to know. Anyway, he then started asking me if there was anything else in the house that needed attention.'

'Oh my God. It sounds like the start of a porno.'

She grimaced. 'Please, don't. Henry is *really* not my type.'

For a wonderful moment, everything seemed normal. We were an ordinary couple sharing a joke.

'Hang on,' I said. 'I thought no one was meant to know about our relationship. You didn't want the whole village gossiping and judging you.'

'I know. I panicked. I was trying to stop him getting into the house.'

'So?' I loved the idea of her talking about me to someone else. 'What did you tell him?'

'Not much.'

'Oh.'

'He asked me if it was serious.'

I perked up. 'What did you say?'

'I told him you're someone I knew at college.'

'And? What was your answer to the seriousness question?'

She let out a small laugh. 'I didn't really answer. My face went pink and I babbled like an idiot.'

'I guess . . . I should be flattered?'

'I'll leave it to you to decide.'

My thoughts returned to Henry. 'Do you think he does fancy you? He's divorced, isn't he?'

'He's never shown any interest in me before. And why wait till I have a new boyfriend? If he was going to make a move, I would have thought he'd have done it ages ago. Plus, he's ancient.'

'I don't know. Maybe he thought you were still grieving, but now you've shown him you're ready to move on . . .'

'Bloody hell. This is the last thing I need.' She went over to the window. 'He's still out there in his car.'

'What's he doing?'

'He's just sitting there, staring at the house.'

I joined her, peeking out at Henry. He kept rubbing his hand across his face like there were ants crawling on it, and no matter how much he tried to brush them off they kept coming back. The affable mask he'd put on when he was talking to Helena had disappeared.

'You don't think . . . he suspects about Lee?' I said.

'No! He's never given me any indication of that.'

The engine revved and there was the crunch of tyres on gravel. We watched Henry drive away and, at the same time, it started to rain. As he disappeared from view, a shudder went through me. It was a horrible sensation. What was the expression? Like someone had walked over my grave. Maybe it was just low blood sugar – I hadn't eaten – mixed with stress. But my confidence that we were going to get out of this was draining away fast.

We couldn't get into Devon's house. She was being uncooperative. It seemed like there was someone turning up at Helena's every ten minutes, threatening to find our hidden guest. I was stuck.

I had absolutely no idea what to do next.

Chapter 17

The rain continued through the afternoon. The hours ticked by. I went downstairs again, collecting Devon's empty pasta bowl and taking her dinner to her. Emptying the bucket, bleaching it and taking it back to her. I tried to persuade her, again, to cooperate, but all she would say was 'I want my money.' That was it.

I picked up the book she'd been reading. *Coves and Scoundrels: A History of Smuggling in Saltdean and Peacehaven.*

'This looks fascinating,' I said with some sarcasm.

She snatched it back from me. 'Actually, it is.'

'Where did you find it? I haven't seen any books in here.'

She nodded at the storage cupboard. 'In there. It was the only thing I could find to read. I thought he'd at least have a stash of grotty magazines.'

I was surprised someone of Devon's generation even knew such magazines existed.

'Are you going to tell me where I can find your laptop?' I asked again.

'Are you going to change the record?'

I gave up. Maybe another night stuck down here would make her change her mind. Perhaps we should make things less comfortable for her . . . It was getting cold. We could turn off the heating. Cut off all the electricity in the basement. Not feed her or change the bucket. But as soon as these words went through my head I recoiled. What was I thinking? I wasn't like that. I was an ordinary man who had found himself in a nightmarish situation. The same with Helena. We weren't evil or cruel. We were good people.

I went back upstairs to the kitchen. The atmosphere in the room was thick, oppressive. To add to the gloom it was getting dark, the relentless rain blocking out the sun and draining light from the world. Helena sat at the breakfast bar.

'We have to get back into Devon's house,' I said. 'She as good as confirmed to me that the copy is on her laptop. All we need to do is find it.'

'It's a shame you lost the house keys.'

'Helena. You'd have panicked too if you'd almost been discovered.'

'Maybe.' She said it like she didn't believe it. Of course, she had been in far more stressful situations than me. But her response irritated me.

'Sorry, I forgot you're the one with experience of—' I stopped myself.

'Go on,' she said. 'Say it.'

'Helena . . .'

'No, come on. What were you going to say? Experience of breaking the law? Being a criminal?'

I tried to take her hand but she snatched it away.

'I was going to say *experience of being in high-pressure situations*, that's all.'

'Hmm.' Again, she clearly didn't believe me. Wasn't mollified.

Silence filled the kitchen. The first awkward silence we'd experienced since we got back together.

'Helena,' I said, needing to fill that silence, 'have you thought about the alternative?'

'What do you mean?'

'I mean, have you thought about giving Devon what she wants? The money. Maybe if you do that, she really will go away and you'll never hear from her again. You'll be free to get on with your life.'

She stood up. 'No! No way. And before you ask, it's not because of the money, even though I don't have anywhere near what she's asking for – half a million, certainly not three-quarters of a million – in the bank. I'd have to take out a massive loan.'

'Or sell the house.'

'Yeah. Which we both know I can't do while she's here, and house sales take ages anyway . . . I could sell the car, some jewellery, some memorabilia Lee had. He's got some old James Bond props that are worth quite a lot, plus some old *Star Wars* junk he found . . .'

My ears pricked up. '*Star Wars* junk?'

She sighed impatiently. 'He and Henry bought an old wreck of a house that, it turned out, belonged to a guy who used to work at the film studio where *Star Wars* was made. He had some old scripts and costumes in a trunk.'

'Oh my God. And they're here?'

She rolled her eyes. 'You're as bad as Lee. They were his babies.'

'Please, don't ever say that.'

'What?'

'That I'm as bad as Lee.'

'Okay. Sorry. I obviously didn't mean it.'

I couldn't help it. The idea of getting my hands on this memorabilia was exciting. 'That stuff must be worth a fortune, right? Couldn't you sell it and use that to pay Devon?'

'No. Lee took it to an auctioneer who specialises in movie stuff. It's not worth anywhere near what Devon's demanding. Like I said, I'd have to get a loan. And anyway, that's not the most important point. If I thought that giving in to blackmail would make Devon go away forever, that I'd be safe for the rest of my life, I'd be tempted. But she'd always be out there, an active volcano, a fault line in my existence. I would never be able to relax. The only way I'll ever feel secure and confident that my life isn't going to go boom is if we can be sure we've deleted all the copies of the recording.'

'Which brings us back to Devon's laptop and the thumb drive.'

'Exactly. I think we should go to the house together. Maybe I can distract Robin while you take a look for Devon's computer.'

'That's not a bad idea,' I said.

'It's the best idea I've got. That either of us has come up with.'

'How are we going to distract him?'

'I don't know, Matthew. We can talk about that on the way. Perhaps you'll come up with something.'

She was still pissed off with me. No, it was worse than that. She was disappointed in me for not coming up with some magic solution to get us out of this. And then, perhaps reacting to the pressure, because I found disappointing her so painful, I did think of something.

'I've got a better idea,' I said. 'We lure him out. Message him as Devon and arrange to meet up. While he's out, we go into the house.'

'That's good. But yet again, we return to the matter of the house keys.'

I swore. Was I ever going to be allowed to forget that I'd left those bloody keys behind? But the desire to solve this problem and impress Helena was making my brain work at double capacity, because I remembered something else. 'The living room window, at the back of the house. It was open.'

'Are you sure?'

'One hundred per cent. If we WhatsApp Robin, tell him it's urgent so he leaves the house quickly, I think there's a good chance he won't remember to close it before he rushes out. Assuming he hasn't already done so, of course. It's a bay window; one that slides up.' I looked her skinny, yoga-toned body up and down. 'You'd be able to fit through, I think.'

Helena vanished inside her own head for a short while, then nodded. 'Okay. It's worth a shot.'

'We should wait till it's dark,' I said. 'Your car is pretty conspicuous. And if we're going to be sneaking into the garden and climbing through a window, I don't think it's a good idea to do that while it's light.'

'Yes. Okay.'

'So as soon as it gets dark, we'll contact Robin, send him to a pub or something on the other side of town, then head—'

'I'll go. You should stay here.'

'What?'

'We know the sound of the doorbell sets Devon off, and it wouldn't surprise me if Henry came back yet again. One of us should stay here, just in case.'

She was right. 'I'll go,' I said.

'No. It sounds like only I will fit through the window. I'll do it.' She fired a glare in the direction of the basement. 'You can babysit.'

Chapter 18

Helena drove past Devon's house slowly, craning her neck to ensure there were no signs of life inside. She had used Devon's phone to WhatsApp Robin shortly before leaving: *Hey, there's something I need to talk to you about. Meet you in the Crown at 9.30?*

Helena had discovered, by scrolling back through Devon's messages, that the Crown – a seedy pub down on the seafront, close to the point where Brighton became Hove – was a place where Devon and Robin drank quite often. From the lack of a car outside Devon and Robin's place, and the presence of a bicycle inside the front door, Helena and Matthew had ascertained that Robin travelled everywhere on two wheels. They reckoned the Crown was a thirty-minute journey from their house by bike, which would give Helena plenty of time to look around, in case Robin turned back as soon as he got there and found no Devon waiting for him.

Robin had replied immediately: *What is it? Can't you come home and tell me?*

Helena and Matthew had already anticipated and discussed this. *No,* Helena had fired back. *I want to meet in public.*

She was confident that would intrigue Robin enough to get him to make the journey across town; and, sure enough, he had again responded quickly. *Okay. See you there. You owe me a drink!*

Robin wasn't the only one who needed a drink, Helena thought as she checked all the lights were out in Devon and Robin's house, then drove on to park in a dark part of the street. When this was all over, she was intending to go to bed with a bottle of vodka.

Except she knew that would be a terrible idea. To go back to drinking. To seeking oblivion in a bottle. Sure, she still drank – had never completely gone teetotal – but not like she had back when she'd started dating Lee.

She had been a mess back then. By the time she bumped into Lee again, on a night out with some girlfriends, she was drinking every day, and not just a glass of wine in the evening. She was getting through at least a bottle of wine every night, two at weekends. No, she hadn't thought of herself as an alcoholic. She'd thought of alcoholics as people who started drinking the moment they woke up, and she always made it through till lunchtime. But she knew now she had been kidding herself. She had been, at the very least, teetering on the brink.

She had been wasted that night – the night she met Lee. She and Shona, her best friend and drinking buddy from the office, had enjoyed a liquid lunch in a wine bar near work, and had only just managed to drag themselves back to their desks, where Helena spent the kind of afternoon that was becoming more familiar: struggling to keep her eyes open at her desk, head throbbing, unable to focus or do any actual work. Endless cups of coffee that only made the buzzing in her head and her veins worse. Instant-messaging Shona for hours, discussing Shona's on-off boyfriend, Luke, and their sex life. Shona kept hinting that Luke wanted Helena to join them for a threesome, and Helena had a horrible feeling that one of these drunken nights it was going to happen. Maybe it would happen tonight, if Helena didn't end up getting off with yet another loser.

There was a point around 4.30 p.m., head pounding, stomach sore, when Helena had vowed to go home, spend the evening in front of the telly with a takeaway; have an early night on her own and hit the swimming pool early the next day. But then 5 p.m. had arrived and Shona was there, like the Pied Piper of post-work London, luring her to another bar – just for one, which became two then three then four.

So yeah, she'd been a mess when Lee 'found' her. And that night in the bar, he'd been kind to her and – oh God it was embarrassing – when she'd invited him back to her place he'd led her outside and put her in a cab, saying he'd call her the next day. Which he did. And over the coming weeks, as they started dating, he'd vowed to help her sort her life out, even though she hadn't asked him to, and she had been so grateful, believing she needed rescuing, and it was only later that she realised how he had manipulated her. She had needed someone to empower her, to lift her up and help her become strong. Instead, he had shamed her and isolated her from her friends. He had encouraged her to leave her job and ghost Shona – 'She's bad for you, Helena' – and all the rest of her friends. He'd pointed out all her flaws and told her he loved her *despite* them. He drank and took drugs in front of her, and taunted her by telling her she was too weak to handle it herself. He was always there, telling her he was protecting her, looking after her, when really he was smothering her, imprisoning her.

He hadn't saved her. Lee had taken her out of her own cage and put her into one he had built.

She had eventually escaped that cage. And she wasn't going back to the one she'd created herself, no matter how shiny and alluring the bars seemed.

She got out of the car and made her way along the pavement to Devon's house, taking in the scruffy front garden Matthew had told her about, the peeling paintwork, the lack of a burglar alarm. She guessed a lot of the people on this street were students, or recent graduates like Devon. Not the kind of people who twitched their curtains or joined Neighbourhood Watch schemes. That made her feel less nervous.

It was easy to get into the back garden, too. There was a low metal gate which wasn't locked, with a high fence beside it that meant anyone looking out of the house next door wouldn't be able to see her as she went through the gate and down the short passage into the garden.

It was overgrown and scruffy there too, with very little lawn, and weeds poking through the paving slabs that took up most of the space. A small shed squatted in the darkness. And there, as Matthew had promised, was the window, and yes, it was open at the bottom. What he hadn't mentioned was that the window was at shoulder height, so she couldn't just climb through it.

She looked around and, spotting a plastic garden chair, carried it over, positioning it beneath the window.

There were lights on in some of the neighbouring houses, TVs flickering, but there was no sign that anyone was peering out.

She stood there for a second. What the hell was she doing? How had her life got to this point? Breaking into someone's house. If she was caught, she would be well and truly screwed. Everything would come out.

But she had no choice. She had to do this.

She climbed on to the chair, put her head through the window, her palms on the frame, and hoisted herself up. There was no graceful way to do this. She hauled the front half of her body through, then dropped head first on to the carpet below, breaking the short fall with her hands. It hurt, but just a little.

She was in.

Now all she had to do was find that laptop.

Chapter 19

I watched Helena drive away, then went back inside. I couldn't relax. I tried to distract myself by turning the TV on, but found myself staring at the pictures without taking anything in. I switched it off and went down to see Devon. I needed to collect her dirty crockery from the dinner I'd taken her a little earlier.

I found her in the home cinema, surrounded by piles of DVD cases. The shelves were half-empty.

'What are you doing?' I asked, even though it was a stupid question.

'Putting it all into alphabetical order. I'm going crazy with boredom down here, all right? I need to keep busy.'

I laughed. Lee had organised everything by category. He'd hate to think of anyone messing up his collection.

She nodded at a pile with the top DVD showing a woman in full S&M gear, brandishing a whip. 'Who'd have thought Helena was into that kind of stuff. Is that what you and her get up to?'

'Very funny.' Although, as she said it, a flash of Helena dressed like the woman on the box entered my head. I was looking up at her, my wrists secured to the bedframe . . .

'Oh my God,' Devon said, her voice dripping with disgust. 'It *is*.'

'Shut up, Devon.' What was wrong with me? I mentally doused myself with cold water. 'These were all Lee's.'

Devon sneered. 'Lee's not the one with a woman locked up in his dungeon.'

Before I could respond, she crouched beside a pile of James Bond DVDs. 'Robin would love this collection. He's always saying he wishes he could afford a UHD player. Whereas Helena has it down here, gathering dust, unappreciated.'

'Have you and Robin ever dated?' I asked.

'Huh. He wishes.'

'He's not, like, an ex?'

She narrowed her eyes at me. 'Why are you asking so many questions about Robin?'

'No reason.'

There was a long pause before she said, 'Robin's my best friend. Probably my only friend.'

This statement would normally have made me feel sympathy, but her tone was so flat it was hard to feel anything. The spiky, aggressive Devon from earlier had retreated. I noticed her eyes kept darting around the room, and she had her arms folded tightly around herself.

She suddenly said, 'Has Helena said anything about this place being haunted?'

I had to check I'd heard correctly. 'Sorry?'

'This place. Is it haunted? Have you heard or seen anything?'

I thought about the footsteps I'd heard outside the first night here, except that had been Devon herself. 'I don't believe in any of that stuff.'

'I should have known. You're not sensitive enough. I feel like Helena would be, though.'

The way she kept looking around, like there were phantoms in the room with us, was creeping me out, despite my scepticism.

'Lee built this place, didn't he?' she asked. 'If I was murdered by my wife, and she stayed in the house I built, I know exactly where and who I'd haunt.'

'Devon. Ghosts don't exist.'

'You shouldn't say that.'

'Why?'

'Because you'll anger him. Make him want to prove they do exist.'

Again, her eyes flicked around the room and she hugged herself tighter. She seemed genuinely chilled. Genuinely afraid.

'You're not trying to tell me you've seen something, are you?'

She nodded very slowly and very seriously.

'What, like an apparition of Lee, shimmering in the corner?'

'Don't be stupid. I've sensed it. A presence. Maybe it's Lee. Or maybe it's one of the smugglers.'

It didn't matter that I knew it was ridiculous: goosebumps rippled across my arms, the hairs standing on end. She was getting to me. I couldn't work out if she genuinely believed this place was haunted, or if she was trying to freak me out. But whichever it was, it was contagious, because I began to think I could sense something too. Something close by, like a figure lurking just out of sight. If there had been a candle in the room, now would have been the time for the flame to flicker.

The book about smuggling was on a nearby chair. There was an illustration on the cover of two men in seventeenth-century garb, holding lanterns as they crept into a cave.

'You need to stop reading this,' I said. I pointed at a stack of horror films. The top film was *The Descent*, a terrifying movie about a group of women who go caving. 'And definitely don't watch that.'

Devon looked at me. 'I know one thing. If Lee is haunting this place, it's you and Helena he'll come after.'

I sighed. 'Goodnight, Devon. Try to get some sleep.' I gestured at the piles of DVD boxes. 'Once you've finished putting these away.'

I almost added: *If all goes well, you'll be going home tomorrow.*

I didn't say it. Because that would have felt like tempting fate.

ω

Upstairs, I still felt unsettled by what Devon had said, and I went round turning on lights to chase away the shadows. *Ghosts.* It was a ridiculous notion, though Devon was half-right. If Lee was going to haunt anyone, it would be Helena and me, though she would definitely be his first pick. I wondered how he would feel if he floated through the wall and found me here. Picturing the displeasure on his face would have made me smile if I hadn't been so sick with tension. I checked my phone to see if there were any messages from Helena, though we had agreed not to text each other just in case there came a point where such messages could be used as evidence against us.

She would be getting to the house now, going inside – presuming the window was open. It was interesting what Devon had said about Robin: that he was her best friend, but that 'he wishes' he was something more. If that were true, their relationship must be agonising for him. To be stuck in the friend zone and having to see that person every day.

Maybe we were doing him a favour, keeping her here for a little while.

Once again, I couldn't sit still. I was desperate to know what was going on at Devon's house. I went upstairs and looked out the front window, even though I knew it was too early for Helena to return in the car.

Someone was standing out the front of the house.

I ducked to the side of the window, then leaned across to peer out. The clouds that had filled the sky earlier had dispersed to reveal the moon and stars, which cast weak light on the ground outside. There was a hedge at the far end of the driveway. The figure I'd seen was behind it, poking their head out, spying on the house. My first thought was Henry, come back to try it on with Helena, but there was no sign of a car. The figure looked too slim to be Henry, too.

Looking closer, I could see the glow of something in their hand. A phone. At the same time I noticed this, a mobile started ringing in the house. The familiar iPhone chime.

It was Devon's phone, ringing in the kitchen.

Whoever was outside, they were phoning her.

I ran down the stairs, trying not to panic. Whoever it was, they had to know, or at least suspect, that she was here. How? What had happened? And who was it?

I reached the kitchen and snatched up Devon's phone. A name filled the screen.

It was Robin.

Chapter 20

Helena took a moment to dust herself down. She took her phone out of her jeans pocket and switched on the torch app, then made her way into the hall. There was no bike there. Hopefully Robin would still be cycling to the Crown.

She went upstairs and found herself on a narrow landing. Both bedroom doors were open and she guessed the third door led to a bathroom. It was obvious from a glance, even in the poor light, which bedroom was Devon's and which Robin's. Matthew had already looked in Devon's bedroom so it made sense to look in Robin's room first. She went in.

The first thing that struck her was the smell. A sour odour, like gone-off milk, mixed with stale weed smoke. Sure enough, there was a pile of clothes, shoved into the corner of the room rather than a laundry basket. The bed was unmade and there were food wrappers on the floor, more dirty clothes, a bedside table on which stood a Coke can that was being used as an ashtray, and a desk on which there was a PC and a laptop.

Helena grabbed the laptop. Was it Robin's or Devon's? The PC was a Windows machine but this was a rather old-looking Apple MacBook. She didn't know anyone who had both a Windows PC and a MacBook – most people she knew stuck to one operating system or the other – and because Devon had an Apple phone, Helena felt confident this was what she had come here for.

Even better, there was indeed a thumb drive inserted into one of its USB ports. She touched it but didn't remove it, unsure if it would cause something – she wasn't sure what – to go wrong. But she was excited. Surely this was what she had come for?

She flipped it open and was confronted by the password-protected lock screen. But, sure enough, there was Devon's name and profile picture.

She'd got it. She could hardly believe it. She sat on Robin's bed, fingers hovering over the keys. She knew she ought to head straight home, where she and Matthew could attempt to get into the laptop, but she was desperate to have a quick look, to see if she could find the backup and check if there was any evidence that Devon had made more backups or sent the file to someone.

What would Devon's password be? Helena realised she knew so little about her. Didn't know the names of any pets she might have had, or her mother's maiden name. Didn't know whether there were any celebrities she was obsessed with, or her date of birth. She thought about it. Why was the laptop in Robin's room? Had Devon told him he could borrow it, or had he just taken it? If it was the latter, he would have needed to have cracked the password too.

There was a notepad lying open on the desk, next to where the MacBook had been. Helena got up and saw that Robin had been doing this very exercise, writing down a list of potential passwords. It filled two pages, with all the incorrect guesses crossed out. He had been trying combinations of names and places – obviously he knew Devon far better than Helena did – and at the bottom of the list he had written *3Stanmer*, which she guessed was somewhere Devon, or perhaps both of them, had lived.

Helena typed it in.

It worked.

The laptop opened to reveal that Robin had been looking at Devon's digital photo collection. The screen was full of thumbnails. Helena was about to leave the app and go hunting through the computer for the recording of her confession, when something in the bottom corner of the screen seized her attention.

A photo of herself.

Next to it was another. And another.

These weren't the unflattering pictures Devon had uploaded to Facebook. Those had included Matthew or the whole group. These were pictures of Helena on her own, all taken during the trip to Iceland. In some of them, Devon – assuming it was Devon who was responsible – had zoomed right in on Helena's face.

There were dozens of pictures like that. Helena scrolled up. Had Devon taken photos of other people in the group too? No, she hadn't. There were the group shots that had been on Facebook. A few pictures of the landscape. All the rest were of Helena – snapped secretly, as if Helena were a celebrity and Devon a paparazzo. It might have made sense if they had been taken after Devon over-heard Helena's confession. But they hadn't. These were all from earlier in the trip.

Ice crept through Helena's veins. What did this mean? What was going on?

While she was trying to make sense of it, something caught her eye: a folder on the left side of the screen labelled *For His Eyes Only*. It was too intriguing to resist. She clicked into it.

The folder was full of selfies of Devon. Helena clicked away immediately, because seeing the gallery of nudes and shots of Devon in lingerie felt intrusive and embarrassing. But even though she exited quickly, the images remained burned in her mind like the after-effects of staring at a light bulb. In all of the photos, Devon had been gazing intently into the camera, a porn-star expression on her face.

For His Eyes Only. Who was the 'his'? Surely not Robin.

Helena would have felt that it was none of her business if it weren't for all the pictures of *her* on this computer.

An alarm was going off in her mind, telling her this meant something.

She snapped the laptop shut and got up. She left Robin's foul-smelling room, relieved to be away from that stink, and went into Devon's bedroom, the laptop tucked under her arm.

Her eyes were immediately drawn to the sketchpad on Devon's desk. Matthew had mentioned it briefly but he'd said he only skimmed it.

Helena opened it at a random page and gasped. She almost dropped the laptop.

The body sketched on the page was familiar. So was the face, rendered in pencil, that stared up at her.

Lee.

Devon's notepad contained a naked sketch of Lee.

Chapter 21

I jumped back from the phone as if it might bite me. What was Robin doing here? Why wasn't he at the pub we'd sent him to? When we'd contacted him he hadn't given any sign that he didn't think the messages were genuine. I had been confident he would go straight to the Crown. But here he was, outside. Spying on the house. Trying to call Devon.

And now, banging on the door?

'Devon?' he called. 'Are you there?'

My whole body froze. I could see it unfolding before me: Devon would hear him, start yelling and shouting, telling him to call the police, and that would be it. Helena and I would be arrested, charged with kidnapping or unlawful imprisonment – not to mention, in Helena's case, murder.

I had to stop that happening.

I rushed to the front door and flung it open to reveal an open-mouthed Robin. In real life, he was even slimmer and shorter than I'd expected, but with a round, baby face. He had his phone in his hand and he took a step back when he saw me. Incredibly, Devon hadn't started making a commotion. Later, I would discover she was in the home cinema watching a noisy movie, but I didn't know that at the time. I was certain I had to get him away from the house.

I pulled the door shut behind me and walked straight past him, motioning for him to join me at the end of the drive. He looked utterly confused but followed me.

'There's someone asleep in there,' I said in a stage whisper. 'Who are you and what do you want?'

He seemed very unsure of himself. 'I'm looking for Devon.'

'Devon? It's about two hundred miles west.'

He stared at me like I was an idiot. 'Hilarious. I'm looking for my friend and I know she's here.'

'Her name's Devon? Don't know anybody who's called that,' I said. 'You're definitely in the wrong place.'

He narrowed his eyes. 'You're lying. She's here.' He turned on his heel and started to march back towards the house.

I hurried around into his path. 'I have no idea who you're talking about. What makes you think this Devon person is here?'

I don't know what my face was doing while I was saying all this. Was it betraying me? I had no experience of lying like this; of trying to appear calm when my heart was attempting, *Alien*-like, to burst out of my chest.

'I know she's here,' he said again.

'I have no idea—'

'I logged in to her laptop and the Find my Phone app. It says her phone is right here.'

'There must be a mistake,' I said, while thinking, *Oh shit*.

'No. There's no mistake. This is the only house in this spot. She's here. I know she's here.'

I tried to think of an explanation. 'Those things aren't always accurate. Maybe she, I don't know, left it on the beach. Have you checked? Also, does this Devon know you're logging in to her laptop and tracking her? It sounds a bit dodgy to me.'

'Stop bullshitting me!'

He shouted it, causing me to take a step back as if blasted by a sudden gale.

'I know who you are,' he said. 'You were in Iceland with Devon. You're in her photos. With that woman, the one with the black hair. The one she's obsessed with. What's going on? I know she didn't write those messages. I know Devon, and that wasn't her voice. Not the way she writes. Why did you try to send me to the Crown? Are you keeping her prisoner?'

My face was definitely betraying my emotions now. Except I must have looked even more stricken and shocked than I felt because he said, 'Oh my God, have you killed her?'

'No. Don't be ridiculous.'

His eyes were almost popping out of his head. 'You have. You've killed her. What was it? A sex game gone wrong?'

'No! Robin—'

'Oh, so you admit you know who I am!'

Shit. I shut my mouth.

'My God, were you in my house this morning?'

My mind was racing, trying to figure out something I could do or say that would get me out of this.

'What have you done to her? What—?'

He was yelling, almost hysterical. I wanted to grab hold of him. Shake him. Slap him. 'Calm down! She's not dead,' I said. 'Nobody's dead.'

'But she's there? In your house?'

It seemed pointless denying it now. I needed to try a different tack. Trying to keep my tone steady and placatory, I said, 'All right, I admit it. She's here. But it's of her own volition, okay? We became friends in Iceland and we told her she could come to stay for a bit. She said she needed to get away for a few days.'

He shook his head, trying to take this in. 'I want to see her. I won't believe she's safe until I've talked to her.'

Once again he tried to get past me. Again, I stood my ground. 'That's not going to be possible,' I said. 'She doesn't want to see you.'

'Let her tell me that herself.' His voice wavered as he said this, became something close to a whine. It struck me that this was why he was here. The story about her trying to get away was plausible. He was here not only, or not predominantly, because he was afraid she'd come to harm, but because he was scared she had abandoned him – this overgrown boy that she took care of, who 'wished' they were in a relationship.

'She'll talk to you when she's ready,' I said. 'Give it a day or two and I'm sure she'll be home. She said . . . she said she wanted a break from you. Now, I think you should go.'

But he wasn't listening. 'Me? What did I do? Just because . . . I told her I was drunk, that it wouldn't happen again. I value her friendship too much.'

Now that was interesting. He'd propositioned her and been rejected. I could use this.

'She needs some space, okay?' I said. 'Go home. I mean, why not go to the pub, have a drink? I'll come with you, if you like. You can tell me all about it.'

He narrowed his eyes at me. 'Why do you keep trying to get me to go to the pub? Why did the message tell me to meet Devon at the Crown? Something's going on.'

'The only thing that's going on is that Devon needs some space.' I put my hand on his shoulder and tried to turn him around so he was facing the end of the drive, where, I noticed, his bike was propped against the gate posts. He shrugged away from me and lifted his phone.

'I don't believe any of this. If you don't let me talk to her, I'm calling the police.'

'Robin, I told you—'

'That's it. I'm phoning them.'

He stabbed at the screen. A nine, then another.

I snatched the phone from him. I didn't stop to weigh up the consequences. I had to stop him from calling the cops. That was all.

'Hey!' He tried to grab it back, but I dodged him, jumping backwards and holding the phone above my head.

'Let's talk about this,' I said. My mind was flying in crazy directions. How was I going to get us out of this?

I only had one idea.

'Come into the house,' I said. 'I'll show you that Devon's okay. You can talk to her. Then I'll give you your phone back.'

If I could get him into the house, down into the basement . . . It would mean having two of them locked up down there. Two of them to testify against us. But we would still be able to let them go as soon as we had destroyed the recordings. It would be their word against ours when it came to both Lee's death and us keeping them prisoner. Maybe it was a terrible option, but it was better than the police turning up here now.

Robin had backed away from me. I could see that he was freaked out. Scared. And he didn't trust me.

'Come on,' I said. 'Just come inside and you can talk to Devon.'

I could almost see his brain whirring. He badly wanted to see her, to find out if she was okay. But he didn't know me. I had just grabbed his phone to stop him calling the police. I had played this all wrong, though in my defence I hadn't known what he was going to do. If I'd foreseen that he would try to call the cops, I would have invited him in as soon as he'd turned up. *In you come and down you go.*

'No way,' he said. 'I'm going to the police.'

He tried to head towards where his bike was parked, and once again I stepped into his path. I grabbed hold of his shirt. He swiped at me and pulled away. I grabbed hold of him again.

He punched me in the face.

It shocked me rather than hurt me, but he hit me hard enough that I went down, falling on to my arse on the concrete. As I fell, I dropped Robin's phone and it skidded away from me.

He snatched it up and started running. I leapt to my feet and sprinted after him. He reached his bike and hesitated for a second, realising he wouldn't have time to mount it without me grabbing him, and just as I lunged at him he shot off in a different direction, looking around wildly. He ran through the passageway into the back garden and towards the stone steps that led up to the terrace. There was a little square gate at the bottom. He sped through and yanked it shut behind him before running up towards the terrace. Presumably he thought he could buy himself a few seconds to call the cops.

I had to stop him. I raced after him and pulled open the gate as soon as he slammed it. I followed him. He was younger than me, he should have been fitter and faster, but I was fuelled by fear and was only slightly more than an arm's length behind him as I pursued him.

He reached the terrace a second ahead of me. There was a table and chairs there, and he darted to the other side of them. He was breathing heavily.

'Robin. Come on.' I was panting too. 'Let's talk.'

'Fuck that.'

He lifted the phone, ready to call the police. There was a fat outdoor candle on the table. I picked it up and threw it at him. It struck his chest and he stared at me, shocked, and I lifted the table, shoving it against his upper thighs. Robin stumbled backwards, colliding with the railing behind him. The impact knocked the phone from his hand and it skidded beneath the table. I reacted fastest, snatching it up. I glanced at the screen to ensure he hadn't managed to make the call, then stuck it in my pocket.

We stood facing each other, either side of the table, chests rising and falling.

'Let's go inside,' I said. 'You can talk to Devon.'

'No. No way.'

He sprinted around the table and charged me, barged into me with his shoulder, and continued running towards the steps. I sprinted after him, arms outstretched, trying to grab hold of him.

We reached the top of the steps, both running fast, and for some reason I will never understand – perhaps the fear that he was going to lose his footing – he paused. Just for a moment. But it was enough. I was still going at top speed. I collided into him.

I dropped to my knees and watched him tumble, his body crashing down the steps, falling into the darkness.

A series of thuds, followed by a sickening crunching sound.

Too shocked to even call his name, I hauled myself to my feet and scrambled after him. I'm not even sure how my legs kept working. The most terrible sense of dread washed over me as I halted and looked down at him.

Robin lay on his side on the concrete. He wasn't moving.

Convinced I was going to throw up, I forced myself down to ground level. I began to shake and my legs almost gave out. Because as I got closer to Robin, I saw that his neck was twisted at an unnatural angle. Even before I reached out to touch him, to take his pulse, to check if he was breathing, I knew it.

He was dead.

Chapter 22

I must have done two hundred laps of the kitchen before Helena got home, pacing, pacing, fighting off a panic attack. Robin was dead. Robin was dead because of me. I was responsible. I had killed him. Round and round it went in my head, looping, looping, and when I stopped to pour myself a drink – thinking that in the absence of a time machine, alcohol was all that could calm me down – my hands shook so much I got more vodka on the counter than in the glass.

I kept hearing the crunch from when he'd fallen; the sound of his neck breaking. I had never even seen a dead body before, let alone been responsible for one.

And no, it didn't even cross my mind to call the police or an ambulance. It was too late for anyone to help him. All I could think about was what was going to happen to me now. To me and Helena and, yes, Devon. There had to be some way out of this.

But I couldn't see what it was.

My only hope was that Helena would know. That, somehow, she would know how to save us.

It felt like hours before I finally heard tyres on the driveway and saw headlights sweep across the front window. I looked out and was relieved to see it was her, not the police or some other person come searching for Robin.

I opened the front door and ran out.

As Helena emerged from the car, we both spoke at the same time.

'Something's happened,' I said.

'I have something to tell you,' said Helena.

We both paused.

'You go first,' she said.

I found I couldn't speak.

She took a step towards me. 'What is it?'

'It's . . .' My tongue was too fat for my mouth. 'I . . .'

She put her hands on my shoulders. 'Is it Devon?'

I shook my head.

'Matthew, take a deep breath. You're shivering. We should get you inside. Come on.'

In the hallway, she said, 'You feel freezing.' She rubbed my arms. 'I think you might be going into shock, you're so cold. Let me run you a bath.'

'No, Helena—'

But she had already gone. I sat on the bottom stair, hugging myself, and listened as she turned the taps on above. A rush of water. I closed my eyes and tried to quell the shivering.

Helena reappeared while the bath was still running. She led me upstairs. Once the tub was full, she led me into the bathroom and undressed me like a child. The water was hot and came up to my shoulders. Finally, I stopped shivering.

Helena sat on the toilet beside the bath and, after a little while, displaying patience I wouldn't have been capable of, said, 'Tell me.'

I told her.

Her hand went to her mouth and she stood up. 'Oh God. Oh Matthew.'

'It was an accident,' I said. 'He just . . . If he hadn't come here. If he hadn't been so difficult. I tried to get rid of him but he

180

wouldn't go, and he was going to call the police and they would have found Devon and—'

Helena had both her hands on her head and was staring at the bathroom tiles.

'Helena, say something.'

At long last, she dragged her gaze from the tiles to me. 'Are you sure? Are you certain he's dead?'

'One hundred per cent.'

'Oh fuck . . . Matthew!'

'I told you. It was an accident. I crashed into him. I was trying to stop him finding Devon. To protect you.'

'You think this is . . .' She stopped herself. Visibly took a deep breath. Then she left the bathroom, saying, 'I need to think.'

I sat there in the water, unable to move, not wanting to leave the warm cocoon of the bath. While I was in here, time was paused. Once I got out, I was going to have to deal with the reality of what had happened.

You killed a man.

Helena came back into the room. She was calmer. She crouched beside the bath and said, 'Listen. It wasn't you. He did it to himself. He was running. He stopped suddenly. You couldn't stop. It was his fault.'

Was that right? It was all starting to become fuzzy.

'He fell,' she said. 'That's it. An accident. But now we have to deal with it.'

I stared at her. She was right. It was an accident. If he hadn't stopped running, I would never have crashed into him and he wouldn't have fallen.

'Matthew, are you listening to me? I said we have to deal with it.'

'Yes. But . . . how?'

She had brought a towel into the bathroom, which she now placed on the edge of the tub. 'Dry yourself and I'll see you in the bedroom.'

She had laid out some clothes on the bed. A black T-shirt, black hoodie, black joggers. I knew that they must have belonged to Lee but I didn't protest. In silence, I put them on. Lee had been shorter than me and stockier, at least when I had known him, and the joggers were two inches too short on the legs and two inches too wide at the waist. The T-shirt swamped me. But it hardly mattered, did it? I pulled them on, noticing that Helena had changed too and was also wearing all black.

'I love you,' I said, sitting on the bed and tying my trainers.

For a second, she looked at me like I had said something in a foreign language, as if this was no time for emotion. In a clipped tone she said, 'I love you too. Now, show me.'

ᴔ

He was lying in the back garden where I'd left him. *Of course* he was lying where I'd left him. This wasn't *Halloween*. He hadn't been miraculously resurrected. He wouldn't be looming up behind us brandishing a knife, wreaking vengeance. I pulled the tarpaulin off and there he was, at the bottom of the steps, stretched out on his front, his head grotesquely twisted. I took one glance then looked away. Helena shook her head and said, 'Oh Matthew,' very quietly.

'What are we going to do?'

'Let me think.' The seconds stretched out. A cloud passed over the moon. 'We can't say we don't know him, that he's just some random person who happened to fall out here, because the police will figure out the link between us almost immediately. We were in Iceland with his housemate.'

Then she told me the plan. It started with us getting him into the car. Before Helena got home I had covered him with a tarpaulin I had found in the garage. Now Helena lifted the tarpaulin away, averting her eyes from his corpse as she did so, then put it in the back of the car, flattening it out so it covered the space where she had already folded down the back seats. Then she reversed the car so the distance between it and Robin's body was as short as possible. After that, the two of us walked through the passageway to the back of the house, not speaking, and stopped at either end of where Robin lay.

I took a long, deep breath.

'What are you waiting for?' Helena said. Her eyes glittered darkly in the half-light as she bent towards the body. She was by his feet, and I was behind his head.

I got my arms beneath his shoulders and tried to lift him. I now understood where the phrase 'dead weight' came from. I could just about get the upper half of his body off the ground. The car seemed a very long way away.

'We can do this,' Helena said. 'We don't have a choice. But we have to be careful not to drag him. Okay?'

Later, I thought perhaps we *had* had a choice. We could have called the police. Handed ourselves in. But I didn't even consider it at the time. All I could think about was trying to make it all go away.

I slid my hands beneath Robin's underarms again and, on the count of three, we got him off the ground.

I couldn't remember how long it was meant to take for rigor mortis to set in, but he was still floppy, which made it harder to lift him. I thought I could smell him too, the first hint of a rotten, gaseous stink, though I don't know if this was my imagination conjuring the stench of death.

He was small and skinny but it still took all our combined strength to get him down the side of the house, and then there was one more Herculean effort required: heaving Robin into the car. Somehow, we did it, the suspension bouncing as his corpse flopped on to the plastic. While I stood there trying not to vomit, Helena lifted the sides of the tarpaulin and wrapped it around his body, concealing him. Then we got into the front seats and just sat there for a minute in silence, gathering our strength. Every muscle in my body ached, and I suspected that later, when the adrenaline subsided, I would hurt even more.

Helena was about to pull out of the drive when I said, 'Wait!'

The headlights had illuminated Robin's bike. I jumped out, wheeled the bike over, then opened the trunk of the car. I paused. The only way to get it into the vehicle was to place it on top of Robin. If he hadn't been beneath the tarpaulin, if I hadn't been able to pretend there wasn't a human being in there, I might not have been able to do it. It would have felt like the last indignity. But I wrestled the bike into the back of the car and quietly closed the boot, wiping my brow with my forearm.

'Have you got his phone?' Helena asked.

'Yeah.'

'We should take Devon's phone too. It's in the kitchen. Get some rubber gloves too. There are a couple of pairs under the sink.'

I didn't question her. I ran into the house, grabbed Devon's phone, rooted around in the cupboard beneath the sink and found two pairs of Marigolds, then went back to the car.

Helena drove slowly and carefully, as criminals always do in movies. No jumping red lights. No speeding. There was very little traffic on the road, but I was still thankful the car had tinted rear windows.

We pulled up outside Robin and Devon's house. Now I was glad for how silent the car was. No engine noise, just the quiet *shush* of tyres on asphalt. There was no one around and all the windows were dark. Because it was a cul-de-sac there was no through-traffic. I checked the time. Quarter to two in the morning.

Helena held up a bunch of keys. 'I found these on Devon's desk, where you left them.'

She was angry with me. I felt the urge to defend myself – I was only involved in all this because I was trying to protect her! – but I managed to bite my tongue. And she must have seen the dark expression on my face, because when she spoke again her voice was softer. 'Just wait here a moment.'

She slipped her rubber gloves on, then got out, leaving the car door open behind her, and walked up the short front path to the house, where she unlocked the front door. Then she came back to the car and opened the trunk. I put my own gloves on – the sight of them, bright pink, covering my hands, was absurd and somehow horrifying – then joined her at the rear of the car. I lifted out the bike and hurriedly carried it inside, leaving it propped up in the hallway where I had seen it the day before. Realising I hadn't been wearing the gloves when I'd put it into the car, I picked up a winter scarf that was hanging by the front door and used it to wipe the frame.

I re-joined Helena by the trunk of the car and took another look around. There had to be at least one insomniac in this street. We had to pray they were watching TV or listening to an audiobook or something. Not peeking out the window.

Carefully, we lifted the tarpaulin with Robin's body inside out of the boot. The journey up the path was only six metres but it felt like it stretched on for ten times that. I was convinced someone was going to appear and ask us what the hell we were doing. I imagined us having to kill that person, and then another would appear and we'd have to kill them too. A never-ending chain of death and concealment. Finally, we reached the house, putting the body down in the hallway, as gently as we could. Helena closed the front door behind us while I removed the tarpaulin. Seeing his face again, that wrenched neck, I gagged. His eyes were open and his flesh was slack. There were spots of blood on his lips. And yes, I could smell him.

'Do not throw up,' Helena whispered. 'Get a grip.'

There were so many emotions whirling inside me. Horror and fear, obviously. A sick pulse of guilt. But somewhere beneath all that, I couldn't help but feel impressed by Helena's coolness. Grateful too. She was helping me fix this. In this moment, I needed her just as she had needed me when she had been hanging from that cliff. Without her, I would have gone to pieces, and I was happy to go along with her, to allow her to tell me what to do. And mixed in with all this, though I would have been loath to admit it, was a warped, giddy thrill. Not over what had happened with Robin – my God, I would have given almost anything to change that – but in the way it connected Helena and me, bound us together. Surely this would bind us *forever*.

With yet more painful effort, we arranged Robin at the bottom of the stairs. This was the plan: it needed to look like he'd fallen here; that he'd tumbled down this flight, not the other, and landed on his neck.

When Helena had told me the plan it had sounded sensible, like it could work. But now, standing and looking down at him, it seemed crazy. Would the police really believe he had fallen down the stairs in his own house and broken his neck? Did the physics work? I tried to see it through the eyes of a cop. We had positioned him on his front so it looked like he had fallen face first, just as he had at Helena's place. The staircase was high and steep. Yes, it seemed like it could work, especially if they believed he was drunk or stoned, had started coming down the stairs at speed and tripped when he was at the top.

Robin was wearing Doc Martens. I unlaced them, which was tricky with the gloves on, and, after a struggle, managed to pull them off. I carried them up the stairs, placing one on the top step and the other just below, lying on its side, so it looked like Robin had left his boots at the top of the staircase and tripped over one of them, knocking them down a step or two as he fell. Then I went into the living room and found the ashtray I'd seen before. It hadn't been emptied and still contained the stubs of several spliffs. I took it up to Robin's bedroom and placed it on his bed. The room smelled of weed already, so it was a plausible scene.

Then I went downstairs and stood over his body again.

'We need more light,' I said.

'Just use the torch from your phone.'

I checked him over. I wanted to ensure there was nothing to make it look as if he'd fallen outside. No dirt. No scrapes that could only have come from brick. Thankfully, the stone steps he had fallen down were quite smooth and clean.

Finally, I took out Robin's phone and held it in front of his face to unlock it. I deleted the recent message exchange between Robin and Devon, where they had arranged to meet in the pub, then checked to ensure Robin hadn't messaged anyone else this evening. He hadn't.

I took the phone up to Robin's room. Handily, Robin had a little pack of sterile wipes on his desk. I used one to clean the phone and placed it beside the ashtray.

We took the tarpaulin with us, went back to the car and slid away from the neighbourhood.

I was charged with adrenaline again. As we left Moulsecoomb, I went over everything in my head, forcing myself to concentrate when what I really wanted to do was put my head out of the car window and scream into the wind. My DNA would almost certainly be on Robin's body and in his house, as would Helena's. There would be traces from the steps on his body too. Particles of dirt. But surely they would see the broken neck, the spliffs, the boots, and come to the most straightforward conclusion. Investigating further would be expensive and time-consuming. The police were always talking about how budget and staff cuts had left them stretched thin. Why would they look for strangers' DNA at this kind of scene?

On top of that, neither my nor Helena's DNA was on file, and nor were our fingerprints. We had never been arrested for anything. We weren't in the database. I was confident nothing would lead them to us. The only risk was if someone had seen us or the car.

The only risk, that was, apart from Devon's phone. It was a big problem. When they found Robin's body, the police would wonder where Devon was. And the easiest way to find someone these days was to trace their phone. Everyone knew that. It hadn't been such a big issue at first, when we'd thought this would all be over quickly. But now? Oh yeah, it was a very big issue.

'Get a grip, get a grip,' I muttered to myself, echoing Helena's words. She gave me the side-eye now, shaking her head slightly. My fists were clenched, knuckles white. *Get a grip* was looping in my head like a stuck record on a turntable, and I thumped myself on the forehead to jolt it loose. It worked. I could think again.

The phone, the phone. We could have left it at her house. We could destroy it. But the police would still be able to see where it had been the past few days. They would be able to triangulate its location and figure out she had been in the area around Helena's house.

If we hadn't just been in Iceland with Devon, dutifully memorialised on social media, nobody would have linked us. But it wouldn't be hard for the cops to figure out that someone Devon knew lived in the area where her phone was last pinged. They would come looking for her.

But Helena hadn't yet explained what she intended to do with Devon's phone. It was still right here, in the car.

We drove past the turning that would take us home.

'Where are we going?' I asked.

'There's something else we need to do.'

We drove for another half an hour, through Peacehaven and Newhaven and Seaford, along the coast towards Eastbourne. But before we reached the town, Helena turned right. Beachy Head Road. Now I knew the answer to my question.

Beachy Head. Probably England's most notorious suicide spot. Helena pulled up on the edge of the car park and handed me Devon's phone.

'You know what to do,' she said.

I looked at the phone. 'But why? What's the plan?'

'I'll explain later. Please, just do it.'

'But . . .'

'Matthew. You fucked up tonight. I don't want to dwell on it, but just trust me, okay? I'm trying to think ahead here.'

I got out of the car and walked towards the cliff. During the day, the view over the Channel would be stunning. These were the highest chalk cliffs in the country. The long-disused Belle Tout Lighthouse was over to my right, and down below, jutting out of the dark churning sea, was the still-operational red-and-white-striped lighthouse.

I stood on the edge of the cliff and threw Devon's phone as hard and far as I could. The darkness swallowed it.

We drove back in silence. My brain was too tired for me to ask Helena to explain her plan. The adrenaline was draining away and my body was crying out for rest. I could tell Helena felt the same. When we got home, she put the tarpaulin back in the garage and said, 'We'll need to get rid of this in the morning. Bleach the steps and clean the inside of the car. I'm going to have a shower.'

I stripped and got straight into bed. I thought I would fall asleep immediately but my head was buzzing, my heart thumping. Helena got into bed too, warm and damp and naked from the shower, and lay beside me in the darkness. We didn't speak. I thought she had gone to sleep but then she reached out for me, kissing me – a light kiss at first, then more intense, and then she was on top of me, straddling me. She reached down and took me in her hand. Pulled me inside her.

We made love wordlessly, with nothing to break the silence but our ragged breathing. My skin had never felt so sensitive; the touch of Helena's fingers sent fireworks erupting across my nerve endings; patterns of blue and black and red danced and whirled behind my eyelids. Helena dug her fingernails into my flesh, clawing at my chest, biting my shoulder, all teeth and nails. Crazed with desire, I flipped her over on to her front and pushed into her from behind, making her cry out, and her hair fell to reveal the back of her neck. There was the scar, a reminder of where all this had started, and the hatred I felt for Lee – this was all his fault, his doing – was like even more petrol being thrown on to this fire. I realised, through the ringing in my ears, that Helena was saying my name, repeating it over and over, her voice muffled by the pillow. We came, her then me, and for a long second my whole body was gone. It was like being catapulted to another place. Everything was obliterated, forgotten: all my troubles, all the things I'd done. The ecstasy of forgetting. Just for a moment.

Chapter 23

Helena was still out for the count when I woke up, though we were no longer entangled; she was curled up in a ball on the far side of the bed.

I got dressed then went down to make coffee, and was shocked to see it was already ten thirty. It was so gloomy outside, the sky above the sea flat and colourless, that I had to put the lights on to be able to see. I stayed away from the kitchen window, not wanting to look out at the spot where Robin had died. As I'd suspected, I ached like I'd spent the whole day pumping iron at the gym, and my head throbbed. A terrible feeling of dread and remorse threatened to overwhelm me. All I could do was push it away. Keep moving.

I made three coffees and took one down to Devon, who glowered at me.

'I'm starving. And *that* needs to be taken away.'

She pointed at the bucket in the corner without looking at it.

'Okay. I'll change it.' I went over to pick it up.

'Helena been beating you up?' Devon said.

'What?'

She pointed at a spot on her face, just below her eye. I touched the same spot on my own face and winced. It was where Robin had punched me. I'd been in such a state since that I hadn't even noticed.

'It's nothing.' I lifted the bucket and turned to go.

Devon said, 'Wait.'

I looked back at her over my shoulder. Even that hurt.

'Tell Helena I want to talk. I've been thinking. Maybe we can come to a deal.'

I blinked at her. 'You've changed your tune.'

An exaggerated shrug of the shoulders. 'I've had a lot of time to think. I don't hate Helena, not really. Or you. There has to be a solution that will work for all of us.'

If only she had come out with this yesterday. Because I wasn't sure if it was still true, now that Robin was dead. Yesterday, it had all seemed simple. We only had to find the copies of the recordings and destroy them, and then we could let Devon go. Now it was more complicated. Horribly, terrifyingly complicated.

'I'll tell her,' I said, and I took the bucket out of the basement, locking the door behind me and going up the stairs.

Helena was in the kitchen, drinking the coffee I'd been meaning to take to her. On the breakfast bar in front of her was a MacBook. An old model with USB ports, a thumb drive plugged into one of them.

'You found it!' I said.

'Uh-huh.'

She looked tense. Angry.

'Hold on. Last night, when you got back to the house, you said something had happened. Then we got swept up in the whole . . . thing. What was it?'

Helena put her coffee down and picked up her phone. 'Look at this.'

She handed it to me and I found myself looking at a photo of a black-and-white sketch of a man. A naked man, reclining on a bed.

'That's from Devon's sketchpad,' Helena said. 'There were lots of pictures like that. Do you recognise him?'

It took a moment. Of course I hadn't seen him in the flesh for twenty years. And I had *never* seen him with his clothes off. But I knew that face; that smirk.

'Lee?' I said, confused. 'What the hell is Devon doing with naked sketches of Lee?'

'On top of that, there are loads of pictures of me on her laptop.'

'Pictures of you?'

'Yep. She was secretly photographing me in Iceland, *before* she listened in on our conversation.'

'What? You're kidding.'

'No, Matthew, I'm not. I'm going to talk to her. Are you coming?'

I followed her as she marched along the hallway and down the stairs to the basement. Then through the door into the den, where Devon was sitting on the sofa, drinking the coffee I'd brought her. Helena stomped straight over to her and held her phone out, one of the drawings of Lee on the screen.

'Are you going to tell me what the hell this is?' Helena demanded.

Devon looked at the phone, then up at Helena. There was no great shock on her face. Of course she had known we were going to go looking for her laptop. She had been expecting us to find this. She put her mug down on the coffee table and pulled herself up straight, flicking back her hair and looking Helena in the eye.

'Yeah, that's right,' she said. 'Lee was my lover.'

Chapter 24

'How did you meet him?' Helena asked, her voice cold.

'He came to the university to give some guest lectures. One of my friends was studying architecture so I went along to keep her company.' Her hand went to her collar, where her skin had flushed pink. It was as if she was seeing Lee again for the first time. 'I met him afterwards in the bar and he gave me his number. We started seeing each other a couple of days after that.'

My tired brain was still reeling. *Devon was Lee's secret lover?*

'When was this?' Helena asked. She'd had more time to process it. Because, of course, she'd known as soon as she'd found the sketches last night.

'November 2019,' Devon replied. 'We met up once or twice a week, all the way until the first lockdown. It was difficult after that. Horrible. But I started seeing him again occasionally when things opened up. We'd go to a hotel in Brighton and spend the afternoon there.'

'*Spend the afternoon.*'

Helena's voice had gone deeper until it was almost a growl. Lee had been cheating on her. I didn't think she was surprised or upset by that in itself, even if it was yet another betrayal of their marriage vows. She was angry because it was Devon. The woman who had turned up on Helena's doorstep demanding money and threatening her had been Lee's mistress. Her presence on our Iceland trip couldn't have been a coincidence. She must have followed Helena. Even with everything else that had happened, this was hard to absorb.

'When did it end?' Helena asked.

Again, Devon looked Helena straight in the eye. 'When you killed him.'

'You were still seeing him when he died?'

'When you murdered him, yes. We'd been planning to meet the following week. I thought he'd ghosted me, spent two weeks feeling shit then saw it on the news. That he was dead.' Her words caught in her throat and her eyes glistened in the artificial light of the basement. 'I couldn't even go to the funeral, even though I was desperate to. I was so upset, I knew I'd end up doing something I regretted.'

'Did you ever come here?' Helena asked. 'To this house? Did you fuck him here?'

'No. You were always at home. He had to come to me.'

Helena took a few steps across the den, before turning back. 'Don't get me wrong, I don't give a damn that he was cheating on me. If I'd known, I'd have given the two of you my blessing. My God, I would have loved for someone else to take him off my hands . . . Not that I'd wish that fate on any other woman.'

'He wasn't—'

'Shut up. Let me speak. How did you contact him? I went through his phone and emails after he died. There were no messages from you or any other women.'

'He had a phone that he used just for me. He told me you would go into a jealous rage if you ever found out about us.'

Helena shook her head. 'A jealous rage? Fuck me. What were you doing in Iceland? If you try to tell me it was a coincidence, I will punch you in the face.'

'Of course it wasn't a coincidence. I thought it was the opportunity I'd been looking for – to get to know you. I intended to befriend you. And, eventually, even if it took months, I thought I could earn your trust. Get you to tell me what really happened with Lee.'

'You mean you suspected Helena of killing him?' I said.

'Yeah. I knew what a strong swimmer he was. There was no way he would have drowned without help. And he told me Helena hated him. That she was crazy.'

'Of course he did,' Helena said.

'Yeah. And you've proved it by locking me up in your basement. Threatening me with violence.'

'Back up,' I said. 'You followed Helena to Iceland so you could befriend her?'

'Yeah.' She kept her eyes on Helena. 'Except I couldn't get near you. The two of you were inseparable the whole trip, being disgustingly loved-up, and all I could do was watch from a distance. That last night, I came to your hut thinking it was my last chance. I was going to pretend to sympathise with you after your fall, see if you needed anything.'

So she hadn't been telling the truth when she'd said she'd come to alert us to the Northern Lights.

'Imagine my surprise when I got to your door and overheard you talking about Lee. Spilling your guts to Matthew. It was so quiet outside I could hear everything you were saying, especially as your window was open. I got my phone out and pressed Record. Huh, I didn't need to befriend you after all. I had it all recorded. It couldn't have gone any better if I'd planned it. It was like fate.'

'Hold on,' Helena said. 'How did you know I was going to Iceland?'

'You posted about it on Instagram. You even included the name of the excursion company.' Devon shook her head. 'For someone with a big secret, you're not very careful about your privacy.'

Helena seemed temporarily speechless. In the gap, Devon said, 'So you've been to my house. I'm assuming you've got my laptop.'

I was about to answer when the doorbell rang above us.

Helena and I looked at each other.

'Do you have your phone?' I asked. 'So you can see who it is?'

She shook her head. At the same time, Devon jumped up from the sofa and ran to the door, banging on it with her fists and shouting, 'Help!'

I grabbed hold of her, putting a hand over her mouth and pulling her away from the door. She was so light—

oh so light, after Robin's corpse

—that lifting her up was easy. She struggled and tried to bite me, but I held firm so she couldn't open her jaw wide enough to snap at me.

'In there,' Helena said.

It took me a second to realise what she meant.

'The freezer?'

'Yes. Hurry. It's the only way to block out her shouting. Trust me, please.' She opened the freezer door. I was hit by a blast of icy air as the interior light came on, revealing mostly empty shelves.

Devon was still wriggling and trying to bite me. I had no choice. I carried her into the freezer. Into the cold.

'I'll be as quick as I can,' Helena said.

She shut the door, locking us in.

Chapter 25

I pulled my phone out of my pocket and switched the torch on, filling the interior of the freezer with weak light. The phone had no reception down here, and the thick walls even blocked the Wi-Fi signal. We were alone. Cut off. Totally reliant on Helena to let us out.

I was wearing jeans and a sweater with a T-shirt under it, and Devon was wearing the hoodie and jeans she had arrived in. We both immediately started to shiver. Devon wrapped her arms around herself and gave me a look that was somewhere between self-pity and loathing.

My first day here, when Helena and I had been watching *Bonnie and Clyde*, I had asked her why they had a walk-in freezer. It wasn't something I'd come across before.

'I thought you only found them in restaurants,' I'd said.

'Yeah, me too. But Lee thought it would be a cool thing to have. He'd go to the butcher's and buy whole pigs and these huge slabs of beef. He put the animals he killed hunting in here too, loads of rabbits, and he and Henry used to go out on Henry's boat sometimes. He'd come home with a net full of fish. When the pandemic happened and everyone started panic-buying and stripping the shelves at the supermarket, he was enormously smug about it. He said we had enough meat to survive for months.'

'But you're vegetarian.'

'Pescatarian. You know I eat seafood. But I think that's one of the other reasons he did it. He knew how much I hated having all these animal carcasses down here. Plus he used to "joke" about how he'd have somewhere to store my body if anything were to happen to me.'

I'd been so happy Helena had killed him. She really had done the world, not just herself, a favour.

'After Lee's death I gave all the meat to this place in Brighton that feeds the homeless,' Helena had said. 'And I've been intending to get rid of the freezer entirely, but the logistics are too daunting.'

As I'd discovered my first night here, the shelves of the freezer were almost empty. There were some Tupperware dishes, a few bags of ice. And now, two living and breathing humans.

'We're going to die,' Devon said.

'No, we're not,' I said. 'We're not going to freeze to death.'

'How do you know she'll let us out?'

'Of course she will.'

'Oh yeah. Helena wouldn't hurt a fly, would she?'

I wondered what Helena was doing and saying in that moment. What if something happened that prevented her from coming back? Devon and I would be trapped. I felt reasonably confident that we wouldn't run out of air, even if every breath depleted a little of the oxygen in here and replaced it with carbon dioxide. The space, I guessed, was big enough for that oxygen to last a while. If we were going to die, it would be the cold that killed us. Hypothermia.

Helena wouldn't let that happen. If she was arrested, she would tell the police we were here.

Wouldn't she?

'You're thinking about it, aren't you?' Devon said. 'Wondering if she actually would leave you in here.'

'No. Of course not.'

She smiled sarcastically. 'Come off it, Matthew. You must wonder every day if you can trust her. After all, she killed Lee. You know what she's capable of. It would solve all her problems, wouldn't it?'

'What? Having two bodies in her freezer?'

It was getting harder to speak now. My face felt stiff, the ice creeping through my veins and into my bones, chilling the marrow.

'All she'd have to do is make us disappear. She could chop our frozen bodies up, do it bit by bit. Probably easy, once we're frozen stiff. Then bury us. Whatever. If anyone came looking for us, she could tell people we'd run off together. Maybe we met in Iceland and fell for each other. Do you have anyone who'd put pressure on the police to search for you?'

Did I? My sister was in New Zealand. My friends were too busy with their families. I didn't have colleagues anymore. Devon was right. I could vanish and no one would miss me.

'My parents don't care about me either,' Devon said. 'They'd probably be delighted if I disappeared. I never even see them.'

'What about your dad's birthday party?' I said. 'It's this Saturday, isn't it?'

She shot me a look. 'Oh yeah. You saw it on my phone. Huh.' There was a pause, like she was figuring out a strategy. 'They only wanted me to go for the sake of appearances. So their old friends won't ask where their wayward daughter is. They don't actually want me there.'

We both fell quiet for a minute. How long had we been in here? It had only been five or ten minutes but it felt like much longer. Who was Helena talking to? What if she couldn't get rid of them? I was getting colder and colder, finding it hard to breathe. And I knew I shouldn't talk, should conserve the oxygen in here, but I felt like I had to contradict Devon, while also reassuring her – and myself.

'Helena wouldn't leave us in here,' I said. 'She loves me.'

Devon laughed.

'What?'

'You don't sound too sure. And I don't blame you. It's *so* obvious she's crazy. Lee told me all about her. He said she was a fantasist.'

'Are you saying you don't believe Helena when she says Lee was abusive?'

'He was sweet and gentle to me.'

I made a disgusted noise. 'Yeah, of course he was. They always are at first. You were just his bit on the side. But I knew Lee. He was an arsehole at university.'

'Actually, I think you were the arsehole, Matthew.'

'What are you talking about?'

'Lee told me how Helena was completely broken when they got together. That she'd been screwed up by this guy she was with at college and had gone off the rails for a few years. Lee rescued her, put her back together again.'

'Oh, come on,' I said. 'That's exactly the kind of sexist, self-serving narrative he would come out with.'

'Matthew, you don't get it, do you? As soon as Helena told us your story in Iceland, I sussed it. You were that arsehole. You were the one who fucked her up.'

'He said that?'

'He never told me your name. But you were her boyfriend at college, weren't you? Who else could he have been talking about?'

I was so cold now that talking hurt my lungs. On top of that, my teeth were starting to chatter. I watched my breath turn the air white between me and Devon, merging with her own breath-clouds. 'Lee was lying,' I managed to say. 'Our break-up was amicable. Everything he told you about Helena was a lie, designed to make you feel better about fucking a married man.'

But Devon smirked. 'I'd be careful if I were you, Matthew. Because maybe she's out for revenge. I think the reason she killed

201

Lee was that she found out he was sleeping with someone else. She was afraid he was going to leave her and she would lose all this. This house. Her comfortable lifestyle. The poor bitch might actually have to go out and get a job. Lee was nothing like the monster she portrayed. He was lovely. Helena's a liar. I bet she doesn't come back.' A beat. 'Are you sure there's not another way to open this door?'

She got to her feet and inspected the door.

'Forget it,' I said, still reeling from what Devon had said. 'It only opens from the outside.'

She sat back down. 'Oh God, I don't want to die in here with you.'

'She's not going to let me die,' I said, my teeth chattering. I sat hunched over in the cold, trying to blow warm air on to my hands.

We sat there in silence, shivering. Why *was* Helena taking so long? Or had it only been a few minutes? I had lost track of time and was finding it difficult to formulate thoughts. Was the hypothermia kicking in already? I examined my hands. Were they turning blue? In the light from my phone, it was impossible to tell. Was I imagining it, or were specks of ice forming in Devon's eyelashes? I blinked and saw that, yes, it was all in my head. But it wouldn't be long before those lashes were thick with frost if Helena didn't come and free us. Should I stand up and move around to generate some heat, or was it better to keep still to conserve energy?

Devon had gone completely still. I was worried she was going to pass out. I needed to keep her talking.

'I don't think Helena's going to want to do a deal with you now,' I said.

'Huh.'

'Do you regret it?' I asked. 'Coming here and blackmailing her?'

There was a pause before she replied. 'I wish I hadn't turned up here without a weapon and without checking she was on her own. I should have told Helena I'd meet her somewhere public.'

I suppose there was something admirable about her refusal to try to appease me. In her place, I might have been doing everything I could to make it seem like it was safe to let me go. I'd be promising to keep quiet. But Devon didn't even seem to have considered it. She was absolutely convinced she was in the right and that there was nothing morally wrong with what she had done, coming here.

I was about to say something along these lines when she said, 'I'm only trying to take . . . what should be mine.'

'What are you talking about?'

Her speech had slowed right down. It took effort to get the words out. 'Lee was going to . . . leave her . . . divorce her . . . and then I was going to . . . move in here. Be his wife.'

'You're deluded,' I said. 'He would never have done that. Not until after he'd killed Helena. Like he killed his first wife.'

She looked at me. 'That was an accident. A fire. You're the deluded one.'

Silence returned. All I could hear was the hum of the freezer. Our breathing.

Devon sat across from me, the defiant expression back on her face. I sat there shivering, my body growing increasingly numb. Something flickered in the edge of my vision. I rubbed my eyes.

Where was Helena?

Devon whispered something, so quietly I couldn't hear her. I pictured Robin, lying at the bottom of his staircase, and then he was here, in the freezer, sitting between Devon and me. His head wrenched to the side, but his eyes fixed on mine. His skin had turned blue and was shot through with black veins. I wanted to ask Devon if she could see him but she had her head down, her arms wrapped around herself, and Robin continued to stare at me. Knowing. Accusing.

He lurched to his feet and slowly, very slowly, he started to shuffle towards me.

I closed my eyes and shook off the hallucination. Helena. Where the hell was she?

Surely she wouldn't leave me here to die?

This is her solution, whispered the little voice in my head. *This is how she's going to get out of the mess she's in. She'll let Devon and me freeze to death*. And then – what? Oh my God, she would store us here in the freezer until she got the opportunity to dispose of us. Bury us in the garden. Dissolve our bodies in acid. Chop us up and store us here forever like we were meat.

Suddenly, I was convinced it was true. Maybe it was the tendrils of ice squeezing my brain. Devon's whispered words making me paranoid. The lack of oxygen. But the phantom Robin was back, his head bent sickeningly, his lips blue and moving, muttering, telling me it was all true. That Helena hated me, that this was her revenge.

I jumped to my feet and pounded on the door of the freezer, as Devon stared and Robin, grinning now, shuffled closer and closer.

'Let me out. *Let me out!*'

Chapter 26

Helena inhaled deeply and laid her palm flat against her clavicle, then exhaled. In through the mouth, out through the nose. It was a calming technique she'd learned in a Zoom meditation class that she'd taken after Lee had died.

It wasn't working.

The doorbell rang again.

'Hold on,' she called as she unlocked the door.

It was Henry. Again. He was right there, on the doorstep, fogging up the spyhole with his breath, and before she had a chance to go outside he had barrelled past her, straight into the living room. He left an invisible trail in his wake: the smell of booze and sweat. Helena checked the time on her phone. It was only 11 a.m.

'I didn't invite you in,' she said as she entered the living room in time to see him collapse on to the sofa. She looked out of the window and saw his Porsche, parked crookedly on the drive. 'Did you drive here, drunk?'

'I need to talk to you.'

His eyes were bloodshot, his speech slurred. Helena had always known Henry liked a drink – Lee used to joke about it all the time, and Henry had got so pissed at their wedding that he'd ended the evening peeing in a plant pot before passing out – but she had never seen him drunk this early before. Had he been up boozing all night, or woken up and reached for a bottle? Her mind flashed to the bottle of vodka in the kitchen, the one Matthew had cracked open last night. It had taken all her willpower not to empty it down her throat. Maybe she should pour herself a glass now. Invite Henry to join her.

She realised he was speaking.

'I've been . . . doing my best. I've been trying. You believe me, don't you?'

'Henry, what on earth are you talking about?'

'I'm stuck in the middle,' he said. 'Between a rock and a hard place.'

He was making absolutely no sense. Then, to her horror, he started to cry.

'Oh Jesus,' she muttered under her breath. Then, 'Let me get you some water.'

She thought about Matthew and Devon downstairs in the freezer. She'd been locked in there herself. She knew how cold it got and how little air there was in there. She had to get rid of Henry. But she also needed to know what the hell he was talking about and why he had come here. She filled a glass with water and took it to him quickly. He gulped it down, dribbling half of it down his front.

She sat beside him and tried not to breathe through her nose. After he'd drunk or spilled most of the water, she handed him some tissues and he blew his nose loudly. He tried to hand her the damp tissues and she shrank away, gesturing for him to keep them.

'Henry, take a deep breath and then tell me. What's going on? What do you need to talk to me about?'

'The Crowleys.'

'The Crowleys?' The name made her insides go cold. She remembered how scared Henry had seemed when he'd seen Jamie Crowley at the supermarket. Again, the idea that the Crowleys had spread the word about her buying Rohypnol shortly before Lee drowned filled her with horror.

'Henry,' she prompted. 'Tell me what's going on.'

He sniffed. 'They want money.'

'What for?' She thought she might be sick. She thought he was going to say that Jamie Crowley had told Henry about the Rohypnol and told him to deliver a message. More blackmail.

Henry wiped his nose on the back of his hand. 'He fucked up.'

'Wait. *He?* Who? You mean Lee?'

'Yeah. Around the start of the pandemic, when all our work ground to a halt . . . things got a little sticky. We needed money and he did a deal with them but . . . there was some monumental bad luck.'

'What kind of deal?'

Henry shook his head. 'I've been trying to appease them, but they're not happy bunnies. They say we've had long enough and if we don't pay up now . . .' He trailed off, leaving her to imagine the consequences.

'Hold on. What do you mean by "we"?'

He looked at her with those pink, watery eyes, and said, 'That's what I came here to warn you about. They've been coming to me first because I was Lee's partner. The so-called bloody money man.' He laughed bitterly. 'But they're going to come for you next.'

'What?'

'You were his wife. You're next on the list. I've managed to hold them off all this time but . . .'

'Henry, how much did Lee owe them?'

'Taking the absolutely terrifying interest rates into account, at the moment it's just over half a mill.'

She stared at him. 'Half a million?' She almost laughed. It was the same amount Devon had come here to ask for. She repeated it. 'Half a million pounds.'

'You have this house. It must be worth a million, easy.'

'Oh my God. Is that why you were so keen for me to put it on the market? Get things moving, get the house valued, and then hit me with the news that a family of local gangsters were going to demand half of it?'

His sheepish face told her she was right.

'Can't you sell *your* house? You have that big place out in the woods, right? It must be worth at least as much as this place.'

He winced. 'I can't. You know it's been in Sally's name since the divorce?' That was his ex-wife. 'If we sold it, all the dosh would go to her. Besides, it's run-down and nowhere near as fancy as this place. You know how much people would pay for this view?'

'Don't you have any other way to raise the money?'

'I can sell my baby. My Porsche, I mean. But that will only raise a fraction of it.'

'For God's sake, Henry. Why couldn't you have got a loan through the bank?'

'I . . . It wasn't exactly a loan. It was a joint business venture that went wrong. I don't really think I should tell you any more, in case the police get involved. The less you know, the better.'

She swore, several times. She guessed it was something to do with drugs. This was all she needed right now. *All* she needed. She felt laughter surging up inside her again and was surprised to hear it burst forth. Hysterical laughter, the kind that comes when you can't take it anymore, when your brain cracks. Even Henry-the-drunkard was looking at her like she was deranged.

'Are you okay?' he asked.

'Oh yeah. Why wouldn't I be?' More laughter burst out of her.

'I'm sorry, Helena. I know this must be a shock. But if I can tell them the money is on the way, they'll leave you alone. If I can say you're selling the house to raise the funds . . .'

She couldn't think straight. All she knew right now was that she needed to get rid of him, let Matthew and Devon out of the freezer. Then she would add this to the list of nightmarish problems she had to solve. Maybe she should sell the house, raise the money. Leave the cash in the middle of a field and let Devon and Jamie Crowley fight over it. She laughed again. Laughed until it hurt.

'I need to think about it,' she said when she had calmed down.

'Helena, there might not be much time.'

She snapped at him: 'I said, I need to think about it. Okay?'

He managed to get to his feet, stumbling and almost falling back on to the sofa. Could she really let him drive like this? What if he had an accident and killed someone? She really wouldn't be able to take having any more innocent deaths on her conscience.

'I'll call you a taxi.'

She phoned the local cab company, who, thankfully, said they would be with her in five minutes. She escorted Henry outside. Out in the damp autumn air he seemed to sober up a little, but they stood in silence for the whole interminable wait for the taxi.

It finally rolled up outside on the road and she put Henry in the back seat. His chin dipped.

'He's not going to be sick, is he?' said the driver.

'No. But I think I might be.'

The driver gave her a curious look then left. For a minute, it crossed her mind that she could get into her car, or even Henry's Porsche, and drive away. Put her foot down and keep going. Leave all of this behind and start a new life somewhere else.

She thought of Matthew, shivering in the freezer somewhere below her feet. Devon too; Lee's secret mistress. She could still hardly believe it, though she genuinely didn't care. She just wished Lee had run off with Devon. Even kicking Helena out and moving Devon in here to take her place would have been better. And that was when it struck her. It was why Devon felt she was entitled to the money she was demanding. Lee had told her he loved her. Had told her that one day all this would be hers.

In a way, Devon was as much Lee's victim as Helena had been.

She stood there for a moment, mulling over her options. Figuring out what to do. Running away now, when there was still a chance she could find a solution to all this – even with the added complication of Jamie Crowley's demands – would be a foolish thing to do.

With a sigh, she headed to the basement – just as Matthew snapped and started banging on the door, pleading to be let out.

She quickened her pace. By the time she reached the freezer door, she was running.

Chapter 27

I sat huddled on the sofa, wrapped in a blanket, still shivering. Helena sat beside me holding a mug of tea, urging me to drink some, but I couldn't hold it because my hands were shaking too much.

'I'm sorry,' she said. 'I couldn't get rid of him for ages.'

'What did he want?'

'It's . . . He was drunk and wasn't making any sense.'

'Did he try it on with you? If he did—'

'No. For God's sake. It was nothing like that. He was rambling, talking nonsense. He's a lonely old man who's been recently divorced and also lost the person who kept their business going.'

'Are you sure that's all it was?'

'Yes.'

I was almost certain she was hiding something, but before I could press her she sat beside me and wrapped her arms around me, pressing her warm cheek against my cold one, rubbing my back through the blanket and whispering apologies. I couldn't feel my fingers or toes but, slowly, I began to thaw, thanks to the heat coming from Helena's body.

Downstairs, Devon would be attempting to get warm too. Helena had given her a thick blanket, along with a hot-water bottle.

'I'm sorry,' I said.

'For what?'

I hung my head. 'Doubting you.'

'Doubting me? Hold on. You didn't think I was going to leave you locked in the freezer, did you?'

'It was Devon. She got into my head.' I shook my head, unable to look up at her. 'I . . . Yes. Yes.' I was whispering now. 'I started to think you were going to leave us there.'

'Oh, Matthew.'

'She told me that Lee said you were "broken" when you and him first got together. That it was my fault.'

She pulled away from me slightly. 'Yours?'

It had all come back to me in a rush. How our relationship had ended. We'd gone to a concert together, the Manics at Wembley Arena, us and a group of friends. Dave – whose reunion had brought Helena and me back together – had been there, and this girl called Melissa. A few others. Helena and I had got separated in the crowd and I'd lost her. I was drunk, carried away by the music, and Melissa had been flirting with me . . . No, that sounds too passive. We'd been flirting with each other. We had our arms around each other, swaying together to the music, heads and lips close, and when I opened my eyes Helena was there, staring at us. I tried to go after her but Melissa stopped me. I let her stop me. After that, Helena didn't reply to any of my texts. When I went round to see her, her housemates told me she didn't want to see me. And that was it. The end of our relationship. We graduated soon after.

'I treated you so badly,' I said. 'And I never apologised. I want to apologise now. I acted atrociously that night. I'm sure there were other occasions when I acted like an idiot too, like at that party in Hampton Court. I'm not going to make excuses – but I just wanted to let you know I didn't kiss Melissa.'

Helena stared at me for a few moments, and then she laughed. 'Do you hear yourself? Did you really think I was still angry with you about that?'

'I wasn't sure.'

She threw up her hands. 'My God, Matthew. With everything else we have to deal with, and everything I've been through, do you really think I'm still pissed off about some girl you might or might not have snogged twenty years ago?'

'Well, when you put it like that . . . But Devon said Lee told her—'

'What? That I was in a bad place when I started seeing him? That I was vulnerable? Yes, I was. I had a shitty job, I was drinking way too much. I was deeply unhappy. But it wasn't because of you. I'd had a string of loser boyfriends. I still hadn't fully recovered from losing both my parents when I was a teenager. I had a lot of body issues. Self-esteem issues. A whole bloody suite of issues! But it wasn't because my college boyfriend was a dickhead.' She shook her head. 'My God, the male ego.'

I tried to interject but she spoke over me. 'Lee was always going on about how badly you'd treated me, and how lucky I was to have found him again. But even if he'd been the perfect husband rather than an utter piece of shit, I don't think you treated me that badly. You were just a typical young bloke. A child in a man's body. And I really hope you don't think I've been planning some elaborate act of revenge against you for what you did to me twenty years ago.'

I tried not to look too shamefaced.

'This is what happens when you let Lee into your head, via that idiot downstairs.'

She reached across and took hold of my hands in hers. 'We're adult beings now, Matthew, and we're very much in this together. Do you really think I would have told you what happened with Lee if I didn't like you and trust you? Do you not think I'm grateful for all your help? Meeting you again is the best thing that's happened to me in years. Maybe in my life. Please don't make me change my mind about you by telling me you don't trust me.'

'I do. I'm so sorry. I just . . .'

'I know. Your head is all over the place. Believe me, I get it. But we have to stay strong and stay united. Okay?'

'Okay.'

I pulled her to me and kissed her.

Helena pulled away from me with a throaty laugh. 'Oh my God,' she said, 'it's like kissing an ice cube.'

'We could go to bed. That would warm me up.'

She rolled her eyes, but was smiling. 'You're unbelievable.' She got up and went into the kitchen, then came back holding Devon's MacBook. It struck me how thin she looked – how she had lost weight over the past couple of days. I had hardly seen her eat. Come to think of it, I had barely eaten too. The realisation made my stomach growl loudly as Helena handed me the computer.

'Do you want some food?' she asked.

'That would be great. Just a sandwich or some toast. And you should make yourself something too. And Devon.'

'Yeah. Of course. By the way, the password is three Stanmer. Three as a digit, capital S, all one word.'

She went back into the kitchen and I opened the laptop, typing in the password. It was the same kind of computer I'd owned a few years ago, and I knew my way around it.

The first thing I did was check the contents of the thumb drive. There was nothing on it except an audio file. I clicked Play and, hearing Helena's voice, immediately stopped it, noted the file name, and ejected the drive. Now I needed to see if there were any more copies on the laptop, or evidence that she'd saved it or sent it elsewhere.

As I searched the computer, cooking smells wafted out of the kitchen. My stomach growled again. When I had finished searching, I got up and carried the laptop through to where Helena was buttering toast, a pan of scrambled eggs still on the hob.

'Ketchup?' she asked. It was so normal. How could things still be so normal?

'Yes please. Are you not having any?'

'The idea of eating anything right now is making me nauseous. Let me take this down. Not that she deserves anything to eat.'

She left the room with the plate before I could respond to that, and she came back almost straight away. She hadn't hung around to chat with Devon. I'd still managed to wolf down half of mine before she returned, though. Helena sat on the sofa beside me just as I finished eating and put my plate aside.

'So?' she said.

'I've searched the whole computer. I even downloaded a program to locate deleted files, emails, et cetera.'

'And?'

'There's one copy of the audio file here, in the Downloads folder. It looks like she Airdropped it from her phone. I can't see any evidence that she emailed it to anyone or uploaded it to any backup services. I went through all the other recent audio files and gave them a quick listen, in case she saved it under a different name or broke it up into other files, and found nothing.'

'So, are you saying the copy on this laptop is the only one?'

'I think so.'

'*Think* so? We need to know for certain.'

'We can't be one hundred per cent sure, but there's no evidence she saved it anywhere else or made a backup. I've checked her cloud and there's nothing in there. I honestly don't think she would have felt the need to make another copy. My guess is that she was going to email this file to the police, if she ever carried out her threat, and didn't feel the need to make a backup. She was sure you were going to go along with her demands, wasn't she? She thought the copies on her phone and computer were all she'd need.'

I navigated to the Downloads folder, where the file was saved. I hit Delete, then emptied the trash. It made a crunching sound—

like Robin's neck breaking

—and I said, 'There. All gone.'

'Can't deleted files be recovered? By the police, for example?'

'Not if we destroy the hard drive. Do you have a hammer?'

She left the room and came back a minute later with a hammer. I placed the laptop on the floor and set about smashing it up. It was a shame. It was a perfectly good computer. Or rather, it had been. Now it was a mess of plastic and metal, in several bashed-up pieces. I put the thumb drive on the carpet and did the same with that.

I handed the hammer back to Helena, a bead of sweat running down my forehead. I wasn't cold anymore.

She stared at the pieces on the floor. 'That's it? It was that easy?'

'I don't know if "easy" is the word I'd use. A man died so we could do that.'

She laid her hand on top of mine. 'I know how you feel, Matthew. I get it. But it was an accident. Also . . .'

'What?'

'The guy was a creep. What do you think he was doing with this laptop? He was going through her photos, probably looking for the nudes she sent Lee. That's sleazy as hell.'

'It doesn't mean he deserved to die.'

'Of course not.'

I closed my eyes and caught a glimpse of Robin's corpse, just as I had in the freezer. That broken neck. I could smell him. Feel his weight in my aching muscles. 'I killed him. I *killed* someone.' I swallowed and looked up at her. 'The guilt. How do you live with it? How do you come to terms with it?'

'What, you think I'm the expert? I've told you. I feel no guilt over Lee. He deserved to die. With Robin – I don't know. Maybe we'll never feel better about it. Maybe you'll see his face on your deathbed.'

'Oh Jesus. How am I supposed to live with it? Helena, I don't know if I can!'

Something flashed in her eyes. Impatience? Anger? She handed me her phone. 'Go on then. Call the police. Tell them you have something to confess. If that's the only way you can live with yourself. I'll take the whole rap. Tell them about Lee, take the blame for locking Devon up. I'll say I forced you to help me.'

'Helena—'

'No. Don't interrupt. This all started with me, didn't it? It's all my fault. You're just an innocent who doesn't deserve any of this.' She nudged my arm with the edge of the phone. 'Go on, call the cops. Put an end to this.'

I snatched my arm away. 'Stop doing that!'

Her eyes widened; nostrils flared. It was the first time I had shouted at her. I could feel it, deep inside of me. A furnace fuelled by stress and guilt. A fire that was ready to come roaring out of me in an explosion of fury. It would feel so good to shout and bang my fists on the counter. And the fire so badly wanted it to happen, for me to let it out.

But I still had enough control to know that, if I started, I might not be able to stop. I managed to keep it down. To shut my mouth. I picked up a glass of water from the side table, downed it and pictured it dousing the fire inside me.

When I looked back at Helena, I saw the fire in her. Still burning.

She got to her feet. When she spoke her voice was twice its normal volume. 'If you're not going to call the police and confess, you need to shut up about it. Stop sitting around feeling sorry for yourself and find a way to live with it.'

She headed for the door. I tried to stand in her way and she pushed past me. I felt the fire roar again, telling me to grab hold of her, stop her from going. It took all my willpower not to do it.

But as she headed through the doorway, I said, 'Wait.'

She paused.

'What are we going to do? About Devon?'

'I don't know, Matthew. Do you have any bright ideas?'

'No. We've deleted the files, but now Robin's dead, I don't know. I don't know what to do.'

She rubbed her forehead. She looked utterly exhausted, leaning against the doorframe.

'You should get some sleep,' I said.

'Where do you think I'm going? Are you coming?'

'I can't. I'm too wired.'

'Fine. If you're staying up you might want to bleach the steps where Robin died. Clean out the car too. And get rid of that.'

She flicked a hand at the mangled laptop, then went up the stairs and shut the bedroom door.

No, scrub that. She *slammed* the bedroom door.

ᛌ

I did as Helena suggested. I found some bleach under the sink and a mop in the utility room, and I went out and cleaned the steps and the surface of the terrace. After I'd done that, I spent an hour vacuuming and cleaning the inside of the car, though no matter how much I did it I wasn't completely confident I'd managed to remove every trace of Robin.

Putting the cleaning stuff away, I found the tarpaulin we'd wrapped him in. That needed to go. I put it in a bin bag along with the rubber gloves we'd used and the smashed-up MacBook and set out for the dump. It was a tight squeeze past Henry's Porsche. I wondered if he and Helena had discussed when he was going to pick it up.

The dump was a ten-minute drive away. I was in and out in a few more minutes, then I drove back towards Saltdean, expecting to find Helena asleep in bed. I was tired now too, and was ready to join her.

But as soon as I went inside, I heard the TV. Helena was up. And walking into the living room, and seeing how pale she was, my stomach lurched.

Oh God. What now?

Chapter 28

Helena was perched on the very edge of the sofa in the living room, staring at the TV and biting her fingernails. Drella was on edge too, shooting past me in a blur of fur as I came in.

'What is it?' I asked.

'They found Robin.'

My entire body went cold, like I was back in the freezer. 'Already?'

She paused the TV then rewound the picture. 'As soon as it came on I hit Record. Watch this.'

She pressed Play and the newsreader on the local news channel said, 'Police in Brighton are appealing for witnesses after the body of a young man was found this morning at a house in Moulsecoomb.'

Then I found myself looking at Devon and Robin's house, which had police tape strung up outside and a small number of onlookers crowded around.

'I'm going to be sick,' I said.

Helena shushed me as the newsreader said, 'The body was discovered after a courier who was attempting to deliver a parcel looked through the letterbox and spotted a prone figure at the foot of the stairs. The police have revealed that the deceased is Robin Barker, a twenty-three-year-old recent graduate who resided at this address.'

A picture of Robin, which I guessed they'd taken from Facebook or Instagram, appeared on screen. He was on the promenade, the pier clearly visible behind him, grinning and eating from a bag of chips. The words 'full of life' popped into my head and lodged there. The news then cut to a shot of a uniformed police officer outside Brighton police station. She said, 'We are trying to locate Mr Barker's housemate, Devon Maddox, to help us with our enquiries. We would ask Ms Maddox to contact Sussex Police as soon as possible.'

They brought up the photo of Robin again and Helena hit Pause.

'They're looking for Devon,' I said, pacing back and forth.

'I know.'

'Oh my God. *The police are looking for Devon.*'

'I know, Matthew!'

Drella had come back into the room and was staring at me from the doorway, like he was watching a wildlife documentary about this crazy species called human beings.

'I can't breathe,' I said.

She glared at me. 'Do you want me to slap you? You need to calm down, okay?'

I took several deep breaths. I could feel myself standing on a precipice, and the ground beneath my feet was oily, slippery. I had to hold on. Helena was losing patience with me and I couldn't blame her. I needed to be more like her. To get hold of my fear and harness it, use it to help get myself – get both of us – out of this situation. I paced around the room, sucking in air.

'In through the mouth, out through the nose,' Helena said. 'It will help.'

I tried it.

'No, slower . . . That's it. Better?'

I nodded, though my heart was still hammering. At least I was finally able to speak.

'Do you think they suspect Devon of pushing him?' I asked.

'I don't know, Matthew. I'm guessing they think it's weird that Robin's lying dead at the bottom of his staircase and the woman he lives with is missing. But we knew this was going to happen. It's why we threw away Devon's phone.'

I stopped pacing the room. 'Did we? Know this was going to happen, I mean?'

'I'm sure I explained on the drive to Beachy Head.'

And I was sure she hadn't.

'You're going to have to explain it again,' I said. 'My head is fucked.'

'Huh. Okay. Think of it as insurance.'

I sat down and attempted to think it through. To follow what Helena appeared to have foreseen even amid the panic of last night. 'The police are going to look for Devon,' I said. 'As we've known all along, the easiest way to do that is to trace her phone. And they'll be able to see the last mobile tower it pinged was near Beachy Head.'

'That's right. And before that, the phone was at her house.'

'But won't they also be able to tell she was *here* before that? And what about Robin? If they check the location history of his phone, they'll see he was here too last night.'

'I know all that.' Her tone bristled with impatience again. 'Which is why I need to call them.'

'You're messing with me, right?'

'No. The cops are going to find out both of them were here, as you said, because of their phone history. We need to pre-empt that so, when they ask, we can give them a logical explanation as to why Devon and Robin were here.' She drew a deep breath and released it through her nose. So she was stressed too. 'This is the story, okay? You need to memorise it. Are you concentrating? Matthew?'

'Of course.'

'Okay. We befriended Devon in Iceland and she told us her housemate, Robin, was harassing her. That she wanted to get away from him, but he was making it difficult.'

I nodded. I could see where this was going.

'When we got back to England,' she said, 'I told her she could come and stay here for a few days while she found somewhere else to live. She gladly accepted. I'm going to make up the spare room so it looks like she was sleeping in there.'

That was good. Yet again, I marvelled at how clever she was.

She went on. 'Then, last night, Robin came here on his bike to look for her after figuring out she might be staying with us. You told him Devon didn't want to talk to him. He was drunk and belligerent but eventually went away. Then Devon felt bad and decided to go home to talk to him. We haven't heard from her since and no, we don't know where she might have gone or if she pushed him down the stairs. But she was angry with him. At the end of her tether. Who knows what might have gone down in that house.'

Drella came a little closer, as if he was really enjoying the show now. Or perhaps he thought I looked like a giant goldfish, with my mouth opening and closing.

'You want the police to think she killed him and then, full of remorse, jumped off Beachy Head?'

'I just want to give them a plausible story they can tell the world. A story that leads them away from here. Maybe they'll think Devon threw her phone off the cliff and ran away.'

Something about this didn't make sense. But I was resisting voicing what it was because it was so awful.

'What is it?' Helena asked. There was a vein standing up on her temple, and her hands, when she tried to hold them still, were shaking. I was half relieved that, like me, she was only just holding it together. The other half was terrified because one of us, at least, needed to stay calm. One of us needed to be driving this bus.

'There's a big problem with this story,' I said, hearing how my own voice was trembling. 'The moment we let Devon go, she'll go to the police and they'll know everything we told them is a lie.'

Helena looked at me, and all the hairs on my arms stood on end. I knew exactly what she was thinking.

'Oh no,' I said. 'Helena. We can't—'

I was interrupted by banging. For a moment, I was sure it was the police. They were here already, bashing down the door, and within seconds we would be face down, handcuffed, under arrest.

But it wasn't the police. It wasn't my heart either, despite what Helena had just hinted at. *The unthinkable.* The banging was coming from below.

'I'll go,' I said.

'I'll come with you.'

Helena stood up, suddenly looking about ten years older than her age, like she was so exhausted she could barely stand.

'You really ought to eat,' I said.

She raised a hand. 'Please. Don't nag me.'

I followed her down the stairs to the basement, where Devon stood just inside the door. She looked like she'd been here for weeks, not just two days. Her hair was greasy and there was a fresh crop of spots on her forehead and chin. She smelled too, of BO and bad breath. The book about smuggling lay at her feet, and I wondered if she'd been using it to strike the door.

'I want to talk to you in private,' Devon said to Helena. She flicked her eyes at me. 'Woman to woman.'

Helena turned to me, indicating that I should go.

I hesitated.

'Go on, Matthew,' Helena said. 'It will be fine.'

I left the basement and waited on the stairs, wondering what Devon was saying. A minute later, Helena came out. Her expression was weary but neutral.

'I'm going to let her have a shower,' she said.

'What? Are you crazy?'

'Maybe I am. Maybe I really am fucking crazy. This situation is enough to make anyone lose their frigging mind, don't you think?'

Her tone, the wild look in her eyes, frightened me. She was supposed to be the strong one. 'Helena . . .'

'She's started her period. She's sitting there with a ball of tissue in her pants and suffering from cramps. She's in pain, she's filthy, she's miserable, and I feel like being kind, okay?'

She was being kind? I thought about the way Helena had looked at me upstairs when I had pointed out that, if we let her go, Devon would contradict our story. What was this? The equivalent of a last meal? I almost opened my mouth to say it, but stopped and performed a mental U-turn. I had to be wrong. Helena was not like that. I must have misunderstood. This was evidence of what I already knew: that Helena was a good person.

'I want you to go upstairs and close all the curtains and blinds,' Helena said. 'Make sure the front door is double-locked.'

'Okay.'

I ran up the stairs and did as Helena asked. Yes, we were compassionate, reasonable people who had found themselves in a terrible mess. We weren't cold-blooded murderers or kidnappers. We were good people. That was why Helena, who kept telling me to get a grip, appeared to be losing her own grip. She wasn't some cold, calculating killer. This kindness was the real Helena. The one who had indicated that Devon might need to die was not.

Helena came through the door into the hallway, Devon trailing behind her. I followed them both up to the ground floor. Devon was slightly bent over, her hand on her belly, but still somehow carrying her customary air of defiance.

'Follow me,' Helena said, leading Devon up the stairs to the first floor. I dithered below, unsure if I should leave them to it, but decided it would be safer to stay with them. Helena opened a cupboard on the landing and took out a towel, handing it to Devon. 'Wait here.'

She went into the bathroom and I watched as she gathered up everything sharp, like her razors, and heavy, including some glass bottles of bath oil, and carried them out.

'There are tampons in the cabinet there,' she said to Devon, nodding towards it. 'I've left the shower gel and shampoo inside the shower. Let me fetch you some clean clothes.'

She went into the bedroom, dropped off the stuff she'd taken from the bathroom, and came back with a bundle of clothes: a T-shirt, a hoodie, some jogging bottoms, clean underwear. She put them all inside the bathroom, then said to Devon, 'There's a spare toothbrush here too. The toothpaste is on the sink. Do you want some painkillers? Are you allergic to anything?'

'Yes. And no, I'm not.'

'Okay. I'll get some for when you come out. Don't lock the door.'

'What?'

'We're not going to spy on you. Just don't lock it, okay? You have five minutes.'

'Five? I need at least fifteen.'

'Ten.'

'Whatever.' It was one of those moments that reminded me how young Devon was. Staring at the floor, her bottom lip stuck out, she looked like she was barely old enough to vote. She went into the bathroom and closed the door behind her. We heard the shower come on almost straight away.

'Oh God, maybe this was a mistake,' Helena said in a low voice, even though Devon wouldn't be able to hear us over the roar of the shower.

I was surprised. 'Why?'

'I've been trying not to form an emotional connection with her. That's why I've been staying out of the basement as much as I can and making you do it. And now she's made me feel fucking sorry for her.' She spat the words out like she was disgusted with herself.

'But that's a good thing,' I said. 'It shows we're not monsters. We're good people.'

She wasn't listening. 'She doesn't deserve sympathy. She got herself into this situation. She had an affair with Lee. She followed me to Iceland and tried to blackmail me, even knowing what I'd been through.' She glared at the bathroom door like she wanted to haul Devon out of there and chuck her down the stairs.

'She doesn't believe it's true,' I said. 'She thinks Lee was a saint.'

'Yeah, of course she does. She only saw his charming side. You know, if she'd been outraged that I'd taken the law into my own hands and gone to the police to report me, I could respect that. At least it would show some integrity. But I don't think she cares at all about the moral aspect of all this. She doesn't even seem to care that Lee is dead. She only gives a shit about herself.'

'Maybe she's the mon—'

'For God's sake, can you stop talking about monsters! I think she feels like she's been robbed. I bet Lee promised her he would divorce me, and that all this – the house, the nice car – would be hers. The blackmail is her way of trying to get what she thinks she's owed.'

An idea came to me. 'Perhaps we should offer her a deal. We tell her what's happened, including how Robin had an accident, and give her money to keep quiet. I could sell my flat in London. You could sell the car.'

'That's just giving in to her blackmail!'

'Maybe. But it might be the only way out of this.'

She shook her head and I could see it in her eyes: flames of hatred. She had swung back to believing Devon had to die.

I scrambled for a solution; some way to dissuade her. 'Maybe it's possible to ensure she's implicated if she threatens to go to the police.'

'Like what?'

'I don't know. But we should talk about it. It's better than—'

The shower stopped, and the sudden silence made me stop talking. We waited for her to dry herself and get dressed. The bathroom door handle turned and Devon appeared. Her hair was wet and the clothes Helena had given her hung off her like she was a child playing dress-up.

'Come on then,' Helena said. 'Let's get you back downstairs.'

Devon didn't move. 'Please. Let me stay up here for a while. I don't want to go back down there.'

'No. I'm sorry.'

'Helena,' I said. 'Maybe this is our chance to have a chat with Devon. See if we can come to a—'

'No.'

'But if we can come to an arrangement . . .'

Helena spoke through gritted teeth. 'Matthew, we can talk about this later.'

But I didn't want to talk about it later. I didn't want to hear Helena say that the only solution was to kill Devon. I wanted her to form the emotional connection she had been trying to avoid. Perhaps Devon would form a connection with us too. After all, the three of us were in this mess. We should work together to find a solution.

'Let's go downstairs and put the kettle on,' I said, 'then sit and talk about it. I bet we can find a solution that suits all of us. Right, Devon?'

I wanted her to be aware of the danger she was in without actually having to say it. But Devon was ignorant. All she did was grunt.

Helena was shooting daggers at me. 'I think we need to—'

Devon shoved past her and ran towards the stairs. Before either of us could react, she was halfway down and moving fast.

I reacted quickest and pelted after her. As I raced down the stairs, Devon reached the hallway and flew at the front door, reaching up to pull back the bolt, turning the handle and yanking at it. The door didn't budge.

I reached the bottom of the stairs. 'It's locked,' I said. 'I have the key.'

Devon looked around, head darting left and right. She tried to dash towards the kitchen, but Helena, who had by now reached the hallway too, blocked her way, a fearsome expression on her face that made me glad she wasn't carrying a weapon. Devon reversed and, charging into me with her shoulder and knocking me back, shot into the living room. I dashed through after her.

Drella was staring wide-eyed at us from the armchair. Devon snatched him up and held him tight against herself. She wrapped her hand around his throat. He struggled, swiping at her hand and drawing blood, which made her gasp and swear. But she held on, wrapping one of the sleeves of the top she was wearing, which Helena had lent her, around Drella's body so his legs were trapped.

Helena came into the living room behind me and gasped.

The cat tried to move his head so he could bite Devon but he couldn't get to her. 'Let me leave or I'll kill him,' Devon shouted.

Helena's eyes were out on stalks. 'Let him go!'

'No. You let *me* go. I swear to God I will throttle him.' Drella thrashed and wriggled beneath the sleeve Devon had wrapped around him, but she held tight, one arm around his body, the other still gripping him beneath his jaw. His green eyes shone with fury.

'Listen,' I said. 'Let's put the kettle on, sit down and—'

'Shut up, Matthew,' both Devon and Helena said at the same time.

'Hurt my cat and I'll kill you,' Helena said.

'You really are an evil bitch, aren't you?' Devon said, backing away towards the TV, which was in standby, its screen blank. Drella emitted a low rumbling growl from deep inside his throat. I was sure that we were going to witness an explosion of teeth and claws at any moment, but Devon wasn't allowing him any leverage. 'You're going to unlock the front door and let me out, or I promise you this cat is dead. I'm going to count to five. One. Two . . .'

Helena looked stricken. Torn. She loved this cat more than anything.

'Three . . .'

Helena launched herself at Devon, who – shocked – stepped backwards and loosened her grip a little. Drella thrashed, got a paw loose and scratched her hand, hard. Devon cried out and let go. Drella leapt on to the sofa—

And must've landed on the remote control, as the TV lit up, blazing bright and loud, the newscaster's voice making all three of us jerk our heads towards the screen.

There, on the TV, was the photo of Robin. Beneath it, the caption POLICE APPEAL FOR HELP AFTER DEATH OF BRIGHTON MAN.

I tried to grab the remote to turn the TV off but it was too late. Devon had seen it.

'Oh shit,' I said.

Her face was slack with shock. 'What?' she said. 'What did you do?'

'Devon, we need to talk.'

'Oh my God. You killed him, didn't you? You killed Robin.'

The three of us stood in a triangle of silence. Drella had fled the room. I didn't know what to do. In the absence of knowing what to say, I picked up the remote and turned the telly off. At least I no longer had Robin's face staring at me.

'What happened?' Devon demanded. 'He came here looking for me, right?'

I moved to take her arm, to escort her back to the basement, but she jerked away from me. She was backed right up against the window, the closed blinds rattling as she bumped into them.

'Get the fuck away from me!' she screamed.

Helena, in the doorway, had gone utterly still, chest rising and falling as she inhaled and exhaled through her nose. The way she was glaring at Devon made me think she was about to do something drastic and, almost unconsciously, I found myself stepping between her and Devon. I'm not sure if Helena noticed what I was doing, but Devon certainly did.

Because, for the first time since we'd taken her prisoner, she looked scared. She must have been able to see the murder in Helena's eyes too.

Chapter 29

I escorted a silent Devon back into the basement. She was unusually compliant.

'I'll be back,' I said, pulling the door closed behind me.

'Matthew,' she said. 'Wait.'

I pushed the door open and looked at her through the gap.

'What happened? With Robin?'

'I don't want to talk about it now.'

'You murdered him,' she said.

'No.' I couldn't leave her statement, her accusation, hanging like that. I stepped back into the room and locked the door behind me.

'Bullshit. You expect me to believe it's a coincidence that he happened to die while I was here? Did *she* do it? I saw how she looked at me. Like I'm next. It's what she does. First Lee, now Robin. The only two men who ever cared about me.'

'I need to go.'

I turned but she grabbed hold of me. 'Please, Matthew. You're a nice guy. You wouldn't hurt me. I know that. But Helena . . . She murdered Lee, now Robin . . . It's going to be me next, isn't it?'

Devon had tears in her eyes. Grief for Robin or self-pity, it was hard to tell. Once again, I turned to go.

'Please don't let her kill me,' she said as I slipped through the door. As I went up the stairs I heard her begging, calling after me. 'Please. Matthew, please.'

I put my hands over my ears.

ω

Helena was in the kitchen, staring into space. Rain soaked the windows; that particular type of grey drizzle you only get by the English seaside. Drella was on her lap.

'Is he okay?' I asked.

'Yeah. A bit shaken but fine, I think.'

Drella jumped down and went over to sniff his bowl before sauntering off.

Helena's phone lay in front of her on the breakfast bar.

'I had a missed call,' she said. Her voice sounded distant. Numb. 'A voicemail.'

'Oh God. Not the police?'

She shook her head. 'You can hear for yourself.'

She handed me the phone, and a familiar, posh voice immediately filled my ears. Henry.

'*Helena. I need you to listen to me.*' He was panting. He sounded absolutely terrified. '*The Crowleys have been round to see me again. If I don't get that money they're going to kill me and then you'll be next. They've given me twenty-four hours. Please, Helena. I'm scared. If we don't pay back the debt we are both fucked.*'

I put down the phone. 'What the hell is he going on about?'

'This is what he came to talk to me about this morning. He and Lee did some kind of deal with this family, the Crowleys, and it went wrong and now they owe them half a million quid. Henry said Jamie Crowley's patience has finally run out.'

'But what's that got to do with you?'

233

'Isn't it obvious? Henry can't pay them so they're turning their attention to the next potential source of recompense. Lee's widow. Me. That's why Henry was so interested when I told him I was thinking about selling the house. He wants me to sell it and give the proceeds to the Crowleys.'

'Or what?'

'What do you think? The Crowleys are like the seaside equivalent of the Krays. They come from a long line of smugglers, going all the way back to when there were mounted customs officers patrolling the beaches.'

I tried to take all this in.

'It never rains, huh?' Helena said, and she began to giggle hysterically. I stared at her until she stopped.

'What are you going to do?'

'I was thinking about following Devon's phone off Beachy Head.'

'Please. Don't say that.'

She hadn't met my eye through this whole exchange. Now, finally, she looked at me.

'I don't know, Matthew. I can't think about this Crowley thing. I mean, there's absolutely nothing I can do about it, is there? I can't sell the house while Devon is here, so I can't give them their money.'

I couldn't get my head round it. How could this be happening at the same time as everything else? It didn't seem possible.

Helena, once again, displayed her spooky ability of reading my mind. 'I've angered the gods. When I took justice into my own hands and killed Lee, they didn't like it. They tried to kill me by pushing me off that cliff. Then they sent Devon. Now the Crowleys. It will be a plague of locusts next. Or boils.' She giggled again.

'It's got nothing to do with any gods,' I said. 'It's just . . . cause and effect. A chain of events.'

'A chain? It's a massive fucking shitstorm!'

As she said that, the heavens opened and the steady drizzle against the window became a downpour, raindrops drumming against the glass like they were trying to shatter it.

'See?' said Helena. 'Seriously pissed-off gods.'

We listened to the rain for a minute.

'Has there been anything more on the news about Robin?' I asked.

'No. But you know they're going to be looking for Devon. They could be checking her phone records as we speak. They might have done it already.'

The weight of unsaid words hung between us.

'We're not killing her,' I said.

'Then she'll have to stay here forever. When I sell the house to pay off Lee's debts, I'll have to explain that she's a sitting tenant.'

'Helena, it's not funny.'

'Oh, I know it's not.'

More silence. The rain kept beating against the window.

'I still think we could do a deal with her,' I said. 'It might be easier now. She's scared of us at last. We can use that fear. If she thinks we're willing to kill her, she's far more likely to agree to something.'

Helena sighed. 'Yeah, she'll promise anything. Of course she will. The moment she gets out, though, she'll go to the cops.' She rubbed her face. 'I am so tired of having this conversation.'

'I can't believe . . . I can't believe you would actually be prepared to do it.'

'Do what?'

I didn't want to say it.

Helena leaned forward and whispered it. 'Kill Devon.' Her voice returned to its normal volume. 'I'm already a murderer.'

'But . . . that was Lee. That was different. He was abusive. You were scared.'

'And you don't think I'm scared now? I can't go to jail. I just can't. And it won't only be me. We'll both get life. We won't see each other again until we're old and grey. Is that what you want? I'm tired of saying this too, but Devon is hardly some innocent girl we abducted on the street. She walked into this fire.'

'But that doesn't mean . . .'

'Do you think I want to? But I haven't heard you offer an alternative that will actually work.'

'What about running?' I said. 'Get out of the UK, find somewhere that doesn't have an extradition treaty?'

She sighed. 'Do you not think I've looked into that? It's ridiculously hard to find out which countries will extradite people despite not having an official treaty. It mostly seems to be places that are in political turmoil or that are hostile to the UK. Places that wouldn't be easy to get into in the first place. And there's also nothing to say you wouldn't be arrested and put in jail there. The days when bank robbers could swan off to Brazil and live it large on the beach are long gone. And I really don't want to spend my life on the run anyway. Do you?'

I looked out of the window at Henry's Porsche, parked on the driveway. I thought about Devon downstairs. The Crowley family out there somewhere. The police, trying to find out what had happened with Robin.

And something came to me. An idea, stirring.

'Matthew, I said, do you not—'

'Hold on. I'm thinking.'

I went over to the window, thinking it through. It could work . . . couldn't it? It depended on . . . But yes, it was possible. There could be a way of using one of the messes we were in to clean up the other.

236

'I'm going to return Henry's car,' I said.

'What, now?'

'Yes. A drive will help me think. I'll call a taxi to bring me home.'

The key to the Porsche was on the counter.

As I picked it up, Helena said, 'You know we need to make a decision about what we're going to do. The clock is ticking, Matthew.'

'I know. That's why I'm going for this drive. When I get back, we'll talk about it, and I promise we'll make that decision. Okay?'

'Okay.'

We hugged. Her body was warm. Then, before I gave in to the temptation to tell her my idea, and allow her to dissuade me from it, I left the house.

Chapter 30

I used the satnav in the Porsche to find Henry's address. He lived about thirty minutes' drive away, on the South Downs, between the town of Burgess Hill and a little village called Plumpton Green.

It was getting dark as I left Helena's place and the wipers squeaked back and forth to clear the last drops of rain. My stomach was in knots but my head was buzzing. I imagined this must be what it felt like to find oneself on the edge of madness, though I wasn't sure which side of the line I was on.

If this worked out, we would be free, Devon would be free, Jamie Crowley would be satisfied, and everyone could get on with their lives. I would have to learn to live with the guilt over what had happened to Robin. I would do whatever I could to be a useful citizen, stop being selfish and devote myself to good causes. I knew it would always be there – that crunch as Robin fell down the steps, the weight of his body as we carried him into his house – but I could still lead a good life.

So what was the plan?

The key, I had realised, was finding a way to guarantee Devon's silence; something that would prevent her from running to the cops the moment she was released. To do that, we needed to have something to threaten her with. A deterrent.

Which Henry could provide.

When Helena had told me about Jamie Crowley, my initial reaction was that we had another problem to deal with. Two separate entities, Crowley and Devon, demanding money. Two threats to Helena's life and freedom.

But what if I could use one to negate the other?

What did Henry want? To prevent the Crowleys taking their pound of flesh, he needed to pay them back the money he owed them. Unfortunately, the only way to get that money was to sell Helena's house, which Helena couldn't do because there was a woman locked in the basement.

A classic catch-22.

But Henry could provide the solution to break that circle.

How?

By vouching for Helena. By countering Devon's accusations about Helena killing Lee.

It was possible because we had deleted the recordings of Helena's confession. Devon no longer had any evidence of Helena's crimes. But *we* had evidence now, in the form of the sketches, that Devon had been sleeping with Lee, plus there would no doubt be people at the college who had seen them together. If Devon went to the police to tell them Helena had murdered her husband, Henry could come forward and say, *No, that's not what happened.* He could testify that Lee had told him that his mistress, Devon, had threatened his life. He had told her he was ending their affair and, in a rage, she had sworn revenge. That if he left her, she would find a way to kill him.

I had a whole alternative timeline worked out. In this fictional version of the truth, on the morning of Lee's death, Lee had called Henry – from the burner phone he used to talk to Devon – and told him he had spent a final night with Devon then told her it was over. She had been furious, telling him he was going to pay, that she wouldn't let him go on without her. Lee had been shaken but told Henry he was going home for his regular morning swim.

Henry wasn't sure how Devon had done it, but maybe she had drugged him? Maybe Lee had taken a coffee with him from Devon's place? She could have slipped something into it.

So why hadn't Henry come forward when Lee had drowned, to tell the police about his suspicion? Well, he hadn't had any proof, had he? It might have been a coincidence. Importantly, he hadn't wanted to upset Helena, who had been a doting wife who worshipped Lee. He didn't want to be the one to tell her Lee was having an affair.

It was only now, with Devon throwing wild accusations around, that he had decided he needed to come forward. Devon was clearly crazy. She had stalked Helena and followed her to Iceland, befriending her and arranging to come and stay at Helena's place afterwards, because she had just broken up with her new boyfriend-slash-housemate, Robin. And now look what had happened. Robin was dead too. Coincidence? Or was Devon in fact a serial killer? It had to be worth looking into, surely?

I could see it all playing out in court. The wronged widow versus the femme fatale. Sexist tropes, yes, but still ones that connected powerfully, that juries would buy into. And with Henry – the well-spoken, privately educated, Porsche-driving pillar of the community – on Helena's side, and with Helena being older, the cheated-upon wife who'd led a quiet life, I was sure I knew who the jury would side with. At the very least, the possibility that Devon had killed Lee would be enough to provide reasonable doubt to get Helena acquitted. And then the police would have to decide whether to charge Devon.

It would work. I was sure of it.

All I needed to do was persuade Henry to go along with it, in return for us paying off the Crowleys and saving his skin. Once he'd agreed, I would go back to Helena and explain it all to her. Tell her that, by selling the house, she would make it safe for us to release Devon.

She would be half a million quid down; that money would go to the Crowley family. But there would be money left over from the house sale. Another few hundred thousand at least. She would be more than fine.

And she would be free.

She would agree to it, I was sure. And if she didn't?

Well, maybe that would show she wasn't the woman I thought she was. If she still thought the only way out of this was to kill Devon, I would . . .

To be honest, I didn't have the foggiest idea what I would do.

This had to work.

There was no alternative.

ω

According to the map on the satnav, Henry's place was in a wooded area close to the Artelium Wine Estate. The directions took me through the village of Ditchling, then north past a golf club. I could easily imagine Henry being a member, which was all good for the story I wanted him to tell and his credibility as an upstanding member of society. No matter that he had somehow got involved with a bunch of criminals and his former business partner had been, to deliberately speak ill of the dead, a piece of shit. Nobody needed to know that.

As the golf course receded behind me, the road grew narrower and the trees thickened. I had never understood the appeal of living somewhere like this. I was a city boy. I liked to be near shops and light and traffic. To me, dark woods were places where children got eaten by witches, where bodies were buried and never found.

I drove into the trees, heading towards the dot on the screen. There were no houses or buildings in sight and the road had narrowed to a single lane that curved and wound its way deeper into the woods. I went slowly, worried another vehicle would come speeding around a corner. A head-on collision was the last thing I needed right now.

After about ten minutes, the satnav said, 'You have reached your destination.'

'Um, I don't think so,' I answered aloud.

I was still on the lane and couldn't see any houses. My headlights illuminated overhanging branches before me. There was a splat of something dead on the road, which at least indicated other cars had been through here. But where the hell was Henry's house? I slowed right down, crawling forward at fifteen miles per hour, and wound down the window so I could crane my neck out. Was that a light shining in the distance? I rubbed my eyes.

Then I spotted it. A sharp turning to the right. I turned on to it and found myself driving through an open gate. The track suddenly ended and I was in a clearing with a large house at its centre.

I parked the Porsche in front of the house, its façade a faded white with ivy creeping in jagged lines towards the roof. I guessed it was at least two hundred years old, probably more. In front of the house were a couple of statues of angels, covered with moss, and a dried-out pond. There was a separate building to the left, possibly a granny annexe. I tried to remember what Helena had told me about Henry. He had been married until recently, but after the kids grew up and left home, his wife had suddenly announced she was leaving him for an antiques dealer from Lewes. Henry had been left alone in the house his family had lived in for generations, though apparently he'd had to give it to his wife as part of the divorce settlement and start paying her rent.

'He lives out there all on his own now,' Helena had said. 'He doesn't even have a dog or cat.'

I wondered how he would react when he saw me on his doorstep.

I got out of the car and approached the front door. There were lights on inside and colours, presumably from a TV, flickered in what I assumed was the living room.

A ceramic plaque on the wall told me this was Magpie Cottage. There was no doorbell, just a large brass knocker. Before knocking, I checked the time. Just before nine o'clock. Not too outrageously late to be calling.

I raised the knocker and rapped on the door.

Chapter 31

Helena was aware of her own exhaustion as she went down the stairs to the basement, carrying a tray containing Devon's dinner. The physical manifestation of stress, seeping into her bones and muscles and joints. She had felt like this after Lee drowned, when she had been waiting for them to find his body and confirm he was dead. Every step was an effort. But it was an effort she needed to make. She had to keep going.

'Devon?' she said as she went through the door with the tray. Where was she? Helena was about to go into the home cinema when the door to the storage cupboard opened and Devon appeared.

'What are you doing?'

Devon didn't reply immediately. She seemed to be thinking about it, like a child who was obviously about to lie. 'Looking for something to read. It helps me relax, okay? And I've finished that book.' She gestured to the book about local smugglers, which lay face down and open on the sofa.

Helena put the tray down on the coffee table. It was a chickpea curry, with naan bread and basmati rice. Mango chutney and poppadoms on the side. A bottle of lager too, which Helena had poured into a plastic cup, in case Devon tried to use the bottle as a weapon. In Iceland, during a group discussion about food, Devon had told them that Indian was her favourite cuisine.

'What's this?' Devon asked with suspicion. 'My last meal before I'm executed?'

'We're not monsters,' Helena said, hearing Matthew's voice in her head.

'Tell that to Robin.'

Helena took a step towards the younger woman, and Devon backed away. Helena felt a thrill run through her, a thrill that shocked her. Is this how Lee had felt when Helena displayed her fear of him? The rush of blood that fizzes through the predator when it faces its prey?

Devon must have seen it on her face because she backed away further.

'Robin was a sleaze,' Helena said. 'Did you know he borrows your laptop when you're not around? He'd worked out the password and got into it. He'd been looking at your photos.'

'That doesn't mean he deserved to die,' Devon said, her voice quieter than normal.

'No. But it's just as much your fault as it is ours. Three of us caused the accident that led to Robin's death. Four if you count Robin himself. Maybe we should include Lee too. If you hadn't been fucking my husband, if you hadn't followed me to Iceland, if you hadn't tried to blackmail me. You're just as much to blame as I am. But do you know what? I'm sick of saying it. I'm sick and tired of this whole situation. All I want is to get on with my life. Lee already robbed me of some of my best years, and now you're determined to rob me of the rest.'

Devon opened her mouth.

'And if you say that's literally what we've done to Robin, I will slap you.'

Devon closed her mouth.

'I don't know what I'm going to do with you, Devon.'

'You could let me go. What if I promised not to tell anyone about any of it?'

'Then I'd call you a liar.'

Devon appeared to crumple. Two days locked up down here, Robin's death, the fear of what was going to happen to her. It had finally got to her. Broken that defiant spirit. It made it harder to hate her, but that predator thrill was still there, and Helena found herself moving closer to Devon.

She pictured herself with her hands around the other woman's throat. Could almost hear Devon choking as Helena squeezed. Saw her body on the floor and felt the rush inside her.

Devon shrank against the back of the sofa.

'Why are you looking at me like that?'

Helena snapped back to reality, looked down at her hands and saw they were curled into claws. Murderer's hands.

She had to get out of this space. Now.

'Eat your dinner,' she said.

She headed for the door. As she reached it, Devon said, 'None of this was personal, Helena. I want you to know that.'

Helena stopped. Turned to look at the younger woman, who said, 'Maybe in another life we could have been friends.'

'Don't be absurd,' Helena said, and she left, slamming the door behind her.

ᚋ

She reached the hallway upstairs. Her skin was tingling and her underarms prickled with sweat. She stood in front of the hall mirror and found herself staring at a stranger. Those weren't her eyes, were they? What had happened to her face? She stepped forward, hardly able to believe what she was seeing: the dark hollows of her cheeks; her bloodshot eyes. It had only been forty-eight hours since

Devon had turned up here, and the stress was devouring her from the inside.

'You're a wreck,' she said to the creature in the mirror, and she wondered why Matthew hadn't told her. Or had he? She couldn't remember. She also couldn't remember the last time she'd eaten anything. He had definitely been nagging her about that. She wondered, too, what he was planning. Why had he been so keen to take the Porsche back to Henry? Did he have some sort of plan? She was still angry with him for thinking she might have been plotting revenge against him, but he was a good man. Better than her, probably. Or perhaps just not as strong as her. Not as willing to do the unthinkable.

Because, if he didn't come home with some miraculous idea to get out of this mess, killing Devon was still the only solution she could see.

She didn't want to do it. Of course she didn't. But hadn't Devon brought it on herself? Wasn't she almost asking for it?

Her thoughts were interrupted by the sound of an engine, and she went to the front window. Headlights were coming up the drive, piercing the darkness.

It was a police car.

She told herself not to panic, dug her nails into her forearm and hissed at herself: 'Get. It. Together.'

She couldn't afford for Devon to hear the cops, so as they got out of their car she unbolted the front door and ran outside.

There were two of them, a man and a woman, both in uniform. She saw how the woman looked her up and down, taking in the state of her: barefoot and sweaty.

'I was doing yoga,' she found herself saying.

'Sorry to have disturbed you so late,' said the male officer. 'We were canvassing this area, and on the way back realised we'd missed this house.'

'We can always call back in the morning,' the woman cop said, giving her colleague a look that told Helena they'd been debating whether to come round in the dark.

'No problem at all.' Just canvassing. That was good. Or was it a ruse? Should she send them away? Or would that look suspicious? Always better to cooperate. It's what an innocent person with little experience of dealing with the police would do. 'How can I help?'

She saw them look past her towards the house, like they were wondering if she was going to invite them in. She grinned at them, hoping she didn't look as insane as she felt.

The female cop said, 'I'm Sergeant Sharma, and this is Constable Wallace. Like my colleague said, we're canvassing the area. We're wondering if you might have seen this man?'

She handed Helena a printout. Of course, Helena knew who was going to be on it, and she tried to arrange her face appropriately. What was the natural emotion? Curiosity. Eagerness to help.

There he was. Robin. It was a nice photo, taken at his graduation ceremony. He was wearing the gown but not the mortar board. Smiling. Dimples in his cheeks.

Yes, officers. I saw him lying in my back garden with his neck broken.

She pretended to study the photo for a few seconds, brain racing. What was the story she had prepared? Devon had come to stay here because Robin had been harassing her. Devon had gone home last night and she hadn't seen or heard from her since. In this version of events, would she know what Robin looked like? No. She would know his name but she wouldn't have met him.

'I don't recognise him,' she said.

'You haven't been watching the news today?' said Wallace.

'No. I never watch the news. It's too depressing.'

'Don't blame you,' said Wallace with a smile.

'According to his phone records, he was in this area last night,' Sharma said, shooting her colleague a disapproving look. 'Between nine and ten. Were you at home?'

If she lied, and the Tesla had been caught on a road camera, they would find out. 'No. I went for a drive.'

'A drive?'

'Yes. I was . . . a little stressed out about something, and I find driving calms me down.'

'I'm the same,' said Wallace.

A roll of the eyes from Sharma. 'Do you live on your own?' she asked.

'Yes. Well, except my boyfriend is staying here at the moment.'

Wallace frowned, clearly disappointed by this mention of a boyfriend. 'Can we talk to him?' he said.

'He's not home at the moment. He's . . . running an errand. And he wasn't here between nine and ten either. He was in the car with me.'

'Okay,' Sharma said. 'Well, we will need to talk to him, so if you could ask him to give us a call.' She handed Helena a card with her name and number on.

'Of course.'

'And you definitely don't recognise the man in this picture?'

Helena shook her head. She was praying they wouldn't say his name because then she would have to admit she had heard it, or come up with a new story. At the same time, she was trying to second-guess the cops' expectations. Wouldn't she ask who he was and why they were looking for him?

'Is he missing?' she asked.

'No,' said Wallace. 'Unfortunately, he's deceased.'

'Oh!' Did she sound sufficiently shocked? She tried to tap into her genuine horror and sadness but wasn't sure what her face was doing.

'But there are some question marks around Mr Barker's movements, and that of his housemate, who is missing.'

'I see.'

Helena felt like she might throw up. Wallace seemed entirely unsuspicious, but Sharma was scrutinising her closely. Oh God, they were about to ask her about Devon. And if they did, there was no way she could deny knowing her, even if she was able to come up with a different story. They were friends on Facebook. They had been in Iceland together. She felt light-headed. Faint. Her brain raced, trying to work out what she was going to say.

Then Sharma's phone rang.

'Excuse me,' she said, answering it and taking a few steps towards the house, a serious expression on her face.

She tried to listen to Sharma's end of the conversation but Wallace talked over her. 'This is a beautiful spot. You're so lucky to live here.' And then he must have remembered something because his face fell. 'Oh. Wait. Your husband . . .'

Helena was saved from having to react by Sharma ending her call and walking back towards them. 'We need to get back to the station,' she said to Wallace. 'There's been a development.' She turned to Helena. 'Thank you for your time. Don't forget we need your boyfriend to call us.'

'Yes.'

They drove off. Helena watched them go, then ran back into the house.

A development.

She speculated. The pathologist had found evidence Robin hadn't died in his house. They had traced Devon's phone to a spot below Beachy Head. Maybe a neighbour had seen something. Whatever it was, things were moving faster than Helena had expected. It was less than twenty-four hours since Robin had died, and she'd thought they'd have longer.

They would trace Devon's phone to this area too. They would discover the link between Devon and Helena and Matthew. And then they would be back.

Next time, she wouldn't be able to stall them outside.

She ran up the stairs, straight to her bedroom. She took her passport out of her bedside drawer.

I don't want to spend my life on the run.

She looked at the passport.

But maybe I'll have to.

Helena sat on the bed and put her head in her hands. And, sitting there, she felt herself grow calm.

She recalled how it had felt just fifteen minutes ago, when Devon had cowered away from her. How strong it had made her feel.

The police were going to come back. They were going to find Devon.

Helena had two choices.

Run. Or . . .

She flipped open the passport and examined her photo. She had been just-married when this photo was taken. She remembered that day clearly. She and Lee had gone together, and on the way home she had looked at his photo and, very softly, laughed. He had looked so serious in it. Like all passport photos, including hers, it was extremely unflattering.

Except Lee had thought he looked good. He was offended by her laughter. More than offended. Upset. And when he was upset . . .

It had been a terrible evening.

And she had escaped him, hadn't she? She had saved her own life by dealing with him, and she had got away with it. Why should she lose the freedom she'd gained because his fucking mistress had turned up to blackmail her? It wasn't fair. It wasn't right.

Why should she run?

She slipped the passport beneath her pillow. She went downstairs to the kitchen. She didn't feel anything except the conviction that this was the only solution. She couldn't wait for Matthew to come back here with a plan, especially as she didn't believe anything he could come up with would work. The way Sharma had been looking at her, that call . . . She was convinced they were going to be back here with a warrant. They would search the house and find Devon, who would tell them everything. About Robin. About Lee.

She couldn't allow that to happen.

She took the largest, sharpest knife from the block on the counter.

She stood there for a moment, practising her breathing. Calming herself down, shutting off her emotions. Matthew would be upset, but eventually he would understand she was doing this for both of them.

It was the only solution.

She gripped the knife and headed towards the basement.

Chapter 32

I knocked on Henry's front door. There was no answer.

I knocked again. Then, when there was still no reply, I went to the front window and put my face to the glass, peering in. I had been right, the TV was on, along with a side lamp, but there was no sign of life. Where was he? The telly was on, so he must be at home. Surely he didn't get many people calling here at night.

So why was he ignoring my knock?

I waited five minutes, in case he was on the toilet or in the shower, then tried again. Nothing.

This was maddening. I had come all the way out here. I needed to talk to him. I wasn't going to turn around and go home without getting what I'd come for. Then I realised: he probably thought I was Jamie Crowley or one of his men, come to carry out whatever threats they'd made against him.

I crouched and called through the letterbox. 'Henry? It's Matthew.' Would he remember who I was? I added, 'Helena's boyfriend.'

Silence.

Perhaps he thought it was a trick. I could picture him inside, hiding, convinced members of the notorious crime family had come to hurt him. I needed to get inside, to show myself and reassure him.

I tried the front door handle just in case he'd left the door unlocked, but no such luck. There were no windows open at the front of the house either. I walked around the perimeter of the cottage to the back door. It was locked too, and there were no open windows downstairs.

I thought about smashing a window with a rock, but I didn't want him freaking out and calling the police. I thought there might also be a chance he had a gun. Did he go hunting? He definitely seemed the type. I really didn't want him reacting to the sound of a window breaking by blasting me with a shotgun, but if I could get inside and call out, let him know it was definitely me, I believed I'd be safe.

Of course, if I hadn't been so desperate, if I hadn't thought there was no other way out of the terrible mess Helena and I were in, I wouldn't have taken any risks. But I *was* desperate.

So when I spotted the wide-open window on the upper floor of the cottage, with a light on inside, I went looking for a ladder. I thought Henry must have one. And there, at the bottom of the small garden – who needs a big garden when you have the whole woods to yourself? – was a shed.

Fortunately, it wasn't locked. I opened the door and shone my phone's flashlight inside to reveal a space crammed full of junk and decorated with thick cobwebs. I was pretty sure some eight-legged nasties scattered as the door opened. But there was a ladder, slid beneath a workbench. I found a large torch sitting on the workbench and switched it on so I could see without having to hold my phone, and pushed aside all the junk that was in the way. I pulled the ladder out and carried it up to the cottage, extending it to its full length and propping it against the wall so it reached up to the open window.

I climbed the ladder and went through the window into the brightly lit room. This was Henry's main bedroom, by the looks of it. The double bed was unmade and striped shirts were scattered across the floor. The walls were covered with pictures of dogs. Paintings of gundogs, some with ducks or pheasants between their jaws.

'Henry?' I called. 'It's Matthew. Helena's Matthew. I need to talk to you.'

No response.

Okay, this was eerie. Where the hell was he? I listened for the sound of a running shower but the house was so silent I could hear a faint whistling in my ears, the mild tinnitus that only hits me when all is utterly quiet.

'Henry?'

I left the bedroom and went along the landing, switching on lights as I went and pushing open doors. A bathroom. A separate toilet. A couple of spare rooms that looked like they had once been Henry's kids' rooms. One was empty apart from an exercise bike and emo posters on the walls: Panic! at the Disco and My Chemical Romance.

I went down the stairs, calling his name again. The house was chilly and damp, as if the heating hadn't been on for months. The place felt abandoned. The empty house in the woods that would eventually be reclaimed by nature. I felt the hairs stand up on my arms and there was a tingle at the nape of my neck, like a ghost was standing close behind me, blowing icy air on to me through dead lips.

I reached the bottom of the staircase, having passed more paintings of hunting scenes, and found myself in the hallway by the front door. I went into the living room to my left and stared at the TV. It was tuned in to an oldies channel, a rerun of an episode of *Murder She Wrote* playing with the volume turned low. There were family photos on the mantelpiece. A younger Henry with his wife and their kids. Tweed and pearls and a pair of happy children with sensible haircuts.

'Henry? Are you here?'

I checked the little dining room, then the kitchen, where the lights were already on. Both empty but there was another sign of life: a saucepan beside the Aga, the remains of a tin of soup drying inside it, and a bowl and plate in the sink. Today's *Times* was on the table, open at the sports pages.

'He's vanished into thin air,' I muttered. I guessed he could have gone for a walk. But in the dark? He didn't have a dog, so it wasn't like he'd had to take some pooch out for a pee. Maybe he had gone out with a friend, in their car, or taken a cab, or even cycled. But why leave the TV on? I supposed it wasn't that unusual for someone to go out having forgotten to turn the telly off. But the saucepan was still a little warm, the smell of soup lingering in the air. If he'd gone out, it hadn't been long ago, and nobody had passed me on my drive through the woods.

Then I remembered: the granny annexe. I looked out the front window and saw that the lights were on inside this other building. Henry must be in there.

Feeling a little foolish for not thinking about checking the annexe before, I went out the front door, leaving it open in case I needed to come back, and walked across the clearing to the other building. Helena had never mentioned Henry having an older relative living with him – an ancient parent, for example – but it was possible. Perhaps the simple explanation was that Henry's eighty-five-year-old mother lived here and he'd made her a bowl of soup and taken it to her. I'd find the two of them chatting and wondering what was going on.

I reached the annexe. It looked like it had been built far more recently than the cottage; it was a small brick building, perhaps twenty years old. Single-storey.

I knocked and the door creaked open.

'Hello?' I called.

I let myself in. There was a short hallway with an open door to the right. I went through.

I stopped dead, trying to take in the scene before me.

Henry was lying on the floor. There was a gaping hole in his stomach; the blue-and-white-striped shirt he was wearing was soaked with blood. His eyes and mouth were both open, in an expression of shock. There was more blood on the carpet around him and all over the chintzy sofa cover.

I stood and stared down at him, frozen by shock. The blood looked wet and there were no flies around. There was an unfamiliar smell in the air: metallic, sulphurous. Everything told me this had only just happened.

And then, from somewhere behind me, a toilet flushed.

Oh Jesus. This had to have been done by one of the Crowleys – finally carrying out their threat – and they were still here.

I needed to run but I was rooted to the spot, the world slowing to a crawl, legs not working, and I heard the bathroom door open and footsteps coming towards me. A man came into the room. He had his head down and a shotgun dangling by his side.

He looked up.

I stared.

It couldn't be. *It couldn't be.*

'Matthew?' he said. He was shaking, and seemed almost as shocked to see me as I was to see him. 'What are *you* doing here?' And then he laughed. 'I suppose you're thinking the same thing.'

He looked awful. There were bags under his eyes and his face was puffy and pale. His hair was badly cut and there was a shaving rash on his cheeks. The clothes he was wearing – presumably borrowed from Henry – seemed way too big for him.

I hadn't seen him for twenty years, except in Helena's photographs, but there was no doubting who he was.

'Lee,' I said.

'That's me,' he said as he raised the shotgun towards me.

Chapter 33

Helena went down the stairs. This time, instead of a tray she carried a knife. She had tried to empty her head of thoughts and her heart of emotions.

She had no choice. Devon had to die. It was the only way to stop the world from discovering she had murdered Lee, and if she had once thought there might be a chance of mercy from a jury, the subsequent kidnapping of Devon and Robin's death had put paid to that.

Running wouldn't work. She would be caught eventually.

This was her only option.

She unlocked the door to the basement and stepped inside, expecting to find Devon in the den, sitting on the sofa where Helena had last seen her. But the sofa was empty.

She must be in the home cinema, Helena thought.

'Devon?' she said quietly, locking the door and moving forward, the knife held behind her back. But the screen was blank and the lights in the cinema were off.

'Hello?' she said.

No response.

She flicked on the lights.

Devon wasn't there.

This didn't make sense. There was nowhere else she could be. For a horrible moment, Helena wondered if Devon could have snuck behind her and escaped from the basement. But no – Helena had locked the door behind her.

Devon had to be hiding. Helena looked behind the cinema sofas, then checked behind all the other chairs, expecting to find her curled up on the floor. But there was no sign of her.

She went back into the den, trying not to panic, trying to make sense of this. Devon *had* to be here. The door had definitely been locked – Helena remembered unlocking it less than a minute ago – and there was no other way out.

Then she remembered. When she'd come down earlier, Devon had been in the walk-in cupboard where Lee had kept all his junk. With relief, she walked across and opened the door, gripping the knife firmly, ready to strike if Devon leapt out at her.

The cupboard was empty.

Helena stared into the space with its boxes and files and tried to make sense of what was happening. Devon couldn't have just evaporated. She had to be here.

Wait. The freezer.

Had Devon decided to kill herself?

It was funny. Helena had come down here intending to slit Devon's throat, but the thought of her lying dead in the freezer, frozen or suffocated, filled her not with relief that she wouldn't have to go through with it, but with horror. It was like being slapped awake. She stared at the knife in her hand. What had she been thinking? Lee had been a monster. He had deserved it. Devon was nothing more than a stupid, greedy young woman. Helena threw the knife aside and ran to the freezer, heart pounding, and wrenched the door open, convinced Devon would be lying there on the floor.

But like the cupboard and the home cinema and the den, the freezer was empty.

Helena stepped back into the den and turned in a circle, unable to believe what she was seeing – or rather, not seeing. She went back into the home cinema to double-check, lifted the blanket on the sofa as if she was expecting to find that Devon had shrunk and was cowering beneath it. She went back to the walk-in cupboard and looked again, peering beneath the shelves.

It was impossible.

But there was no denying it. No escaping the facts.

Devon was gone.

PART THREE

PART THREE

Chapter 34

'Sit down,' Lee said. 'Over there. That armchair. Keep your hands where I can see them.'

'I don't have a weapon,' I said.

'No? What about a phone? Of course you do. Toss it here.'

I did what he said, pitching my phone to Lee, who fumbled it before managing to get hold of it properly, sticking it in his back pocket. He seemed almost as on edge as I felt. A cocktail of nerves and adrenaline. Henry's body was at my feet. I tried not to look at him but I could smell him now. The stench of death, growing worse by the second.

'What happened?' I asked, indicating Henry's body with my eyes.

'Henry told me Helena had a new bloke,' Lee said, not answering my question. 'I didn't realise it was you, though. That you were the Matthew she's shacking up with. What happened? Come sniffing around the moment you heard I was gone? Wanted to see if you could fuck her life up again, huh?'

'I was an amateur compared to you.' Maybe it was the shock. My hatred for him. Or maybe I'd gone past the point where I was incapacitated by fear and come out the other side. But I wasn't scared of him.

He sneered. 'Of course she's told you a lot of bullshit about me.'

'I've literally seen the scars, Lee. You scalded her with boiling water. You kept her prisoner in that house. You cheated on her with Devon.'

His eyebrows went up. 'You know about that? I bet you don't know what Helena tried to do to me.'

'Oh, I do, Lee. I know everything.'

He stared at me, shocked. He was still pointing the shotgun at me. His hands were shaking. I would have preferred him to be calm and cocky. Not the ball of nervous energy that stood before me.

'Well. Fucking hell. What happened? Talk in her sleep, did she? Or has she found religion?'

I wasn't going to give him the pleasure of hearing about her brush with death in Iceland. Instead, I said, 'She loves me. She wanted me to know everything.' I shook my head. 'Jesus, when she finds out you're still alive . . .'

He licked his lips. 'It's going to be *delicious*.'

'How? How are you still alive? What happened?'

Again, he didn't answer me. His eyes darted around the room. 'I want to know what the hell you're doing out here. And how you know about Devon. Don't tell me she turned up and told Helena we were shagging? Stupid cow.'

'It's a long story,' I said.

'I don't care how long a story it is,' Lee said. 'Why don't you start by telling me what you're doing here.' When I hesitated, he got to his feet and jabbed the nose of the gun into my shoulder. 'Come on. Don't sit there thinking about it, trying to figure out what to say. Tell me or I'll start shooting bits of you off. What shall we start with? A foot?'

He pointed the shotgun at my right foot.

'Okay! I came here because Henry told us the Crowleys were after Helena. I had a plan I was going to put to him that I hoped would get Helena and me out of this . . . this mess we're in.'

When I mentioned the Crowleys, Lee – who had taken a step back, but was still close to me, with Henry's body by his feet – smirked.

'Wait. Was that not true? About the Crowleys being after Helena?'

He couldn't hide it. A smile spread across his face.

'Was that a complete lie?'

'Half a lie,' Lee said. 'They might be a bunch of criminals, but they're not complete monsters. They don't go after people's *widows*.'

'So . . . what? Why did Henry tell Helena she needed to sell her house?'

I thought Lee was going to explode. '*Her* house? It's my house! I designed it. I built it.'

I put my palms up. 'I don't understand.'

'Can you not figure it out? The plan was to get Helena to hand over the money, but we were never going to pass it on to Jamie Crowley. It was for me.'

'So you don't owe Jamie Crowley money?'

He rolled his eyes.

'You do owe him money? And . . .' I tried to figure it out. 'You faked your death? Because of the Crowleys?'

He tucked the gun under his arm and did a slow hand-clap. 'Bravo, mate. You've got it.'

'But how? It was your body that was fished out of the water. The police confirmed it through your DNA. How did you do it?'

He tried to grin but it came across as more of a sneer. It struck me again how terrible he looked. Pasty and bloated, his skin sallow and his hair thin and greasy. If he'd been in hiding for nine months it hadn't done him much good. I couldn't deny it: the state he was in made me happy.

'Do you know how boring it's been, stuck out here for months? I've had no one but Henry for company. I haven't been anywhere, seen anyone. No fun, no sex, not even any work. I've been sitting on my arse watching box sets. This is proving to be a very exciting day. Now you can make it even better by telling me exactly what the hell's been going on and how you know about Devon. Come on, Matty. Fill me in.'

I glanced at Henry's body.

'Don't mind him,' Lee said. 'He's not going to tell any tales.'

With the shotgun resting in his lap, his finger still on the trigger, I didn't feel like I had any choice. I told him everything, as succinctly and emotionlessly as possible, though even my flat retelling didn't stop him from reacting like he was watching a blockbuster movie. The word, I believe, is *Schadenfreude*. I started by telling him how Helena and I had met again at the college reunion, then about Helena's near-fatal fall in Thórsmörk, her confession, Devon turning up . . . Our attempts to find the backups of the recording. Lee howled with glee when I told him about Robin.

'I met that little twat when I was shagging Devon,' he said. 'He obviously had the hots for her. Knowing she was screwing me nearly killed him.' He guffawed. 'And then you finished him off.'

Finally, I relayed the plan I'd come here with, which made him chuckle again.

'So Devon is still locked in the basement?'

'She is.'

'And this plan involving the Crowleys and Henry . . . that's all you had?'

I nodded.

'And Helena thought it would work too?'

I paused, which made Lee clap his hands together and say, 'She didn't know, did she? You hadn't told her.'

'I wanted to talk to Henry first.'

'Wow. This has almost been worth all the months I've been stuck here. I can see Helena wringing her hands. The anguish!

Except . . . Helena's already killed once. Or, at least, she thinks she has. Hasn't she considered bumping Devon off?'

Again, my hesitation told him everything.

'Oh my God. I love it.'

I couldn't hold back my disgust. 'You don't care about Devon either, do you?'

He shrugged. 'She had a nice, young body.'

'You're foul. I might have been a dick at college, but at least I grew up. You haven't changed at all, have you?'

'Who wants to grow up? Matthew, I'm officially dead. I can be whoever I want to be. Whatever age I want. I can invent my own history.'

'Maybe. But you're stuck in a cottage in the woods a few miles from where you lived before. Why haven't you bought a new identity for yourself and moved to the Bahamas? It's not like anyone's going to be looking for you.'

He frowned.

'Come on, Lee,' I said. 'I've told you everything. Now it's your turn. How did you fake your death? And why kill Henry?'

His right hand was resting on the gun again. With his other hand, he scratched the stubble on his chin. Then he stood.

'Get up.'

'What?'

'Come on, outside. Keep your hands where I can see them.'

He nudged me with the gun and forced me to leave the annexe, following me out into the clearing. I was terrified. Was this it? Was he going to kill me?

The moon had come out while I'd been in the annexe. Out here, Lee looked even worse than he had indoors. He was grinning again and it struck me, more than it had inside the cottage: he was unhinged. After all these months of isolation, he was a coiled spring.

'What are we doing?' I asked.

'I have to see her.' A cool breeze blew across the clearing, stirring leaves around our feet. 'I want to see the look on her face when she realises I'm still alive.'

'What? Lee, that's—'

'Mad? Do you think I give a fuck? Do you?' He took a menacing step towards me.

'No, I—'

'I can't stay here anymore. Someone will notice Henry's missing and come out here to investigate. I need to do what you said before. Disappear. Properly this time. And you and that bitch are going to help me.'

He gestured at Henry's Porsche.

'You can drive.'

I moved towards the driver's door, my hands still in the air. Lee went round and slid into the passenger seat, keeping the shotgun trained on me as I sat behind the wheel.

'How did you do it, Lee?' I asked. 'How did you fake your death?'

He showed me his teeth, which under the dome light looked like they hadn't been brushed for weeks. 'What, you think you might want to fake yours too?'

It wasn't a bad idea. It really wasn't.

He thought about it, then nodded. 'Fine. Drive, and I'll tell you on the way.'

Chapter 35

DECEMBER 2021

Lee sat in Henry's kitchen, drinking tea and waiting for Jamie Crowley to show up. The house was bloody freezing, the only warmth in this room coming from the Aga, but Henry – hunched over his laptop at the ancient kitchen table – had beads of perspiration on his wrinkled brow. He was going through their recent accounts, trying to make the numbers add up, and every so often he would emit a groan of frustration, laced with despair.

'We're screwed,' he said.

They had been screwed for a while. A series of bad investments, the pandemic, half the cheap labour they used buggering off home to Poland after Brexit, soaring costs, supply problems. It was a terrible time to be a property developer and they had run out of money six months ago, with several projects left uncompleted, unable to pay their men's wages. The bank had turned down their latest loan request and Henry's wife had cleaned him out in the recent divorce.

Yeah, they were screwed.

The sound of a car engine came from outside. Henry got up and went over to the window. 'He's here.'

Lee got up and went out through the front door, into the clearing in which Henry's cottage stood. Jamie was getting out of his black Land Rover, dressed in a brown leather jacket, his bald head pink in the cold air. Lee had known Jamie since they were kids. He'd been one of the worst bullies at school and Lee had figured out at an early age that befriending him was the best form of protection, even though his family had warned him not to get chummy with the Crowleys.

Now Jamie came striding towards him, legs wide in the cowboy gait he'd always had, trying to look like he had massive balls. Behind him, someone else got out of the car. Another man, whose name Lee couldn't remember, but he was one of the Crowleys' foot soldiers, a drug dealer and enforcer who Jamie and his family used for unpleasant tasks they didn't want to dirty their hands with.

'Lee,' said Jamie. 'You know Kyle?'

Kyle. That was it. He was in his twenties and hadn't grown up around here. Rumour had it that he was a drifter who had followed a girl here and decided to stick around after she introduced him to the Crowleys. He always wore a baseball cap, and had acne scars on his cheeks.

They all went into Henry's kitchen and sat around the oak table that had apparently been passed down through the generations. It was Christmas week but you wouldn't know it. Henry hadn't bothered to decorate. Since his divorce, Henry had said, he didn't see any point celebrating.

'I'm going to get straight to the point,' Jamie said. He wasn't in the festive spirit either. 'Have you got my money?'

Lee and Henry exchanged a glance that made Jamie let out a disappointed sigh.

'What happened?'

Lee had no option but to tell Jamie the truth.

A couple of months earlier, Lee had seen a business opportunity – something that would help boost their revenue during this downturn in the property development market.

One morning, on his swim, he had watched a dinghy full of migrants pass him then land on the beach. The migrants had scattered and Lee, who had passable French, had got talking to the guy who operated the dinghy. This guy was part of a huge operation that smuggled refugees or migrants or whatever they were – Lee wasn't interested in the political reasons these people had for coming here – into the UK every day.

'Is that all you smuggle?' Lee had asked.

From there, a plan had been formed. As well as bringing over refugees, the French gang who ran the operation were very interested in the idea of bringing across drugs from mainland Europe, stuff that had a big mark-up when it hit British shores – everything from cocaine to painkillers. But they needed money to kick-start the arrangement, to procure the drugs, and Lee was cash-poor – that was the whole reason he was interested in doing this. Unfortunately, being cash-poor meant he needed a partner, and Jamie Crowley, Lee's old schoolmate, was the obvious candidate.

Jamie hadn't needed much persuading. It seemed like easy money, and it appealed to his idea of himself as the descendant of the smugglers who had once ruled this section of the coast. Henry wasn't involved in the deal but he knew about it and provided the venue for discussions. Everything was shaken on. The money was handed over to the French gang on the beach, taken back to France, and the first consignment of drugs was loaded on to a dinghy along with a dozen refugees.

And then tragedy had struck. There was an unexpected storm. The dinghy sank. Four of the refugees drowned. It was awful. But what was most awful from Lee's point of view was that the drugs he had paid for were now at the bottom of the English Channel.

When he went to his contacts in France, they'd shrugged and told him it wasn't their problem. They weren't in the business of offering refunds.

'So that's it,' he said now, in Henry's kitchen. Several steaming mugs of tea sat between them; Henry had even put out a plate of mince pies, his one concession to Christmas. 'The bastards are refusing to cough up.'

'Right,' said Jamie, with no emotion.

'Right?'

'Sometimes these things don't work out. That's business. This one didn't work out for you, Lee.'

Lee laughed nervously. 'Jamie, we've both lost out.'

'Er, no, I don't think so. How much of that cash was yours? Let me answer that: none of it.' Jamie stood up. 'Now, we're old friends so we can treat it as a business loan, but loans have interest, and in the two weeks since I handed over the cash the amount you owe has gone up from this' – he showed Lee a figure on his phone, then tapped in another – 'to this.'

'That's outrageous,' said Henry.

'Did anyone fucking ask you?' Jamie snapped.

Henry shrank back. Lee knew he hated this. He was terrified of Jamie and was only going along with it because, well, he pretty much did anything Lee asked. Henry was a weak man. Always had been.

'This time next week the debt will be this.' Jamie showed Lee another, even higher figure. 'Now, in order to stop the debt spiralling totally out of control, I've taken the liberty of putting together a repayment schedule. Kyle.'

Kyle took a scrunched-up sheet of paper from his pocket and handed it over. There were a couple of stains on it.

'Kyle here will be back Monday to collect the first instalment,' Jamie said.

'And if I can't pay?' Lee asked.

Jamie moved surprisingly fast. He had his hand around Lee's throat and Lee flat on his back on the table in the space of a second. Mugs fell and shattered and hot tea sprayed everywhere. Jamie's spittle landed on Lee's face as he said, 'You think we're mates, don't you, Lee? The truth is, I've always thought you were a twat. You make one late payment and it will give me great pleasure to put a bullet in your stupid pretty-boy face and bury you in these woods.'

He squeezed. Lee tried to fight but Jamie was too strong. Lee could feel his eyes bulging, the life leaving his body as his lungs were starved. This was it. He was actually going to die and there was nothing he could do about it.

Jamie let go at the moment Lee thought he might pass out.

'Happy Christmas,' Jamie said, and he and a grinning Kyle walked out.

ꞷ

Lee had spent the next week trying to work out exactly what he was going to do. He knew Jamie wouldn't hesitate to follow through on his threat, and Lee felt increasingly desperate, taking out his frustration and fear on Helena. He cursed Henry, who, thanks to his divorce, was unable to help him out. He fantasised about getting revenge on the gang across the Channel who had taken the money and sunk the merchandise.

He was starting to regret not taking out a big life insurance policy on Helena, but after what had happened with Lisa – and the big pay-out that had followed when their house burned down – he had always known it would be unlikely he'd get away with it again. When Helena died, he didn't want anyone accusing him of bumping her off for the money. No, it would purely be for pleasure. But, shit, if he'd known this was going to happen, he might have taken the risk.

Jamie wanted the first instalment by Monday, the 27th. Lee sold a watch and Henry flogged some old medals of his dad's to help out, so Lee had enough to make that first payment. Then he drove out to Henry's and waited for Jamie, thinking he might be able to reason with him again. If Jamie invested more money, he'd make back what he'd lost within a couple of months. Lee would forego his cut until they were all square. Jamie might just go for it.

But Jamie didn't turn up; only Kyle. He swaggered in stinking of dope, giggling to himself. Lee handed over the money, telling Kyle he wanted to talk to Jamie, and Kyle said, 'He's gone up to London for the night with Mrs Crowley.' Then he chuckled. 'Bruh, I don't know what *your* missus is up to.'

'What are you talking about?'

'Your wife. Black hair, fit, looks like she spends a lot of time at the gym. That's her, yeah? Christmas Eve, she bought a load of roofies from me in the park.'

'*Roofies?*'

Rohypnol. The so-called date rape drug. Lee couldn't believe what he was hearing. He produced his phone and showed Kyle a photo, convinced Kyle would admit to making a mistake. 'This woman?'

'Yeah. That's her. She was totally shitting herself when she handed the money over, so I guess it's not something she does very often. Come to think of it, she's the first woman . . . Mate, you should see the look on your face.'

Kyle took the cash from the shell-shocked Lee, got into his car and drove away, still smiling. Lee stood in the clearing for a minute, thinking. It was getting dark already, the low winter sun retreating at the end of what had been another depressingly short day. By the time he went inside, it was pitch-black.

Henry was at the kitchen table, going over their accounts again.

Lee walked up to him and said, 'I think Helena's planning to kill me.'

Henry laughed. 'What, by feeding you too many biscuits? I've noticed you've put a few pounds on lately, old chap.'

'No, I mean she's actually planning to kill me.'

He told Henry what Kyle had said. Part of him was actually quite impressed with Helena's gumption. He'd never imagined she had it in her. 'I knew something was up. The last week or so she's been watching me like a hawk. My routine. I've seen her watching me when I go for my morning swim. It all makes sense. I bet she's planning to put it in my morning coffee. How long do roofies take to kick in? Twenty minutes? Thirty?'

'How should I know?'

But Lee wasn't listening. 'The drug kicks in while I'm in deep water, I fall unconscious. Bye-bye, Lee.' He shook his head, then checked something on his phone. 'Yeah, it says here Rohypnol only stays in the blood for twenty-four hours. By the time the police do the pathology report there'll be no trace of it. Fuck me. Hels, you dark horse.'

'But why would she want to kill you?'

It was a question that didn't need to be asked. Henry knew exactly why Helena would want to kill Lee, who had always been open with Henry about his marriage. He didn't tell Henry exactly how badly he treated Helena, didn't go to work every day and detail the ways he'd found to torment his wife the night before, but he'd made plenty of little comments, and Henry had heard Lee talking to Helena on the phone many times, ordering her around, acting like she was something he'd found on his shoe. Henry knew about Devon too, and the women before her. Henry never said anything, though Lee had often suspected that Henry fancied Helena and fantasised about rescuing her. But when it came to it, Henry's loyalty lay with his business partner.

Henry had opened a bottle of red wine. He took a sip now. 'My God, Lee. You've got two people who want you dead. Lucky Helena bought the stuff from Kyle or she might have saved Jamie a job.'

Lee stared at him.

'What is it?' Henry asked.

'What you just said. Helena saving Jamie a job. This is it.'

'Sorry, old bean. You've lost me.'

Lee paced the room. It was crazy. But the more he thought about it, the more sense it made.

Jamie was going to kill him. The first payment he missed, or even if Jamie got bored of the arrangement or decided Lee had looked at him funny, he would carry out his threat.

This was a way out.

'It's a golden opportunity,' he said at last. 'This is a way for me to disappear, get Jamie off my back.'

'What, by *dying*?'

Lee found that hilarious. He laughed for two minutes straight. Eventually, he caught his breath and said, 'Don't be a dickhead. I'm going to make Jamie and everyone else *think* I'm dead.'

'This is mad,' Henry said. 'Wouldn't it be easier not to accept the spiked coffee and sell your house to pay off the debt?'

'That will take too long.' It would be humiliating too. Selling the house, having to explain everything to Helena, being forced to move somewhere small and shit. He'd rather the world think he was dead than see him fail.

'I'll lie low here for a while,' he continued. 'It's the perfect place to hide. No passers-by. No visitors. I can stay in your granny annexe and we can carry on working together, with everyone thinking it's you doing it all, until things pick up and we start making a profit again. At which point I can pay for a new identity and start again, somewhere else.' He flashed back to Jamie with his hands around his throat. 'I can't stress how appealing that is right now.'

Henry stared at him like he was nuts. 'There has to be another way.'

'Can you think of one?'

Henry couldn't.

Over the next twenty minutes, they figured out a plan. Or rather, Lee figured it out. Henry kept protesting, saying it was too risky, too insane. But Lee wouldn't back down. They would make it work. He didn't have a choice.

Before Lee headed home – to the woman who wanted to kill him – Henry said, 'Don't you think Jamie will come after me for the money?'

'Why would he? You had nothing to do with the deal. Jamie won't bother with you after I'm gone. There's just one more thing we need to make this work.'

'Which is?'

Lee rubbed his chin. 'A body.'

Chapter 36

I had listened to the story with a kind of incredulity. At the same time, I was gripped. Lee might be a tosser but he was very good at painting a vivid picture, of making me see the whole thing in my mind's eye. I could finally see how he must have been able to charm Helena at the beginning of their relationship.

We were halfway to Saltdean, the world pitch-black beyond the car windows, except for the moon hanging over the rural landscape. We could have been two old pals out for a drive, if it weren't for the shotgun Lee was cradling and the knot of foreboding in my stomach. I wished I could get a secret message to Helena to warn her, but of course that was impossible.

'You needed a body?' I repeated back to him. 'Someone who looked like you?'

'Yeah, of course. A white man, the same height and build as me, around the same age. Without any tattoos or obvious distinguishing features. I knew if we weighed the body down on the seabed, it would be nice and rotten before it was found. I looked it up on Google. The skin would go black and green and crabs and fish would nibble on the flesh.'

'Christ.'

'Yeah. And it would have been me if Helena had got her way.'

'So who was it? Let me guess, you found some poor homeless guy who no one would miss.'

Lee actually looked offended. 'Fuck me, Matthew, I'm not an animal. No, I found someone who deserved it. The guy who brought the refugees over on the dinghy, the French bloke I'd talked to about expanding our operation. He wasn't on the dinghy that sank, but he was on the next one, and do you think he gave a shit about either the lost drugs or the lost lives? Do you want to know what he said? "They know it's a risk when they get on the boat."'

I swallowed. I had tried not to picture the scene when the dinghy had sunk. The horror of it. These people – Lee and the Crowleys and the traffickers – were the lowest of the low.

'And this trafficker looked sufficiently like you?'

'As if he'd applied for the part. Right age, build and height. Even had the same hair colour – dark brown. No tattoos as far as I could see.'

We turned on to the coast road and I saw Lee's gaze fall upon the sea. 'I waited for him on the beach the next morning,' he said, his eyes far away. This was where it had all happened. 'I knew a crossing was due today. A yellow dinghy, carrying a dozen migrants. The moment it landed, they scattered, leaving the French guy standing by the dinghy, getting ready to make the return crossing.

'I went up to say hello, then had the plastic bag over his head in an instant. Pulled it tight around his throat before he could get his fingers beneath it. He struggled like crazy. I had to kneel on his back and use every fucking ounce of strength to stop him getting the bag off. It took forever.'

I listened with rapt horror.

'Then I got Henry to come and pick him up in his boat, which was a right performance because Henry was so freaked out, having to deal with a corpse. But we did it. Stored the body in the hold, wrapped in tarpaulin, and took it back to the harbour.' He grinned. 'This was the really clever bit: I'd brought along a brand-new toothbrush, identical to the one I used at home, and stuck it in the French guy's mouth, brushing the insides of his cheeks and tongue, getting plenty of DNA on it.'

It was ingenious. I had to admit it.

'You weren't worried someone would come looking for him?'

'Nah. I figured the rest of the gang would think he'd decided to stay in England, make a new life for himself. Or maybe there'd been a fight with the human cargo. They certainly weren't going to go to the police about his disappearance, were they?'

Lee didn't sound so charming now. They way he'd described suffocating the French trafficker had chilled me, even if the victim was hardly someone deserving of sympathy. It drove home to me that even though Lee and I were both responsible for other men's deaths, I wasn't like him. And I would never be like him.

'So . . .' Lee said. 'The morning arrived. I texted Henry using my burner phone. *Today's the day. Be ready.*'

Lee still appeared to be in a trance as he told his tale. 'His text came back straight away. He was using a burner too. *I'm ready.* I'm not afraid to admit that I was a little nervous; there was a chance I could actually die. If I misjudged the timing, or if Henry got held up . . .'

He waved a hand as if these worries were unimportant now.

'I waited for Helena to come out of the bathroom – she looked like she was about to have an embolism – then went in and switched my toothbrush with the one that had the dead French guy's DNA all over it.'

'What did you do with the old toothbrush?'

'Put it in a bag, along with the burner, and hid it under a bush outside for Henry to collect later. But before that, I waited for Henry to drive to the marina and text me to let me know we were all good. Only when I got that message did I go downstairs and drink my coffee. Specially prepared by my loving wife.'

He smirked. 'I told Helena to make sure she had breakfast ready when I got back and she promised she would. She looked so scared and excited. Mate, it took all my self-control not to give the game away.' A shake of the head. 'I wanted to vomit up the Rohypnol on the beach but I couldn't. I needed her to think her plan had worked.'

Which she had. She really had.

'I told Henry to meet me about three hundred metres east from where I started my swim. There's a spot there that can't be seen from my house, just past where the cliffs jut out? Gotta hand it to him – he was waiting in the exact spot at the exact time. Ready to help me into the boat.' He chuckled. 'The drug was starting to have an effect by then. I felt as dizzy as fuck and like I wanted to go to sleep for a week. Henry took the boat out further, and that was when the drug really started to kick in. I could barely talk, was slurring my words so badly I wasn't making any sense. But Henry knew the plan. He headed further east, then south, into the Channel.'

'And the cliffs still blocked the view from your house.'

'Exactly. Man, by the time we got to the spot I could hardly stand up. But I managed to help get the French bloke's body to the edge of the boat.' He mimed lifting a heavy object. 'We tied an anchor around his waist to make sure he sank and stayed on the seabed, and I put my Rolex on his wrist, which would have been a sad moment if I wasn't so fucked up by that point. I took off my trunks and put those on him too. And then, *heave*, into the sea he went – *plop!* After that, I lay down and zonked out. I was gone in seconds.'

It was like watching a movie. I could see it all. One thing Helena and Lee shared was a gift for telling a story.

'The next thing I knew,' Lee told me, 'I was in Henry's car, in the clearing outside the cottage. And from that point, it all went exactly as I'd planned it. I went back three weeks later, in the dark, dived down and cut the anchor from the body. The tide did the rest, carrying it to shore. Google had been right. The flesh had decomposed so the guy was unrecognisable. They had to take a DNA sample to identify him and, as I knew they would – I've watched enough true crime documentaries – they used my toothbrush to source my DNA.'

'Except it wasn't your DNA on the brush. It was the French guy's.'

'Yep.' I had never seen anyone look so pleased with themselves.

We were almost in Saltdean now. I felt like I'd stumbled into a horror movie. I was about to deliver my girlfriend's dead husband to her, resurrected.

He drummed his free hand on the dashboard and bounced in his seat, so much that I was worried the shotgun he was holding – butt in the footwell, muzzle angled towards my face – might go off. It struck me that I had now heard this story from both sides, Helena's and Lee's. I was the only person on the planet who knew what had happened.

Except I still didn't know everything, did I?

'Why did you shoot Henry?' I asked.

He ceased jiggling in his seat. 'That's the part of the plan that didn't work out.'

'With Jamie Crowley, you mean?'

'Yeah. That wanker. He stopped hassling Henry for a while, because he thought I was dead. But I'm guessing business for the Crowleys hasn't been great either, because a couple of months ago he and Kyle came out to Henry's – I was in the annexe, so they didn't see me – and told him they were collecting old debts. Crowley said they'd decided that, as my partner, and as someone who was privy to the deal with the French, Henry had liability. Henry's been freaking out ever since, because he didn't have anything to give them.'

'So that part of your plan didn't work out either? Rebuilding the business?'

He gave me a filthy look. 'It's been harder than I thought. Do you know how difficult it is to get into the zone when you're hiding out in the woods? Plus Henry kept fucking things up, turning up to meetings with alcohol on his breath, generally being a useless twat. We were just starting to make some progress – Henry found an old warehouse with a lot of potential for conversion into flats – when Jamie turned up asking for money.

'I told Henry not to panic, that Jamie was just trying it on, but he was terrified. He decided the best way to get his hands on the money was by scaring Helena into selling the house and handing it over.' When Lee had died, I reminded myself, his mortgage protection insurance had paid off the mortgage so any sale would be pure profit. 'He only told me that tonight. Told me he didn't think she was going to go for it, that she was acting weird. He was totally freaking out.' He curled his lip. 'He came over to the annexe, drunk, raging at me, calling me every name under the sun. A whole new Henry, driven over the edge. He had this gun with him, was swinging it around, and then he pointed it at me and told me he was going to call Jamie, hand me over and get the Crowleys off his back.'

I could picture it. 'What happened?'

'I told him I'd rather die and he said "Fine" but he couldn't do it. Same old Henry, after all. Couldn't do what had to be done.'

'So you got the gun off him and shot him?'

He shrugged with one shoulder. 'Yeah. It's a shame. Old Henry did a lot for me.' For a moment, I thought he was going to start crying. But he perked up, staring out the window as we entered

Saltdean. 'It feels so weird to be back. All I've seen for the last nine months is the inside of that granny annexe and the woods.'

We were almost there. I was driving as slowly as I could. 'Lee. What exactly is the plan here?'

'I've been thinking about that. Helena can sell the house, just as in Henry's plan, and give me the money. It belongs to me, after all.'

'And you'll use that to disappear?'

'Exactly. In the meantime, I can hide out in the basement.'

I turned my head towards him. 'Have you forgotten what I told you? About Devon? She's in the basement. The police are going to come looking for her any minute.'

'I thought you and Helena already had a story figured out to explain her and Robin's movements? A story that ends with Devon jumping off Beachy Head.'

'But that's not going to work if Devon's still there!'

Lee showed me his dirty teeth. 'That's easy to fix.'

The way he said it sent a chill crawling through me. 'You're saying you'll kill her.'

'It's what you want, isn't it? This way you won't even have to feel guilty about it. Think about it, Matthew. It solves everything.'

'And you would let me and Helena walk away? After what she tried to do to you?'

He patted my shoulder. 'Yeah, of course. All I want is the money, and I need you alive to get it for me. And I certainly wouldn't want to set off a manhunt after that. Plus I'm still excited about seeing the look on Helena's face when she clocks me.'

I didn't believe him for a second. There was no way he'd let us live once we were no longer useful. He'd find some way to finesse it so there'd be no 'manhunt'.

'Oh look, we're here,' he said. 'Home sweet home.'

I turned on to the driveway. Lee sat beside me, rubbing his hands together at the thought of this reunion, and then the front door opened and Helena emerged.

I quickly got out of the car and closed the driver's door behind me, wanting to be right next to her when she saw Lee. To warn her.

'Helena—'

She spoke over me. 'It's Devon. She's gone. She's gone!'

Grabbing her shoulders, I opened my mouth to warn her about what was about to happen. But it was too late. Lee opened the door on his side and got out, pulling himself up to his full height and standing there, smiling over the car at Helena.

She was so intent on telling me that Devon was gone – which was something I was going to have to worry about in a moment – that she didn't see him straight away.

Until he cleared his throat.

At last she looked his way.

And I saw the shock and horror in her eyes, as everything she'd believed for the last nine months crumbled away.

Chapter 37

Helena pulled away from me and staggered like she'd been shot. She put a hand out to search for something to hold on to and I grabbed hold of her, keeping her upright.

She tried to speak but nothing came out. All she could do was stare at Lee with her eyes wide and her mouth open.

'Boo!' he said, then laughed as he came around the front of the car towards us. I was forgotten in this scene. It was all about them. Helena and Lee. The man she'd married. The man she thought she'd murdered. 'This makes it all worthwhile. The nine months stuck out at Henry's place. All. Worth. While.'

Helena jerked away, still gawping at Lee, who was standing there with the shotgun in his arms. Her chest was rising and falling so rapidly I was worried she was going to have a heart attack. 'But,' she said. 'But . . . How? *How?*'

'He's told me the whole thing,' I said. 'I'll explain it all later.'

'Look on the bright side, darling,' Lee said. 'You're not going to go to prison for my murder now. Except . . . did you say Devon's gone?'

Helena didn't respond. Was she going into shock?

'Hey,' I said, gently putting my hands on her shoulders. 'You need to stay calm. Tell us what's—'

Lee stepped up and snapped his fingers in front of her face. 'Hey. What did you mean, "Devon's gone"?'

She blinked several times before her eyes focused. 'You really are alive.'

'Living and breathing.'

'But the body . . . Whose body was it?'

'No one important.' He looked her up and down. 'Gotta say, Hels, you're looking good. A bit skinny maybe, but apart from that, looks like being a widow suits you.' He guffawed. 'But you still haven't told us what the hell is going on.'

Her attention returned to me. 'I went down to the basement to . . . see her. And she's not there.'

'What do you mean?'

'I mean, she's *not there!*'

'You let her escape,' said Lee, shaking his head.

'No! The basement door was locked the whole time. It's like she's evaporated.'

'Show me,' I said.

'Show *us,*' said Lee.

I followed her towards the house, with Lee just behind us, carrying the shotgun. We went in through the front door. Drella was there, sitting on the floor in the hallway, but he bolted the moment he saw Lee, who didn't appear to notice. He was too busy looking around. 'I love what you've done with the place.'

'Nothing's changed,' said Helena.

'Exactly. Although I see you've got rid of the wedding photos.'

'I burned them,' she said, though I knew this was a lie. 'I should have burned you too. Watched the whole thing, to make sure you were really dead.'

For the first time, Lee's irritating grin slipped and I saw a flash of anger. 'Maybe next time,' he said, his voice flat. But he raised the shotgun a little, to remind us who was in charge here. My mind was racing. Could I risk dashing to the kitchen to grab a knife? No, that wouldn't work. All I could do, for now, was go along with Lee's demands. Try to find Devon. Stay alert and look for an opportunity.

Helena's lip curled. 'I'm not afraid of you anymore.'

'Please,' I said, stepping between them. 'Can we focus on Devon? Try to figure out where the hell she's gone.'

'Yeah, Helena,' said Lee. 'Concentrate, dear.'

I thought she might launch herself at him. I gently took her arm and she allowed me to lead her towards the basement. The three of us went down the steps to the bottom door, which Helena had had the presence of mind to lock behind her when she'd come out.

We went through.

'You've been keeping her locked in here?' Lee said.

Helena ignored him, but gave me a look that told me she was not happy I'd told Lee about our situation.

'I've searched the whole space,' she said. 'Including the freezer.'

Lee was walking around slowly. 'Man, I've missed this place.' He put his head into the home cinema. 'I've been stuck watching films on this shitty thirty-two-inch piece of crap at Henry's.'

'Better than the eternal torment you should be facing,' Helena muttered.

'Did you look in there?' Lee asked, pointing to the storage cupboard.

'Of course I did.'

'I wonder.'

He walked past us and opened the cupboard. 'Devon's quite smart,' he said. 'If she's been locked down here for a few days, there's a good chance she found it.'

'Found what?' I asked.

He went to the back of the cupboard, which was just about big enough for three people to cram into, and leaned the shotgun against the wall. Frustratingly, his body blocked it so there was no way I could grab it.

It struck me that most of the boxes and crates that had been piled up on the back wall had been moved to the side. Lee rapped on the wall and the resulting noise told me there was a hollow space behind it.

'Stand back and give me some space,' he said, and looking past him I realised the back wall was in fact a sheet of boarding. Lee hooked the tips of his fingers into a gap on the far left of this boarding, where it met the side wall, and pulled. The boarding came away. He pulled some more, and exposed a gap big enough for a person to squeeze through.

'What the hell?' Helena said.

Lee pulled the board out further and I saw there was a large space behind it: dark and cobwebby, with unplastered stone walls, and about the same size as the cupboard.

'Follow me,' he said, picking up the shotgun and preparing to squeeze through the gap. Then, 'Wait. We're going to need a torch. There should be one in that box there.'

He pointed to a box on the second shelf on the right. I checked and there was indeed a torch. I turned it on and held it out to Lee. He had the gun in one hand, gripping the barrel, and he shook his head. 'You hold on to it.'

I thought about striking him on the head with it, and he must have seen it in my eyes because he jabbed the gun at me.

'You first,' he said. 'Get a move on.'

I squeezed through the gap, with Helena following me, then Lee. There was, I saw, a strap attached to this side of the fake wall, which Devon must have used to pull it back into place. We stood close together in the unfinished space. It was cold in here, but dry.

The rough walls had a slightly chalky texture, and I was reminded that this space, the whole basement, had been dug out of the cliff on which the house stood.

'This is great,' said Helena. 'A hidey-hole behind the cupboard. But I can't see Devon.'

'Shine the torchlight down there, Matthew,' Lee said. 'At the bottom of that wall.'

I did as he commanded. It took a moment for my eyes to adjust to the shadows, but then I saw it: another gap, this time running beneath the wall. A crawlspace. I crouched to take a better look and saw that it was actually more of a slither space, as to get through it one would have to get down on one's belly. The thought of it made my flesh crawl.

'Where does it lead?' I asked, a tremor in my voice.

'You're gonna love this,' he said. 'You know this whole area was once used by smugglers, right? When I tore down the old wreck that used to be on this land so I could build this place, want to know what I found?'

'Tunnels.'

'Yeah,' he said, sounding a little annoyed that I had stolen his thunder. 'Smugglers' tunnels, a whole frigging network of them, leading up from the beach to the cliffs. It's how they used to evade the riding officers and get all the shit they were smuggling off the beach. Over time, all the tunnels were lost. Sealed up.'

'So Devon could have escaped to the beach,' Helena said.

'Maybe,' he allowed. 'But the slopes are pretty bloody treacherous. I think it's more likely she'd have ended up in the Smuggler's Arms.'

The closed-down pub that was less than half a mile from here.

'The tunnels lead there?' I said.

'Yeah. I mean, it's a bit of a maze and she'd have to be lucky to find her way there this quickly . . .'

'You've been down there?'

I was picturing Devon emerging into the pub, escaping, going straight to the cops. And right then, even though I knew it would lead to me and Helena going to jail, I couldn't see any other way we were going to survive this. I'd rather be in prison than dead. I needed to keep Lee talking. To give Devon more time.

Lee answered my question. 'Yeah. I poked around in them when I was building this place. I always thought being able to access them might come in handy, which was why I built the cupboard the way I did.'

'Are these tunnels mentioned in that *Coves and Scoundrels* book?'

'Yeah, they are. Why? Don't tell me you gave it to Devon to read?'

'She found it in here.'

'That's hilarious,' said Lee. 'The old wreck I knocked down is mentioned in that book. There's even a map of the tunnels. I guess that's what made Devon go looking. She really isn't just a pretty face.'

'Can we please stop talking and go and find her?' Helena said. I gave her a sharp look – I was trying to buy Devon more time! – but it was too late.

'Yeah,' said Lee. 'Go on, Matthew.'

'Me?'

'Well, one of you needs to. You want Helena to do it?'

The thought of being down in those dark tunnels made my whole body clench up.

'Not too scared, are you?'

Of course I was scared. But, ridiculous as it was, I didn't want Lee to see it. Didn't want Helena to see it either.

'Of course I'm not.'

'Good,' said Lee. 'Hels, you and me can go to the Smuggler's Arms and wait there, in case Devon gets there before Matthew finds her – if she hasn't already.'

Helena's face was shadowy in the torchlight, but I could see the disgust there and hear it in her voice. 'I'm not going anywhere with you.'

'Do you want to find her or not?'

'What if she comes back out this way?' I asked. 'Shouldn't one of us wait here?'

'Oh, send me on to the pub alone, maybe? Do you think I'm a mug, Matty? On with you. Me and the wife will just have to lock the cupboard behind us and Devon won't be able to get out this way.'

Neither would I. Once I was in the tunnels, the only exit would be through the pub. I swallowed hard.

Lee pointed the gun in Helena's direction, which made my stomach flip over. 'The pair of you are starting to piss me off. We need to find Devon. It's the only way this plan works.'

'What plan?' Helena asked, eyeing the gun nervously.

'I'll tell you when we get to the Smuggler's. Matthew, get into those fucking tunnels.' He nudged Helena with the shotgun. 'Let's go.'

She shot him a look of contempt but backed out through the gap, back into the cupboard. Lee followed. A moment later, I heard the cupboard door shut and the key turn in the lock.

I stood there with the torch, then got down on my knees.

I had no choice.

Chapter 38

I got down on to my belly and commando-crawled through the gap. I was aware of the great weight of rock above me, terrified it would collapse, crushing me. But after a few metres, the gap widened and I was able to get on to my hands and knees. A little way after that, I found myself crawling around a corner, and there, stretching ahead of me and into the darkness, was a man-sized tunnel.

I got to my feet and pointed the torch along the shaft of the tunnel, revealing the chalky walls and rough floor. It was about three feet wide and six feet high, so it scraped the top of my head, causing me to stoop slightly as I walked. I couldn't stop thinking about spiders. Rats too. But there was no sign of any life. This wasn't like the tunnels in the video games I'd played, with skeletons of lost explorers around every corner and cryptic messages scrawled on the walls. It was long and dark and smelled stale. There was also a slight gradient, with the tunnel sloping downwards.

I took deep breaths and tried not to think about what would happen if the batteries in this torch died. Did Devon have one, or had she come down here in complete darkness? I wondered if Lee was exaggerating Devon's cleverness. Maybe he had mentioned the tunnels to her during their affair and she had been searching for the entrance to them all along, her fear that Helena was going to kill her giving her extra motivation to find them.

After a few minutes I came to my first fork. One path sloped steeply downwards, presumably towards the beach. Hopefully the other path led to the Smuggler's Arms.

The darkness that surrounded me, the weight of the rock above me . . . I needed to get out of here. I was hardly even thinking about finding Devon now. I felt like I was swimming underwater, running out of oxygen, desperate to get to the surface. With the exit behind me locked, all I could do was keep going forward.

But after I'd been down there ten minutes, I started to get used to it; a little, anyway. Enough to start worrying about Devon. Because if Lee found her before I did, he was going to kill her. He was going to kill all of us. With three of us against him, we might stand a chance.

'Devon! It's Matthew.' My voice echoed back to me through the tunnels. 'You need to let me find you. Otherwise you're going to get hurt.'

My voice bounced back: *Get hurt, get hurt, get hurt . . .*

'Devon?' *Devon, Devon, Devon . . .*

There was no response. I picked up the pace again. Before too long, I reached another fork. This time, both paths were on the same level. Left or right? I tried to picture where I was, in which direction the pub would be, but it was impossible. All I could do was guess. I went left, following the internal compass that told me this path led inland.

Where was she? Had she already reached the pub and escaped? The nearest police station was miles away, but she might have flagged down a passing car or run to one of Helena's neighbours.

I hurried through the tunnels, calling her name.

'Devon. You're in danger!'

It echoed back to me: *Danger, danger, danger.*

And in the silence that followed, I heard it. Up ahead of me: footsteps.

Chapter 39

Lee insisted on driving to the Smuggler's Arms even though it was just a ten-minute walk from the house.

'Don't want anyone to see this, do we?' he said, gesturing to the shotgun.

Helena drove. She was glad it was a short, straightforward journey, because she was trembling so much that a more complex drive would almost certainly have ended with a crash. But perhaps that wouldn't be such a bad thing. She could speed into a wall, unfastening Lee's seat belt at the last second. Watch him hurtle through the windscreen.

He looked sideways at her from the passenger seat.

'It was a good plan,' he said. 'You were unlucky, that's all. I only found out about it because you bought the roofies from one of Jamie Crowley's guys. Henry told me you put on a good act at the funeral, spilling crocodile tears all over the place. I was going to ask him to video it – I would have loved to have seen all the weeping and wailing over me – but decided people might wonder what he was doing.'

She didn't speak. Couldn't speak. Her insides were red with hatred and black with fear. Lee was going to kill her; she was certain of it. Her and Matthew and Devon. He was going to murder everyone who knew he was still alive. Then he would take whatever he could easily sell or pawn from the house and disappear.

She couldn't see how she was going to survive this. She couldn't even call the police and confess everything to save herself, as Lee had taken her phone.

'I should have found another way to kill you,' she said, almost to herself. 'One where you died right in front of me. I should have slit your throat in your sleep.'

Lee laughed. 'Sure, Hels. And spent your life in jail.'

'Right now, I think it would have been worth it.'

They pulled up outside the Smuggler's Arms and got out of the car. Lee made Helena go first, directing her through a gap in the rickety fence that surrounded the dilapidated building.

'This used to be the most popular pub in the village,' Lee said as he looked around the shut-up pub for a way in. He was talking in a hushed tone, inspecting the boarded-up doors and windows, not wanting to alert Devon to their presence if she was in there. There was nobody around and the only sounds came from the distant waves. No people. No traffic. Even the gulls were quiet. The moon was out, casting light on to the empty building.

They went round to what used to be the beer garden. Helena wondered if she could run, but dismissed the idea immediately. She wanted to find Devon as much as Lee did. Even more.

'Ah, here we go,' he said. The boards on one of the windows had come loose at the edges. He leaned the gun against the wall, grinned at Helena as if daring her to make a move, then pulled away the rotten boards.

'You first,' he said.

Before this week, Helena had never entered a building by climbing through a window. Now she had done it twice. Lee had instructed her to grab another torch on their way out of the house, and she turned it on now, sweeping it around what used to be the lounge area. The room stank of mould and damp but, beneath those top notes, Helena was sure she could detect the odour of beer and cigarette smoke, clinging on after all these years.

The torch picked out a shard of glass, presumably from a broken beer bottle, just within reach of where she'd landed. She glanced back at the window then grabbed the shard, tucking it into her jacket pocket a moment before Lee came through the window, still clinging to the shotgun. He was bigger and less agile than he'd been in his previous life. All those months without his daily swim. He'd piled on the pounds.

'Right,' he said. 'Follow me.'

Lee had already told her that the entrance to the tunnels was in the cellar, and the door to the cellar was behind the bar. Stone steps led down into the dark space, and a cobweb dragged across Helena's face as they descended. She snatched at her cheek, convinced an enormous spider must be on her flesh, pieces of cobweb on her lips.

She shone the torch around the cellar, revealing exposed brick and a few empty beer kegs that had been left behind when the pub went bankrupt.

'The entrance to the tunnels wasn't a secret when I was a kid. I remember people talking about it. I have this really vague memory of my dad bringing me down here to take a peek.' He shook his head. 'Of course, after the world went health-and-safety mad they had to put a stop to it.'

'Fascinating.'

Lee ignored her. 'Now, where is it? I'm sure there was a hatch. Ah, here we go.'

There was a pile of plastic crates in the corner. Standing back, he indicated for Helena to move them aside. And there it was. The hatch.

'Lift it,' he said.

She had no choice but to do as he said. The hatch opened surprisingly easily and she peered down into the space that had been revealed. A vertical shaft with a metal ladder bolted to one wall, leading down into darkness.

'Now what?' she asked, looking back at her despised husband.

'We wait.'

He pulled up a couple of old chairs and positioned them beside the hatch.

'So,' she said. 'How did you do it?'

She listened as, over the next five minutes, he boasted about what he'd done. From the drug deal gone wrong to the toothbrush bearing a dead man's DNA. He was immensely pleased with himself, even if it was surprising to hear how scared he was of Jamie Crowley. It was unlike Lee to admit any vulnerability. If only she could call Jamie now, tell him Lee was still alive, bring him here and get him to finish the job she'd tried to do nine months ago. She was shocked to hear that Crowley had never been after her, that it had been Henry's attempt to get the money to protect himself. She didn't feel sad to hear Henry was dead. Not only had he tried to scare her, he'd helped Lee. She'd always thought he was a decent man, deep down. Turned out he was just like his business partner.

'So what is this plan that you mentioned to Matthew?' she asked when he'd finished.

'It's simple,' he said. 'With Devon, we're going to finish what you set up when you chucked her phone off Beachy Head. Then I'm going to lie low while you sell the house, and I'll take the money and disappear.'

'All the money?'

'Don't try to negotiate, Helena. You tried to kill me.'

'Only to stop you killing me. Like you murdered Lisa.'

He waved a hand. 'You're going to get out of this with your life and your freedom. You can go and live with Matthew. You'll be fine.'

She thought about it. He was lying. He wouldn't risk keeping her and Matthew around, taking the chance that they would expose him or even kill him. She was sure her initial instinct was correct: he was going to murder all of them, take whatever jewellery and money he could get his hands on, and vanish. The police thought he was dead. Escaping wouldn't be hard. Much as it would gall him to abandon the house, he had fucked everything for himself by killing Henry, and now this – grabbing what he could and disappearing – was his best, really his only, option. But first he needed to find Devon, and stop her going to the police and bringing them to the house before he was ready to go.

She eyed the shotgun in his lap.

'Did you hear that?' he said, standing up.

'What?'

'Listen.'

And she did hear it. There was someone in the tunnel beneath them, coming closer. Lee put a finger to his lips and stood back.

Devon's head appeared through the hatch. She blinked several times, eyes adjusting to the light, and then took in the scene before her.

'Lee?' she said. '*Lee?*'

At the same time, from beneath them came a second set of footsteps, moving fast, and Helena heard Matthew call out, 'Devon? Devon, stay where you are.'

But Devon ignored him. She was staring at Lee with wonder. 'You're alive! Oh my God, you're alive.' She scrambled up the ladder and into the cellar, glancing quickly at Helena before returning her attention to Lee. 'How? Oh, Lee . . .'

She ran towards him, rapt with joy and relief, and he swung the barrel of the shotgun upwards. 'Stop.'

She lurched to a halt, a puzzled frown on her face, which was smeared with dirt and sweat. There were cobwebs in her hair and her clothes were filthy. 'I don't understand.'

'Back up,' Lee said. 'Against that wall.'

'But Lee, it's me. Devon. The one you love.' She pointed at Helena. 'It's her you ought to be pointing a gun at!'

He bellowed at her, 'Get up against that wall!' Then, in a quieter voice: '*Love*. Give me strength. I loved your body, yeah. But I was starting to grow bored of even that.'

And then Matthew appeared through the hatch.

Chapter 40

I took in the scene. A horrified Devon backing up against the wall in the face of Lee and his gun. Helena a couple of metres away, standing beside a chair. Old beer barrels. This was the cellar of the Smuggler's Arms.

I continued up the ladder until I was standing next to Helena. If the hatch was the central point of a clock, Helena and I were at six, Lee at three and Devon at twelve.

'You bastard,' Devon said to Lee. 'What, are you going back to *her*?'

He laughed. 'Sorry, Dev. But I can't have you knowing I'm still alive.'

Devon reached out for him. 'I promise I won't tell anyone.'

He jabbed the shotgun at her. 'Stay back.'

Helena appeared frozen. She was breathing heavily, her body coiled with tension. Lee adjusted the shotgun so it was pointing at Devon's chest. She still seemed stunned by his betrayal. The scales falling away from her eyes. Too late. Much too late. I watched as he put his finger on the trigger.

'There has to be another way,' I said. 'Lee—'

And then Devon was rushing at him.

I will never forget the expression on her face. Not hurt. *Fury.* And the look I will forever associate with Devon: defiance. As she flew at him, she let out a cry, a roar, her hands outstretched like she was going to grab the shotgun, and for a split second I thought she was going to succeed.

Then Lee pulled the trigger and there was an explosion of red, and I instinctively brought my hands up as if the blast were directed at me.

When I lowered my hands I saw Devon's bloody body on the floor.

Lee appeared to be temporarily shocked by what he'd done. He let the gun droop, just for a moment, but it was long enough.

For the first time in my life, I acted on pure instinct. All the anger and frustration and pain of the past few days suddenly ignited inside me, and I leapt at him.

I smashed into him, shoulder first, driving a deep grunt from him as he staggered back. He tried to regain his footing and lift the gun at me but I crashed into him again, this time driving a fist into the side of his face, and he went down on to his back, still gripping the shotgun.

I threw myself down on to him, grabbing his arms, trying to wrestle the gun from his grip. I felt crazed. Powerful. He fought back, trying to get enough leverage to swing it at me. But then Helena was there, and she had something in her hand, something sharp: a shard of glass. She slashed at Lee's knuckles with it and he screamed and loosened his grip on the gun. I snatched it from his grasp but stumbled as I tried to stand, falling on to my rear.

Helena grabbed the shotgun from me and pointed it at Lee.

He had pushed himself into a sitting position, cradling his bleeding hand with the other. When he saw Helena aim the gun at him, he looked afraid for a second, but then he smiled.

'You're not going to do it,' he said, the smile twisting into a smirk.

305

Helena was panting and her hands were shaking.

'Come on,' Lee said. 'Let's talk it through.'

'Shut up!' she yelled.

'Helena,' he said, using the old, smooth voice I remembered from college. '*Think*. Devon's dead. We can go ahead with this now. We can all get on with our lives.'

'Stop talking!' The gun was trembling in her hands. I could see her chest rising and falling. Her voice came out strangled, high-pitched. 'I *know* you, you bastard. You're lying. I can tell,' she said with a wild, jittery laugh, 'because your fucking lips are moving.'

'Hels, I promise. We're all going to get out of this, and then you and Matty can live happily ever after. Just put the gun down.'

She wavered. For a second, I thought she was going to do as he asked. And then I saw something harden in her eyes. In the same moment, she stopped shaking. 'No.'

'Hels . . .'

'No.' Her voice was flat now. Quiet. She'd made her mind up.

Lee heard it too and he shook his head, disbelieving. All the smoothness in his voice was gone, replaced by desperation. 'You can't *kill* me. I'm—'

She blasted him in the chest.

He went down, twisting as he fell beside Devon.

I got to my feet. Helena stood there, still breathing hard, gripping the shotgun until her knuckles turned white. I crouched beside Lee and felt for a pulse. Then I did the same with Devon.

'They're both dead,' I said.

Helena moved closer to Lee's body, the gun still pointed at him. 'Are you sure?'

'He's definitely dead this time,' I said. 'I promise.'

She dropped the gun and sank to her haunches. I was numb. I had seen so much death in, what, twenty-four hours? Robin. Henry. Devon. Lee.

I felt sorry for all of them except one.

But there was no time to dwell on it. No time to mourn or feel guilt.

'We need to hide them,' I said.

Helena looked up at me. She had been staring at her hands. They were coated with Lee's blood from where she had slashed his knuckles. There was more blood pooling around his body from the gunshot.

To the new me, the instinctive Matthew, who had seen so much death but who was still here, still alive, it seemed obvious what we needed to do.

I shuffled over to Lee and, trying not to look at his face, took hold of him beneath his armpits, and dragged him across to the hatch that led down to the tunnels. He was so much heavier than Robin had been, and it took all my strength to begin to move him the six feet to the hole. But then Helena got up, seeing what I was trying to do, and helped. Between us, we tipped him, head and shoulders first, through the hatch.

Let him fall.

He landed with a thud, and I went down the ladder to drag his body a little way into the tunnel before returning to the pub cellar and doing the same with Devon. We were more gentle with her body, lowering it rather than letting it drop, which was easier because she was a lot smaller and lighter than Lee, but still, we at last had to let go. The impact made the same dull sound as Lee's body had, just quieter.

I remembered passing that last fork on the way here, close to the pub. I went to explore now and found that it was perfect. The tunnel beyond it sloped steeply downwards. Presumably it would eventually lead to the beach, where the entrance to the tunnels had likely long been sealed and hidden.

Who knew these tunnels were here? The book Devon had been reading was twenty years old. Helena had been living above them for years and hadn't known they were here. Lee had only known because he had demolished the house that used to stand here. It was the perfect hiding place.

Nobody was going to be looking for Lee. Everyone thought he had died nine months ago.

And Devon? Well, we had already resolved that one by throwing her phone off Beachy Head. Her body wouldn't be found in the sea beneath that cliff, but that wasn't too unusual.

This would be their final resting place.

We worked for the next few hours. We dragged their bodies down the tunnel to the top of the slope, then pushed them down into the darkness, Lee first then Devon. I went down after them, to check where they lay. It was dark and cold. I placed the shotgun alongside them then stood there for a moment, feeling like I ought to say a few words. But what was there to say?

I knew that over the coming days and weeks I would build a wall around the truth. I would slowly convince myself that Devon had died because of her own actions. If she hadn't had an affair with Lee. If she hadn't recorded Helena's conversation. If she hadn't blackmailed us.

Protecting myself from the truth about Robin's death was harder. He was still an innocent victim, no matter how I rearranged the facts. All I could do was remind myself it had been an accident.

After hiding the bodies, we followed the tunnel back to Helena's house and fetched bleach and water, which we used to clean up the blood in the pub cellar. Finally, we covered the hatch in the cellar as best we could before leaving the Smuggler's Arms and driving home.

On the way, Helena said, 'We're going to have to seal up the entrance to the tunnels in the basement. You told me you're handy. Think you'd be able to build a proper wall at the rear of that cupboard?'

'Yeah. How hard can it be?' At that moment, I felt like I could do anything. 'I think we should try to buy the pub, too. If I sell my flat in London, and maybe you could release some of the equity in your house . . .'

'It's a good idea.'

'We can buy it and leave it closed. Or maybe convert it into a house. We just won't ever be able to let anyone else into the cellar. And you won't ever be able to sell your house. You're going to have to stay here forever. It's the only way to protect the secret.'

We had reached her house. It was the middle of the night. The quietest hour. All I could hear, far below us, was the sea clawing at the pebbles on the beach.

'Me, or us?' she said.

'Us,' I replied. 'If you want me, of course.'

I looked at her and she looked at me, and I'm sure we were both thinking the same thing. That we had no choice. We were still only a few weeks into our renewed relationship, but we were stuck together, bonded by our shared crimes and secrets. She had power over me and I had power over her, like two countries with nuclear warheads aimed at each other. To go to the police, to admit what we'd done, would be mutually assured destruction. All the while we loved each other, it was fine. But what about the future? What if one of us fell out of love? If love turned to hate, if one of us cheated, if we had a terrible argument?

It wasn't just a bomb. It was a time bomb.

But it was what we had. It was our foundation.

I pulled her into an embrace.

'Let's try to lead a really boring life from now on, shall we?'

'Sounds perfect. The less eventful the better.'

'No more secrets.'

'No more lies.'

We got out of the car and walked up to the house, hand in hand.

Epilogue

Six months later

Ryan Barker had been meaning to unpack the box containing his big brother's possessions for ages. His parents had brought it back from Robin's house in Moulsecoomb shortly after his death, along with his bike, and put everything in Robin's old room. The room had long ago ceased to be Robin's bedroom. His mum had turned it into a home gym, with an exercise bike and a set of barbells, but she never went in there anymore. It was as if Robin's old possessions held some kind of demonic power. She couldn't go near them.

So it was left to Ryan to deal with them. And one day, bored during the Easter holidays, Ryan decided today was the day to finally tackle this task he'd been putting off.

Ryan was seventeen and Robin, who had been six years older, had been his hero. He'd introduced him to video games. Taught him how to shut himself away when Mum and Dad were fighting. He'd even bought him his first alcoholic drink. Robin had been brilliant at impersonations, and stuck up for his little brother when their dad was being a wanker.

His only flaw, as far as Ryan could see, was that he'd been in love with that stupid girl he lived with. Devon. Even her name was annoying. Ryan had met her a couple of times and she'd been quite cute, but she was stand-offish and stuck-up. Worse, she had absolutely no interest in Robin but kept stringing him along because she liked the attention. Loved having a guy who worshipped her. When Robin had told Ryan that Devon was shagging some older, married guy, Ryan had tried to talk some sense into his brother. But Robin hadn't listened. He'd just waited patiently for Devon to get tired of this married man. But even when the older guy died, Devon hadn't been interested in Robin.

And then she'd killed him.

The police, who had found footage of Robin on a traffic camera, riding his bike towards Saltdean the evening he had died, speculated that it had happened during an argument. These friends of Devon's, who she'd met in Iceland, had told the cops that Robin had been stalking her, harassing her, which was ridiculous. It wasn't harassment. He loved her! But they believed that he had cycled to the house of these friends and persuaded Devon to meet him nearby. After that, they believed, she had gone home with him, where she had either caused or witnessed his death, before taking her own life – which indicated she had killed him and been racked by remorse. They'd found her phone, its innards destroyed by sea water, at the bottom of Beachy Head. Her body, apparently, had washed away. It was mad. One of those bizarre double deaths his mum liked to read about in her true crime magazines. Several journalists had been in touch about it, but Mum and Dad had told them where to go.

Ryan went into what had once been Robin's room, and there, on the floor in the corner, next to the exercise bike, was the box. It was actually, Ryan now realised, more of a crate, the plastic kind you'd buy at Ikea for storage. It was depressing how little stuff Robin had owned. His clothes had been put into black bin liners, and apparently most of the household items in the shared spaces had belonged to Devon, so her family had taken them. Most of Robin's remaining possessions had been digital. Games and software and apps. Thousands of photos stored on a hard drive. The police had taken his phone after his body was found, and Ryan wasn't sure if they'd sent it back yet.

The rest was in here. The crate. Ryan carried it into his own bedroom, placed it on the bed and sat down to go through it.

There was Robin's iPad and charger. Ryan would plug that in later and see what was on it. He had a few novels; Robin had never been a big reader. There were a few framed photographs. Mum and Dad and Ryan. Gritting his teeth to stop himself from crying, Ryan set them aside. Next he came across a few notebooks and flicked through the first one. One page contained a list of what looked like passwords, but there was nothing else interesting. There was a Swiss Army knife and an old watch that didn't work anymore. A bag of foreign currency. Some pens and a torch. Robin's degree certificate and passport. It was depressing. Ryan looked around his own room. What would be salvaged if he died? What would be left behind?

In that moment, he made a vow not to waste his life. He was going to make an imprint on the world, so that when he went – in eighty years, hopefully – there would be keepsakes. Objects that he had created or collected that meant something, and that would be meaningful to others.

He reached the bottom of the crate. That was it. All Robin's stuff.

He began to put everything back, except the iPad, which he plugged into the wall. He put one of the framed photos on the shelf. This one was of the whole family. The four of them. He gazed at it for a little while and wiped his cheek with the back of his hand. Gritting his teeth had stopped working.

Then, as he was putting the notebooks back into the crate, something fell out of one of them.

It was an envelope. Someone had written KEEP SAFE on the front.

Ryan sat back on the bed, holding the envelope. Strange. It didn't look like Robin's handwriting. If he had to guess, he'd say it was a woman's writing. Devon's?

Could this have something to do with Robin's death? There was something small and hard inside the envelope.

He ripped it open and found a USB thumb drive.

Okay, this was getting weirder. KEEP SAFE. What if it was a sex tape or something? Had Robin and Devon actually hooked up at some point? As much as Ryan didn't want to see his brother doing it, he had to know what was on the drive.

He grabbed his laptop and inserted it.

It took a few seconds for the laptop to recognise the thumb drive and open it. But when the window opened on screen, Ryan saw there was a single file on there. Not video, but audio. According to the timestamp, it had been created in September last year.

He double-clicked it and a woman's voice came out of the laptop's speakers.

'*I came up with the plan after watching a documentary on TV . . .*'

She went on for about ten minutes. Ryan listened to the whole thing, then sat there, stunned.

He had just listened to a woman confess to the murder of her husband, a guy called Lee. Was it for real? Who was the woman? And who had she been talking to? It was a man, one who had interjected occasionally and made sympathetic noises.

Ryan listened to it again. The woman mentioned Saltdean. That was where Devon had been staying, the police had said, the night Robin died. Staying with the people she'd met in Iceland.

He went on to Google and searched 'Lee drowned Saltdean 2022' and found it straight away. Lee Davidson. He found an obituary. His wife was called Helena.

Yes, that was the woman Devon had been staying with. That was the woman on the recording.

Not a grieving widow. A *black* widow. A murderer.

Ryan felt sick with excitement. This was huge. He googled Helena's name and found pictures of her. As far as he could tell, she had got away with it. He listened to the audio for a third time, making sure it didn't sound like some kind of creative writing exercise. But no, he was sure it was real, and Devon had recorded her even though they were friends. Shit, had Devon been in on it? Ryan wouldn't put it past her.

He ejected the thumb drive and was about to take it downstairs to show his parents when he realised they would make him go to the police.

And maybe that wasn't the best use of this opportunity. Helena Davidson looked rich. Ryan would be willing to bet Lee had left her loads of dosh. On the recording she'd said she'd killed him because he was abusive, but she probably did it for the life insurance.

This recording could be worth a fortune.

Ryan made up his mind. He wanted to make something of his life. Having money would give him a big head start. On top of that, this Helena woman might know exactly what had happened between Robin and Devon. He was willing to bet it was all tangled up together in a single knot.

Before going to the cops, he was going to give Helena a choice. Tell him what she knew about Robin's death and hand over a nice sum of money, or Ryan would give this recording to the police.

Before leaving the house he made a copy of it and saved it on his laptop. Then he went downstairs and got his bike out of the garage. Saltdean was only a thirty-minute cycle ride from here.

His heart thudded with excitement.

His life was about to change.

What could possibly go wrong?

Letter from the Author

Thank you for reading this book. It goes without saying that I hope you enjoyed it and would love to hear from you. You can email me at mark@markedwardsauthor.com or contact me through my Facebook page, @markedwardsauthor, or on Twitter, where I'm @mredwards.

For a bonus chapter from *Keep Her Secret*, which delves more into Matthew and Helena's past, please visit my website: www.markedwardsauthor.com/free – you'll also get a box set of free short stories.

The rest of this letter contains spoilers so please don't read it until you've finished the novel.

Firstly, I should point out that I have taken some liberties with the geography of Saltdean. The cliff on which Helena's house sits does not exist. And although there really were smugglers' tunnels in that area, as in much of Sussex – including in Rottingdean – the ones in this book are invented.

This novel was inspired by a tale told to me by a friend, Karis Harrington, who also happens to be the talented illustrator and designer who I have collaborated with on several projects. A few years ago, Karis was travelling alone in the mountains of New Zealand when she slipped and almost fell to her death. Luckily, her backpack hooked on a rock and she was able to haul herself to safety. Her brush with mortality lodged in my memory, especially as I tried to imagine what must have gone through her head, during and immediately afterwards.

This idea combined with another I'd been playing with for a while. I have long wanted to write a book about a good person who finds him or herself in a terrible predicament because of a mistake they made, and a secret they would do anything to protect. I have also long been a fan of noir movies like *Double Indemnity* and *Body Heat*, and books like *A Simple Plan*. In November 2021 I went on a trip to Iceland and, seeing the glorious mountainous landscape there, all of the above came together in my mind. I started to plan and write *Keep Her Secret* almost as soon as I got home.

I am grateful to a number of people who helped me with research, including some of my fellow authors. Elly Griffiths gave me the out-of-print book *The Saltdean Story* by Douglas D'Enno, which was invaluable for research into smuggling in the area. Caroline Green helped me brainstorm the early parts of this book and made several brilliant suggestions. I owe Neil Lancaster several pints for helping me with questions about policing and DNA, and Tony Kent graciously answered my daft legal enquiries. Ruth Ware helped me find the perfect location for Henry's house in the woods. I would also like to thank my companions on that Icelandic trip – Ed James, Fiona Cummins and CL Taylor – who, along with Luca Veste, gave me a couple of lines that somehow made it into this novel. You should read all the books of all the authors above.

More thank yous:

Rob Mackintosh gave me a huge amount of helpful advice about mountain rescue and hiking equipment, and talked me through the cliff-fall incident with great patience. Any errors are, of course, my own – though I also blame the Chris Pratt doll I used to enact the scene at home. Oh, and thank you to Clare Mackintosh for introducing me to her husband (you should read her books too).

My editor Victoria Oundjian helped me transform this book at an early stage, demanding more twists and making me kill several subplots. This novel would be far inferior without her.

It would also be a much lesser work without the skills and talents of my long-suffering editor in Seattle, David Downing. This one was less painful than the last few – it couldn't have been *more* painful – but David still put me through my paces.

My copy-editor, Gemma Wain, rescued me from several embarrassing errors and at least one hilarious typo. Copy-editors are the unsung heroes of the publishing process and mine deserves a medal.

My agent Madeleine Milburn was supportive and enthusiastic as always, and I would like to say thanks to her and everyone at the agency.

Several readers have the dubious honour of having characters in this book named after them: Robin Barker, Kathy Leed and Julia Joss, who was the winner of an auction to raise funds for the people of Ukraine.

Speaking of readers, I would also like to thank all the regulars on my Facebook page, as well as those who chat with me on Twitter and Instagram. It's lovely to see so many familiar names and faces every year, including many readers who have been with me since day one. I appreciate all the cheerleading.

Finally, huge thanks to my family: my children, Ellie, Poppy, Archie and Harry, and the most important person of all, my wife Sara. I know how lucky I am – and not just because she doesn't have any dark, deadly secrets.

At least, I don't think she does . . .

Thanks again for reading.

Mark Edwards
Wolverhampton, October 2022

Free *Short Sharp Shockers* Box Set

+ Bonus Chapter From

Keep Her Secret

Join Mark Edwards' Readers Club and get an exclusive bonus chapter from *Keep Her Secret*, delving more into Matthew and Helena's past. You will also get a free collection of four stories, including *Wish You Dead*, *Kissing Games*, *Consenting Adults* and *Guardian Angel*. Get it all now at www.markedwardsauthor.com/free

About the Author

Photo © 2022 Tim Sturges, Express and Star

Mark Edwards writes psychological thrillers in which scary things happen to ordinary people.

He has sold 4 million books since his first novel, *The Magpies*, was published in 2013, and has topped the bestseller lists numerous times. His other novels include *Follow You Home, The Retreat, In Her Shadow, Because She Loves Me, The Hollows* and *Here to Stay*. He has also co-authored six books with Louise Voss.

Originally from Hastings in East Sussex, Mark now lives in Wolverhampton with his wife, their children and two cats.

Mark loves hearing from readers and can be contacted through his website, www.markedwardsauthor.com, or you can find him on Facebook (@markedwardsauthor), Twitter (@mredwards) and Instagram (@markedwardsauthor).

Follow the Author on Amazon

If you enjoyed this book, follow Mark Edwards on Amazon to be
notified when the author releases a new book!
To do this, please follow these instructions:

Desktop:

1) Search for the author's name on Amazon or in the Amazon App.
2) Click on the author's name to arrive on their Amazon page.
3) Click the 'Follow' button.

Mobile and Tablet:

1) Search for the author's name on Amazon or in the Amazon App.
2) Click on one of the author's books.
3) Click on the author's name to arrive on their Amazon page.
4) Click the 'Follow' button.

Kindle eReader and Kindle App:

If you enjoyed this book on a Kindle eReader or in the Kindle
App, you will find the author 'Follow' button after the last page.